Chicano Sketches

Chicano Sketches

Short Stories by Mario Suárez

Edited by Francisco A. Lomelí

Cecilia Cota-Robles Suárez

Juan José Casillas-Núñez

The University of Arizona Press   Tucson

The University of Arizona Press
© 2004 The Arizona Board of Regents
All rights reserved

Library of Congress Cataloging-in-Publication Data
Suárez, Mario, 1923–1998.
Chicano sketches : short stories / by Mario Suárez ;
edited by Francisco A. Lomelí, Cecilia Cota-Robles Suárez,
Juan José Casillas-Núñez.
p. cm.
Includes bibliographical references.
ISBN 0-8165-2404-1 (pbk. : alk. paper)
1. Mexican Americans—Fiction.   2. United States—Social life
and customs—20th century—Fiction.   I. Lomelí, Francisco A.
II. Suárez, Cecilia Felicia Cota-Robles.   III. Casillas-Núñez, Juan.
IV. Title
PS3569.U155C48   2004
813'.54—dc22
2004006903

Publication of this book is made possible in part by
the proceeds of a permanent endowment created with the
assistance of a Challenge Grant from the National Endowment
for the Humanities, a federal agency.

Manufactured in the United States of America on acid-free,
archival-quality paper containing a minimum of 30%
post-consumer waste and processed chlorine free.

13 12 11 10 09 08   7 6 5 4 3 2

In memoriam:

Dr. Ruth Keenan

Dr. Cecilia Cota-Robles Suárez

Contents

Foreword

Conversations of My Father

Most of the things that our parents try to teach us disappear later in the faded memories of childhood. Looking back, I realize that when my father tried to lecture me or "teach" me about life, I was usually unmoved. I don't have memories of being taught how to drive or fish. I don't remember talking to him about boys or school. What I remember most about my father was his conversations. I can remember one of the conversations he had when I was about ten years old. I was sitting at a bus stop in the middle of Mexico City with my family.

"Dad's met a new friend," my brother Francisco reported as my mother impatiently waited for him to finish his conversation so we could continue our vacation. As we sat, the gentleman my father had just met was completely engaged in conversation. My father's eyes were shining on that warm afternoon, as if he were speaking with an old friend he hadn't seen in years. We learned later that the gentleman knew someone who knew someone who was related to someone in my father's family. Like a skilled athlete passing the baton to a teammate, my father would always find a way to connect with fellow human beings. His ability to take this scary and crowded element called humanity and tame it was his greatest gift.

My father used his gift to create a collection of stories. In his stories he was able to shape images of those he met at the bus stop, the barbershop, or the coffee shop. The new friends my father met were the molds for characters in his stories. These people were not always the royalty of society, and their stories were not always like those in fairy tales of faraway places. In one of his stories, he describes some of the people in a place called El Hoyo, where he grew up. Reading the story is like peering into the windows of those who lived in Tucson, Arizona, in the 1950s. In "Señor Garza," a barber and his array of clients are drawn and shaded with the harsh realities of everyday life. I am certain that my father did not sit in the barbershop with a notebook taking notes as customers came and went throughout the day. Instead, he was probably chuckling about what had happened last night at the neighborhood bar. Not all artists carry a pouch of materials to create a landscape. In order to develop a great story, one needs only the ability to see human beings with all of their dimensions. The backdrops for my father's works of art were not seascapes and mountaintops, but instead places like dance halls, dirt roads, and local bars. His palette contained the dreams, disappointments, and laughter of all those who were lucky enough to be taken in by his welcoming smile.

The stories that my father wrote came from his skill as a writer and his ability to draw from the people around him. Unlike the painter who sits in the background and creates, my father had an ability to delve inside the worlds of the people around him to create his works. He was a master of inviting ordinary people into his world and making them permanent characters in the sketchpad he carried in his mind. Through these sketches (a word he used to describe his stories), my father was able to teach the reader about his world and his culture.

The stories my father wrote make available a culture and a history of the Chicano that the reader would never be able to understand as a casual observer. As the first writer to use the word "Chicano" in print, my father was able to share with the reader a world full of richness, pride, and pain. However, he did not consider himself a scholar. He was too much a man of the neighborhood to think of himself as a man of the world. You would rarely find him in a room full of fellow professors philosophizing about the fate of mankind. My father was much more likely to be found in the donut shop talking to a new friend.

The memories we carry of our parents can provide us with valuable lessons about the world. The memories of my father with his seemingly endless conversations remind me that to know the world is to know how to explore the hopes and dreams of its inhabitants. My father is no longer with us, but his stories remain as priceless portraits of everyday heroes leading fascinating everyday lives.

Laura Suárez

Introduction

Mario Suárez, Biography and Background

Mario Suárez (January 12, 1923–February 27, 1998) represents a unique case of an early Chicano author who remained faithful to his original purpose by creating a distinctively Chicano literary space. His ultimate goal was to portray and describe the people whom he knew intimately from a barrio in Tucson called El Hoyo, generally considered an urban wasteland. This so-called underside of America inspired him to pay close attention to the people's mannerisms, their language, customs and habits, racial composition, aspirations and complexes, eccentricities, as well as normative tendencies, history, and folklore. Along with Fray Angelico Chávez, author of *New Mexico Triptych* (1940), Suárez figures as the most important short story writer of Mexican descent from the mid-twentieth century, with his distinction resting on his mild-mannered realism filled with humor, irony, and pathos about the quirky, the virtuous, the deviant, the mischievous, or the mysterious characters who emerged and thrived in or around an ordinary barrio. He set out to fictionalize and re-create such a place of ignored characters because he believed their human story was worth telling, and he hoped that American literature would eventually include them or at least recognize their existence.

Suárez, the ever adept observer, concise short story writer, polemical essayist, aspiring novelist, committed educator, informed activist, and determined editorialist, does not stand out as a prolific writer. He preferred to be succinct and meticulous, a perfectionist with a focus on starkness over detail, yet more interested in human character than pure craft. Born and raised in the Chicano barrio of Tucson, he came from a family with five children: Rubén (named for the famous modernist Nicaraguan poet Rubén Darío), Graciela, Leticia, and Eugene, with Mario as the oldest. His father, Francisco Suárez, originally from Chihuahua, and his mother, Carmen Minjares, from Hermosillo, were directly influenced and shaped by the immigrant experience, arriving in the United States shortly after the Mexican Revolution in the early 1920s. His father, a tailor, and his mother, a seamstress, carved out a meager life for the family while living in a modest apartment in Tucson. Mario Suárez studied in the local schools (Safford Elementary School, Safford Junior High School, Tucson Senior High School, and eventually the University of Arizona), delivered the newspaper *Arizona Daily Star* at the age of eight or nine in El Hoyo, and later did odd jobs like painting and golf caddying to earn extra money. Shortly after finishing high school, he joined the navy, serving with a coast patrol stationed in Lakehurst, New Jersey, working partly on blimps, and spent some unforgettable times in nearby metropolitan New York. In late 1943, he was sent to Brazil as a radioman, where he served the remainder of his military duty until 1945.

Soon after returning from overseas duty, Suárez faced extraordinary responsibilities when his father died and he took charge of the family. Despite the demands, he enrolled at the University of Arizona, majoring in English, but later switched to a Spanish major while concentrating on folklore. He completed his BA diploma in 1952. Not known as an outstanding student, he nonetheless eagerly explored new subjects, discovering the likes of William Shakespeare, Jonathan Swift, François Voltaire, Vicente Blasco Ibáñez, John Steinbeck, Mariano Azuela, Benito Pérez Galdós, and others. Literature became his central focus, observation his natural inclination, and folklore his inspiration. It was at this time that he began to write his first sketches with the intention of writing about what he knew best: common folks doing ordinary things. His freshmen English teacher, Dr. Ruth Keenan, is to be credited for discovering his talents, and becoming a key mentor who corrected his rough drafts and demanded greater finesse in telling stories. Thanks to Dr. Keenan's unwavering compassion and encouragement, Suárez learned the art of creating short stories. He submitted his earliest sketches to the *Arizona Quarterly* in summer 1947 when the journal sought southwestern themes and motifs. To his surprise, the journal accepted his first five stories: "El Hoyo," "Señor Garza," "Cuco Goes to a Party," "Loco-Chu," and "Kid Zopilote."[1] This marks his first cycle of productivity, including two other sketches in 1948 ("Southside Run" and "Maestría")[2] and one in 1950 ("Mexican Heaven").[3] He also received significant input and guidance from other University of Arizona professors, such as Richard Summers and Frances Gilmore, a distinguished folklorist at the time. Thus, he slowly developed a personal style and a flair for writing. In the middle of his studies, he ventured to New York in 1949 to test the market and publishers' interest in Chicano topics, hoping to promote the idea of a novel on barrio characters. He returned highly disappointed but not defeated. On his return, he met Cecilia Cota-Robles, whom he later married in 1954. They had three children: Francisco Amado (1955), Mario Miguel ("Mike") (1956), and Laura Harriet (1957). In 1957 he received a John Jay Whitney Foundation Fellowship to further hone his writing skills.

Inclined to observe local urban politics, Suárez discovered that raising a family and handling work demands required a balancing act. For a short time in the early 1950s, he worked for Alianza Hispano Americana Insurance, which was intended to benefit local Latinos but did not. He resigned from his post because of the company's fraudulent practices, dedicating himself to research for legislator Frank Robles, who, along with Suárez, exposed the corruption surrounding such institutions. In addition, between February 14 and June 6, 1958, he served as contributing editor to a Hispanic newspaper in Tucson called *P-M*,[4] short for *Prensa Mexicana*, or *Mexican Press*. Using the pen name "El Gavilán" (the hawk), he produced provocative and combative investigative articles in both Spanish and English. The articles demonstrate his sharp eye for defending the underdog while defying questionable social practices in business, politics, and community services. In the process he idealistically denounced wrongs and demanded corruption be curbed, but his piercing writings drew a warning from then governor Howard Pyle: Cease the attacks or face reprisals against your family. Numerous hot issues emerged at the time regarding urban renewal, and Suárez's barrio became a target, eventually falling victim to the demolition of downtown Tucson. Suárez reassessed his options

in the difficult circumstances. Although he served as assistant manager in several finance companies, he considered his growing family
and realized his opportunities in Tucson were limited.

In 1958, the Suárez family moved west to California, pulling a trailer
with a 1952 Plymouth. They settled for a year in Whittier, then moved
to the suburb of La Mirada, near Los Angeles. He quit his new finance
company job in 1960 and again pursued his secondary teaching credential. His participation in local grassroots political activities, as part of
the burgeoning Chicano movement, started with his joining an East
Los Angeles chapter of MAPA (Mexican American Political Association). Here he performed invaluable community service, supporting
crusades for local justice and civil rights and assisting in political cam-
paigns and other community-based activities. On completing his secondary teaching credential at California State University at Fullerton
in 1972, he opted for working in a Chicano research firm in education
instead of teaching. Later in 1966 he was hired to develop a tutorial
reading and writing program at Claremont College, where his princi-
pal role was to create and make available new reading curricula for the
needy. Such work gave him a deep sense of personal satisfaction because he could combine, for the first time, his social commitment with
his English skills. As one of the poverty programs in the heart of East
Los Angeles, the reading and writing tutorial aimed at providing direct assistance to a wide range of disenfranchised people. However,
again Suárez's strong sense of ethics and his unconditional honesty
conflicted with local practices. He sardonically accused some of the
leaders of the organizations of being "poverty pimps."

Suárez's social commitment in the late 1960s and early 1970s developed into a unique brand of cultural and educational militancy while
advocating for his community and the voiceless and powerless. He continued to polish his literary sketches, but the only ones published during this period were "Las comadres" in 1969 and "Los coyotes" in 1972.[5]
His main activity, besides teaching and developing curricula in education and Chicano studies, was writing editorials, polemical essays, and
op-ed pieces for such newspapers as *Herald-Dispatch*, a local African
American newspaper, and *La Raza*, a Chicano paper in Los Angeles. He
also contributed short stories to a Chicano vanguard journal called *Con*

Safos, plus he lent his pen to numerous social causes through journalism, newsletters, organizational announcements, wide-ranging manifestos, pamphlets and brochures, mimeographed reports, and many other informal political grassroots publishing venues. He witnessed the Chicano Moratorium demonstration of August 1970, when police attacked the protestors, reminding him of the dangers involved in politics.

By 1970 Suárez transitioned into university teaching, working at California State Polytechnic University in Pomona, California, until his retirement in 1990. There he distinguished himself for imparting basic critical skills, while also teaching about Chicanos' place in American society, particularly encouraging and challenging students to pursue excellence. As a full-time professor, he offered students a relevant form of education he had never had, emphasizing an interdisciplinary perspective through history, literature, education, and culture. He was especially known for promoting high standards and for instilling an ability to articulate personal opinions. He taught in multiple areas, including Chicano literature, Southwest history, Mexican history and culture, writing skills, and Chicano studies in general. His deep commitment to education continued through the 1980s, though he sought to return to writing sketches about the characters he fondly remembered. He maintained an active political and cultural agenda until his long sickness in the mid-1990s. He died on February 27, 1998, in San Dimas, California.

Mario and Cecilia, students at the University of Arizona, 1949.

Mario in 1950.

Mario and Cecilia going on honeymoon in Tucson, 1954.

Mario,
Miguel,
Laura,
and
Francisco
in La
Mirada,
California,
1969.

Laura, Miguel, Cecilia, Francisco, and Mario in a family portrait, 1980.

The Stories

El Hoyo

rom the center of downtown Tucson the ground slopes gently away to Main Street, drops a few feet, and then rolls to the banks of the Santa Cruz River.[1] Here lies the sprawling section of the city known as El Hoyo. Why it is called El Hoyo is not clear. It is not a hole as its name would imply; it is simply the river's immediate valley. Its inhabitants are *chicanos* who raise hell on Saturday night, listen to Padre Estanislao on Sunday morning, and then raise more hell on Sunday night. While the term *chicano* is the short way of saying *Mexicano*, it is the long way of referring to everybody. Pablo Gutiérrez married the Chinese grocer's daughter and acquired a store; his sons are *chicanos*. So are the sons of Killer Jones who threw a fight in Harlem and fled to El Hoyo to marry Cristina Méndez. And so are all of them—the assortment of harlequins, bandits, oppressors, oppressed, gentlemen, and bums who came from Old Mexico to work for the Southern Pacific, pick cotton, clerk, labor, sing, and go on relief. It is doubtful that all of these spiritual sons of Mexico live in El Hoyo because they love each other—many fight and bicker constantly. It is doubtful that the *chicanos* live in El Hoyo because of its scenic beauty—it is everything but beautiful. Its houses are built of unplastered adobe, wood, license plates, and abandoned car parts. Its narrow streets are mostly clearings which have, in time, acquired names. Except for the tall trees which nobody has ever cared to identify, nurse, or destroy, the main things known to grow in the general area are weeds, garbage piles, dogs, and kids. And it is doubtful that the *chicanos* live in El Hoyo because it is safe—many times the Santa Cruz River has risen and inundated the area.

In other respects living in El Hoyo has its advantages. If one is born with the habit of acquiring bills, El Hoyo is where the bill collectors are less likely to find you. If one has acquired the habit of listening to Señor Perea's Mexican Hour in the wee hours of the morning with the radio on at full blast, El Hoyo is where you are less likely to be reported to the authorities. Besides, Perea is very popular and to everybody sooner or later is dedicated The Mexican Hat Dance. If one has inherited a bad taste for work but inherited also the habit of eating, where, if not in El Hoyo, are the neighbors more willing to lend you a cup of flour or beans? When Señora García's house burned to the ground with all her belongings and two kids, a benevolent gentleman conceived the gesture that put her on the road to solvency. He took five hundred names and solicited from each a dollar. At the end of the week he turned over to the heartbroken but grateful señora three hundred and fifty dollars in cold cash and pocketed his recompense. When the new manager of a local business decided that no more Mexican girls were to work behind his counters, it was the *chicanos* of El Hoyo who acted as pickets and, on taking their individually small but collectively great buying power elsewhere, drove the manager out and the girls returned to their jobs. When the Mexican Army was en route to Baja California and the *chicanos* found out that the enlisted men ate only at infrequent intervals, they crusaded across town with pots of beans, trays of tortillas, boxes of candy, and bottles of wine to meet the train. When someone gets married, celebrating is not restricted to the immediate families and friends of the couple. The public is invited. Anything calls for a celebration and in turn a celebration calls for anything. On Armistice Day[2] there are no fewer than half a dozen fights at the Tira-Chancla[3] Dance Hall. On Mexican Independence Day more than one flag is sworn allegiance to and toasted with gallon after gallon of Tumba Yaqui.[4]

And El Hoyo is something more. It is this something more which brought Felipe Ternero back from the wars after having killed a score of Germans, with his body resembling a patchwork quilt. It helped him to marry a fine girl named Julia. It brought Joe Zepeda back without a leg from Luzon[5] and helps him hold more liquor than most men can hold with two. It brought Jorge Casillas, a gunner flying B-24s over Germany, back to compose boleros. Perhaps El Hoyo is the proof that those people exist who, while not being against anything, have as yet failed to observe the more popular modes of human conduct. Perhaps the humble appearance of El Hoyo justifies the discerning shrugs of more than a few people only vaguely aware of its existence. Perhaps El Hoyo's simplicity motivates many a *chicano* to move far away from its intoxicating *frenesí*,[6] its dark narrow streets, and its shrieking children, to deny the bloodwell from which he springs, to claim the blood of a conquistador while his hair is straight and his face beardless. Yet El Hoyo is not the desperate outpost of a few families against the world. It fights for no causes except those which soothe its immediate angers. It laughs and cries with the same amount of passion in times of plenty and of want.

Perhaps El Hoyo, its inhabitants, and its essence can best be explained by telling you a little bit about a dish called *capirotada*. Its origin is uncertain. But it is made of old, new, stale, and hard bread. It is sprinkled with water and then it is cooked with raisins, olives, onions, tomatoes, peanuts, cheese, and general leftovers of that which is good and bad. It is seasoned with salt, sugar, pepper, and sometimes chili or tomato sauce. It is fired with tequila or sherry wine. It is served hot, cold, or just "on the weather" as they say in El Hoyo. The Garcías like it one way, the Quevedos another, the Trilos another, and the Ortegas still another. While in general appearance it does not differ much from one home to another, it tastes different everywhere. Nevertheless it is still *capirotada*. And so it is with El Hoyo's *chicanos*. While many seem to the undiscerning eye to be alike, it is only because collectively they are referred to as *chicanos*. But like *capirotada*, fixed in a thousand ways and served on a thousand tables, which can only be evaluated by individual taste, the *chicanos* must be so distinguished.

Señor Garza

Many consider Garza's Barber Shop as not truly in El Hoyo because it is on Congress Street and therefore downtown. Señor Garza, its proprietor, cashier, janitor, and Saint Francis, philosophizes that since it is situated in that part of the street where the land decidedly slopes, it is in El Hoyo. Who would question it? Who contributes to every cause for which a solicitor comes in with a long face and a longer relation of sadness? Who is the easiest touch for all the drunks who have to buy their daily cures? For loafers who go to look for jobs and never find them? For bullfighters on the wrong side of the border? For boxers still amateurs though punchy? For barbers without barber shops? And for the endless line of moochers who drop in to borrow anything from two bits to two dollars? Naturally, Garza.

Garza's Barber Shop is more than razors, scissors, and hair. It is where men, disgruntled at the vice of the rest of the world, come to air their views. It is where they come to get things off their chests along with the hair off their heads and beard off their faces. Garza's Barber Shop is where everybody sooner or later goes or should. This does not mean that there are no other barber shops in El Hoyo. There are. But none of them seem quite to capture the atmosphere that Garza's does. If it were not downtown it would probably have a little fighting rooster tied to a stake by the front door. If it were not rented to Señor Garza only it would perhaps smell of sherry wine all day. To Garza's Barber Shop goes all that is good and bad. The lawbreakers come in to rub elbows with the sheriff's deputies. And toward all Garza is the same. When zoot suiters come in for a very slight trim, Garza who is very versatile, puts on a bit of zoot talk and hep-cats[7] with the zootiest of them. When the boys that are not zoot suiters come in, he becomes, for the purpose of accommodating his clientele, just as big a snob as their individual personalities require. When necessity calls for a change in his character Garza can assume the proportions of a Greek, a Chinaman, a gypsy, a republican, a democrat, or if only his close friends are in the shop, plain Garza.

Perhaps Garza's pet philosophy is that a man should not work too hard. Garza tries not to. His day begins according to the humor of his wife. When Garza drives up late, conditions are perhaps good. When Garza drives up early, all is perhaps not well. Garza's Barber Shop has been known, accordingly, to stay closed for a week. It has also been known to open before the sun comes up and to remain open for three consecutive days. But on normal days and with conditions so-so, Garza comes about eight in the morning. After opening, he pulls up the green venetian blinds. He brings out two green ash cans containing the hair cut the preceding day and puts them on the edge of the sidewalk. After this he goes to a little back room in the back of the shop, brings out a long crank, and lowers the red awning that keeps out the morning sun. Lily-boy, the fat barber who through time and diligence occupies chair number two, is usually late. This does not mean that Lily-boy is lazy, but he is married and there are rumors, which he promptly denies, that state he is henpecked. Rodríguez, barber number three, usually fails to show up for five out of six workdays.

On ordinary mornings Garza sits in the shoeshine stand because it is closest to the window and nods at the pretty girls going to work and to the ugly ones, too. He works on an occasional customer. He goes to Sally and Sam's for a cup of coffee, and on returning continues to sit. At noon Garza takes off his small apron, folds it, hangs it on the arm of his chair, and after combing his hair goes to La Estrella[8] to eat and flirt with the waitresses who, for reasons that even they cannot understand, have taken him into their confidence. They are well aware of his marital standing; but Garza has black wavy hair and picaresque charm that sends them to the kitchen giggling. After eating his usual meal of beans, rice, tortilla, and coffee, he bids all the girls good-bye and goes back to his barber shop. The afternoons are spent in much the same manner as the mornings except that on such days as Saturday, there is such a rush of business that Garza very often seeks some excuse to go away from his own business and goes for the afternoon to Nogales in Mexico or downstairs to the Tecolote[9] Club to drink beer.

On most days, by five-thirty everybody has usually been in the shop for friendly reasons, commercial reasons, and even spiritual reasons. Loco-Chu, whose lack of brains everybody understands, has gone by and insulted the customers. Take-It-Easy, whose liquor-saturated brain everybody respects, has either made nasty signs at everybody or has come in to quote the words and poems of the immortal Antonio Plaza. Cuco has come from his job at Feldman's Furniture Store to converse of the beauty of Mexico and the comfort of the United States. Procuna[10] has come in, and being a university student with more absences than the rest of his class put together, has very politely explained his need for two dollars until the check comes in. Chonito has shined shoes and danced a dozen or so boogie pieces. There have been arguments. Fortunes made and lost. Women loved. The great Cuate Cuete[11] has come in to talk of the glory and grandeur of zoot suitism in Los Angeles. Old customers due about that day have come. Also new ones who had to be told that all the loafers who seemingly live in Garza's Barber Shop were not waiting for haircuts. Then the venetian blinds are let down. The red awning is cranked up. The door is latched on the inside although it is continually opened on request for friends, and the remaining customers are attended to and let out.

Inside Garza opens his little National Cash Register, counts the day's money, and puts it away. He opens his small writing desk and adds and subtracts for a little while in his green record book. Meanwhile Chonito grudgingly sweeps and says very nasty words. Lily-boy phones his wife to tell her that he is about to start home and that he will not be waylaid by friends and that he will not arrive drunk. Rodríguez relates to everybody in the shop that when he was a young man getting tired was not like him. The friends who have already dropped in wait until the beer is spoken for and then Chonito is sent for it. When it is brought in and distributed, everything is talked about. Lastly, women are thoroughly insulted although their necessity is emphasized. Garza, being a man of experience and one known to say what he feels when he feels it, recalls the ditty he heard while still in the cradle and says, "To women neither all your love nor all your money." The friends, drinking Garza's beer, agree.

Not always has Señor Garza enjoyed the place of distinction if not of material achievement that he enjoys among his friends today. In his thirty-five years his life has gone through transition after transition, conquest after conquest, setback after setback. But now Señor Garza is one of those to whom most refer, whether for reasons of friendship, indebtedness, or of having never read Plato and Aristotle, as an oracle pouring out his worldly knowledge during and between the course of his haircuts.

Garza was born in El Hoyo, the second of seven Garzas. He was born with so much hair that perhaps this is what later prompted him to be a barber. At five he almost burned the house down while playing with matches. At ten he was still waiting for his older brother to outgrow his clothes so that they could be handed down to him. Garza had the desire to learn, but even before he found out about school Garza had already attained a fair knowledge of everything. Especially the knowledge of want. Finally, his older brother got a new pair of overalls and Garza got his clothes. On going to school he immediately claimed having gone to school in Mexico, so Garza was tried out in the 3B. In the 4A his long legs fitted under the desk, so he had to begin his education there. In the 5B he fell in love with the teacher and was promptly promoted to avert a scandal. When Garza was sixteen and had managed to get to the eighth grade, school suddenly became a mass of equations, blocks, lines, angles, foreign names, and headaches. At seventeen it might have driven him to insanity, so Garza wisely cut his schooling short at sixteen.

On leaving school Garza tried various enterprises. He became a delivery boy for a drug store. He became a stock room clerk for a shoe store. But of all enterprises the one he found most profitable was that of shearing dogs. He advertised his business and it flourished until it became very obvious that his house and brothers were getting quite flea ridden. Garza had to give it up. The following year he was overcome with the tales of vast riches in California. Not that there was gold, but there were grapes to be picked. He went to California. But of that trip he has more than once said that the tallness of the Californian garbage cans made him come back twenty pounds lighter and without hair under his armpits. Garza then tried the CCC camp.[12] But it turned out that there were too many bosses with muscles that looked like golf balls whom Garza thought it best not to have much to do with. Garza was already one that could keep everybody laughing all day long, but this prevented almost everybody from working. At night when most boys at camp were either listening to the juke box in the canteen, or listening to the playing of sad guitars, Garza trimmed heads at fifteen cents. After three months of piling rocks, carrying logs, and of getting fed up with his bosses' perpetual desires of making him work, Garza came back to the city with the money he had saved cutting hair and through a series of deals was allowed a barber's chair in a going-establishment.

In a few years Garza came to be a barber of prominence. He had grown to love the idle conversation that is typical of barber shops, the mere idle gossip that often speaks of broken homes and forsaken women in need of friends. These Garza has always sought and in his way has done his best to put in higher spirits. Even after his marriage he continued to receive anonymous after anonymous phone call. He came to know the bigtime operators and their brand of filthy doings. He came to know the bootleggers, thieves, love merchants, and rustlers. He came to know also the smalltime operators with bigtime complex and their shallowness of human understanding. He came to know false friends that came to him and said, "We're throwing a dance. We've got a good crowd. The tickets are two dollars." And on feeling superior, once the two dollars had fattened their wallets and inflated their conceit, remarked upon seeing him at the dance, "Damn, even the barber came." But in time Garza has seen many of these grow fat. He has seen their women go unfaithful. He has seen them get spiritually lost in trying to keep up materially with the people next door. He has seen them go bankrupt buying gabardine to make up for their lack of style. Their hair had cooties but smelled of aqua-rosa. The edges of their underwear were frilled even though they wore new suits. They gave breakfasts for half of the city to prove that "they had" and only ended up with piles of dirty dishes. Garza watched, philosophized, cut more hair, and of this has more than once said in the course of a beer or idle conversation among friends, "Damned fools, when you go, how in the hell are you going to take it with you? You are buried in your socks. Your suit is slit in the back and placed on top of you."

So in time Garza became the owner of his own barber shop. Garza's

Barber Shop with its three Koken barber chairs, its reception sofas, its shoeshine stand, wash bowls, glass kits, pictures, objects to be sold and raffled, and juke box. Second to none in its colorful array of true friends and false, of drunks, loafers, bullfighters, boxers, other barbers, moochers, and occasional customers. Perfumed with the poetry of the immortal Antonio Plaza, and seasoned with naughty jokes told at random.

Soon the night becomes old and empty beer bottles are collected and put in the little back room. Chonito, who has swept the floor while Garza and his friends have consumed beer, asks for a fifty-cent advance or swears with the power of his fourteen years that he will never sweep the shop again, and gets it. Lily-boy phones his wife again and tells her that he is about to start home and that he is sober. Rodríguez, if he worked that day, says he has a bad cold which he must go home to cure, but asks for an advance to buy his tonic at Tom's Liquor Store. Then the lights are switched off and Garza, his barbers, his friends, and Chonito, file out. Garza, not forgetting the words he heard while in the cradle, "To women neither all your love nor all your money," either goes up the street to the Royal Inn for a glass of beer or to the All States Pool Hall. Then he goes home. Garza, a philosopher. Owner of Garza's Barber Shop. But the shop will never own Garza.

Cuco Goes to a Party

One night Cuco Martínez decided not to go home right away. Every night he hurried home from work because his two brothers-in-law did it and thought it right. The brothers-in-law believed that if a man got up very early in the morning and cooked his breakfast, it was right. The brothers-in-law believed that if a man came straight home from work, it was right. The brothers-in-law also believed that if a man worried about the price of household needs and discussed them with the wife, it was right. Maybe it was right. But only to his two brothers-in-law. To Cuco it was very boring. So tonight he would not go home right away. If his brothers-in-law wanted to be henpecked and do so, it was all right with him. Where he came from men did as they pleased, and here, as long as his name was Cuco Martínez he would do the same thing. When Cuco walked out of Feldman's Furniture Store at six o'clock he did not direct his steps toward his home in El Hoyo as he usually did. He walked up the street to Garza's Barber Shop. It was already closed but Garza and his friends were inside. When Cuco was let in, Garza, who was shaving, said, "Happy are the eyes that greet you, Cuco."

"The feeling is mutual, Garza. And what is new with you?" asked Cuco as he sat down with two of Garza's friends on the long reception sofa and began thumbing through a magazine.

"Cuco," said Garza, "today is Lily-boy's birthday and I hope you will join Procuna, Lolo, and myself in honoring him."

"I will be glad to," said Cuco.

So when Garza was through shaving, when the lights were put out, and when the door was locked, Lily-boy, who was to be the honored one, Garza, Procuna, Lolo, and Cuco walked up the street to the Royal Inn. When they got there it was not yet very full of customers because it was at the time when most men were at home eating supper. The bartender was wiping glasses in anticipation of a good night. The juke box was

still silent. Lolo, who walked in ahead of everybody, promptly found a
good table and the five friends sat down and ordered beer. Cuco went to
the juke box and soon the gay rhythm of El Fandango[13] was filling the
air. Garza ordered more beer and Lolo, who is sometimes very poetic,
toasted to Lily-boy. Lily-boy was wished eternal happiness. Whether he
deserved that kind of happiness was questionable. He was also wished
a thousand happy years. Whether Lily-boy really wanted that many was
also questionable. "Bottoms up," said Garza. The friends drank. And
drank. After a few hours the table was so littered with bottles that Lolo
began to wonder how much he could get for them should he decide
to go into the bottle-collecting business. Lily-boy went to the phone
booth to tell his wife that he would soon be home and that he would
arrive sober. Lolo, who was the king of the jitterbugs and an up-and-
coming prize fighter as well, was thinking of challenging everybody.
He looked across the table to see which one of his companions would
make a good match. When Lolo realized that these were no fighters, he
looked at a little group of drunks, and on seeing that they did not look
like good potential foes, he shouted a few obscenities at them and continued drinking his beer. Garza was trying to brush off a little drunk
who was sure that he had seen him somewhere and Garza was trying
to convince him that it had probably been at Garza's Barber Shop. Cuco
was saying to Procuna, "I think that if I had my way about most things
I would go to Mexico City and see a full season of bullfights. I sure like
them. I truthfully believe that there is nothing as full of emotion as a
good bullfight. I remember having been at bullfights from the time I
was about eight years old. I used to go with my father. But what I remember best is when I say Silverio Pérez makes such a beautiful kill
that that supreme moment has lived with me ever since."

"Why, Cuco?" asked Procuna.

"Well," continued Cuco, "Pérez is not a good killer. He is a good
bullfighter but he is not a good killer. But this bull, which was as big as
a house, knocked him down. When Pérez was on the ground the bull
almost gored him but luckily, when he got up, only his pants were torn.
Silverio was so mad that he picked up the *estoque* with which he would
soon kill the bull and, in his rage, slapped the bull across the face. Silverio Pérez was mad. Then he lined himself up with the left horn. He

sighted the bull. The two met. Collided. For a second there was but a mass of enraged animal and embroidered silk. But in the end Silverio Pérez was alive, though shaken, and the bull was dead. Yes, Procuna, Silverio Pérez is great."

"How about Armillita,[14] Cuco, is he any good?" asked Procuna.

"Is he any good? You ask me. Is he any good? Why—, he is the *maestro* of *maestros*. He is the teacher of teachers. When Armillita wants to be good he can do the impossible. He is great. I saw him perform in the Mexico City arena. He was magnificent. Each time the bull passed by his body it seemed that the great Armillita would end up on the horns of the bull. Yet he was as much at ease in the midst of it all as we are here, drinking beer. There is no doubt. Like Armillita there are not two."

Soon Cuco got up to demonstrate, with the aid of his coat, how the bulls were passed. Procuna acted as a bull, and Cuco told his friends how the different passes were executed. He explained how in the art of bullfighting things must be done with delicacy and finesse. Cuco waved the coat and Procuna, the bull, charged. He charged true and straight and Cuco passed him with grace and charm. He charged again. And again. Each time Cuco passed him with all the known passes in the art of bullfighting. Each time Procuna, the bull, charged he came so close to Cuco that he almost bumped him. But he didn't. After a fine exhibition of cape work Cuco drank some more beer. Then he stood in front of the table of the companions and to Lily-boy, who was the guest of honor, dedicated as the *matadores* do in Mexico City, the death of the bull. Once again Cuco took the coat and Procuna, the bull, charged. The bull was getting tired. Soon Cuco realized this and went through the motions of killing him. By this time half of the people in the Royal Inn were crowded around Cuco. Procuna, who had been a good bull, got off the floor, dusted himself, and drank some more beer. Garza was proud of them. He hugged both of them. Lolo, who was very anxious for a bit of excitement, challenged Lily-boy to a fight. Lily-boy was very drunk. He, too, was willing to fight. He feared no man, so he was willing. So Lolo and Lily-boy went out into the alley followed by a big crowd to fight it out. After a while Lily-boy and Lolo, who had shaken hands after their fight, came back to drink more beer. Lily-boy had merely sat on top of poor little Lolo. But still it had been a great fight. By this time, Garza, who has always been a good barber and better philosopher, was thinking of turning into an impresario. He was thinking of organizing a bullfight at the edge of the Santa Cruz River. He was also thinking of promoting a few boxing matches. Lily-boy once again went to the phone booth to tell his wife that he was about to start for home. Lolo was challenging Garza. Lolo was bribed into silence with another beer. Cuco was telling Procuna more about fighting bulls. Every now and then one of them would get up to execute a pass. Lily-boy was getting so drunk that he was looking for the phone booth in the men's room. After he came back to the table and had another beer he was looking for the men's room in the phone booth. Garza, in truth, was having a hell of a time keeping his friends on their feet. Lolo was insistent about fighting Lily-boy again. He wanted a re-match. Mike, the bartender, gave them a red drink on the house. After all, they had been very good customers. They had broken no chairs and upset no tables. Very soon Mike decided that they deserved another drink on the house. When the second drink went down the throats of the friends they began to drop. Soon the only ones left standing were Procuna, who was executing passes, and Garza. Garza realized that it was late so he bought Procuna another bottle of beer and told him to keep an eye on things while he went for the car to take the friends home. He well realized that if the authorities saw them in their present condition it would be taken for granted that they had been drinking. Garza went for the car and Procuna, who was left in charge, fell asleep on the shoulder of Lily-boy. When Garza came in for his friends he first woke Procuna. Together they carried Lolo, the king of the jitterbugs, feet first to the car. Then they carried out Cuco, a very nice young man, and put him in the car. Last but not least, they tried to awaken Lily-boy, who was very fat, and who had to hurry home to cut his birthday cake. Finally he had to be carried to the car, too. After the three friends were piled into the back seat and the doors closed, Procuna jumped into the front seat with Garza and the car started toward each of their respective homes. Lolo, the king of the jitterbugs, woke up long enough to say that he was hungry. Garza, who cannot stand anybody being hungry as long as they are with him, told Lolo to shut up and go to sleep. Garza turned toward the Hacienda Café. When they got there the only ones that were able to get out to eat were Procuna and Garza. Lolo did not wake up, so Garza thought it best for him to sleep. After a hot meal and a singeing cup of coffee Garza and Procuna decided that they were still too sober, so they went across the street to the Gato Blanco Café.[15] They drank a few beers. They shook hands with a few friends and then went back to the car. When they got going again Lolo was taken home first and put to bed because he was training for his next fight and needed rest. Cuco then decided that he did not want to go home right away. He wanted to get out of the car for certain universal necessity. So Garza patiently stopped the car and Cuco remedied his need. Then he was taken home. Lily-boy was taken home. He was a little bit late to cut his birthday cake but at least he was home. After Procuna, who had to go to school the next day, was dropped off at his house, Garza started for his own. After all, it had been a gay party. Lolo had fought Lily-boy. Cuco had fought many bulls. Procuna had executed passes and had consumed a lot of beer. Garza was happy that his friends had been happy and with a smile on his lips and very glassy, tired eyes, drove home. Tomorrow he had to go to work.

The next day, in the early afternoon, Procuna dropped around to Garza's Barber Shop with his schoolbooks under his arm. Garza was putting the finishing touches on a customer when he came in. When he saw him, he said, "My great Procuna, how are you?"

"Fine, Garza, and you?" asked Procuna with a tired voice. "I thought I was going to go to sleep in class today. But wow, I sure had a wonderful time last night."

"Yes. I guess we all did. When you and Cuco started you were fighting little bulls. By the time you got the free drink from the bartender you were fighting bulls from La Punta about five years old," said Garza.

"How about Cuco, has he been in?" inquired Procuna.

"Well, Procuna, I am going to tell you," said Garza.

"Tell me what," said Procuna.

"Well, Cuco was in here a little while ago and just went out to eat with Lily-boy. He is sad. In fact, he is very sad," said Garza.

"Why in the hell should he be sad today? He was very happy yester-day," said Procuna.

"Well, last night he lost his underwear," said Garza.

"And—?" inquired Procuna.

"Just that poor Cuco has been at odds with his in-laws and they found this as an excuse to turn his wife against him. Poor Emilia," said Garza, "but I think the damned in-laws are talking her into getting a divorce from Cuco." Garza brushed off the customer's neck and took off the linen apron. He rang up seventy-five cents in a cash register and continued, "Yes, that is the way it is. Cuco really loves his wife too. It is only that his in-laws do not give him a minute of peace."

At that moment Lily-boy and Cuco walked into the barber shop. Lily-boy put on his barber's apron and Cuco sat down in the reception sofa. He looked very sad. He did not want to talk about anything. He picked up a magazine and began to thumb through it. Looking up, Cuco said, "Yes, Garza, I guess it was all a mistake for me to get married in the first place. The only thing that worries me is that Emilia is going to have a child. I really planned to stay married to her. But I guess I will just wait until it is born and then go back to Mexico."

"And her?" asked Garza.

"She will keep the child and I will go back by myself."

Then Cuco once again began to look through the magazine for a little longer and then, without saying anything, got up and walked out of the barber shop. The friends, Procuna, Lily-boy, and Garza felt sorry for him. He was a good young man. They felt somewhat guilty for having got him so drunk that he had to go and lose his underwear.

Cuco Martínez was not very gay after that. Every day he went home to hear the nagging ways of his in-laws. Cuco was not understood. At first he had been something new but now nobody seemed to like him any longer. The brothers-in-law told him that he was a no-good fancy storyteller that should have stayed working for the railroad. They told him that he would always be but a rest room cleaner at Feldman's Fur-niture Store. That he was so stupid that he should not expect to ever make over thirty dollars a week. That he was nothing but a no-good drunk and that they did not see how Emilia had ever fallen in love and consented to marry him. Every day the same thing happened. Cuco got mad and said nothing. He knew that conditions would change. As soon as the child was born he would leave. Because he loved Emilia very much, he realized he could not stay long enough for her to dislike him for the same things his brothers-in-law did. He would return to Mexico. That is the way he would have it.

Loco-Chu

very morning Loco-Chu[16] is on Congress Street asking for nickels. Truthfully, a nickel is not much to give anybody, much less to Loco-Chu. But almost everybody is very tired of giving them to him. Loco-Chu will accept dimes and even pennies but his passion is nickels. When people see him coming, walking as if in a daze with his battered hat pulled well over his eyes, with his shredded tie, his old coat and very patched trousers, they cross the street to avoid him. To be seen close to him is an excuse for someone to say, "I saw you with your relative." So most people try to avoid poor Chu. If one chooses to remain on the same sidewalk until he passes, he is sure to say to him, "Go away, Chu. Go away." Sometimes he does. But sometimes he does not and will follow, pointing, grunting, and cursing. This, most people find very annoying, so Chu almost always gets the nickel he demands. Then he smiles. Music is on his mind. He pulls his hat farther down over his eyes and throws back his shoulders. He pulls up his trousers. He walks very happily, puffing on a snipe of a cigarette, into the Canton Café[17] because it seems that it is the only restaurant that will accept his small trade. "Coffee," he says. The saliva begins to drip from the corners of his mouth. "Coffee. I have money. I have money. Coffee." In order to avoid difficulties within his establishment, Lin Lew brings him coffee and gives him old doughnuts and pieces of cake or pie. Lin Lew never charges Chu. After eating the pastries and drinking some of the coffee, spilling the rest on his vest and part on the fly of his trousers, Chu gets up and walks out. He wanders up and down Congress Street some more. He goes by Garza's Barber Shop and makes faces at the customers. He makes dirty signs with his hands. He grunts and shouts nasty words. Garza, the barber, then leaves his customer, goes to the door with any old newspaper and a nickel and says to Chu, "Extra, Chu. Go sell it." And Chu happily takes the nickel and the paper and goes up and down the street hollering, "Extra! Extra! Paper! Five cents. Extra paper!"

By noon Chu sometimes has as many as a dozen nickels. He tinkles them and he is happy. He has music on his mind. He then defies everybody. He will insult even without provocation. Once again he goes to the Canton Café and sits down. "Food," he shouts, "I want food!" And Lin Lew goes to the kitchen and brings him a dish of rice or a bowl of soup. As Chu eats, leaving food all over the floor and all over the counter, he smiles. He bares his teeth and says with words coming from his heart, "*Buena comida*. Good food." Lin Lew nods and is happy that Chu is content. After eating, Chu automatically gets up and goes to the back room. He emerges with a bucket of hot water and a mop and goes to work. He hums as he glides the mop over the floor and underneath the tables. When he is through he puts the mop away, empties the dirty water, and leaves. Lin Lew smiles, breathes freely, and feels more than paid. In the afternoon Chu walks past Garza's Barber Shop again, puffing his snipe, and repeats his nasty signs. He goes by the Pastime Penny Arcade and cusses at the top of his voice at the zoot suiters seated along the window sill like crows on a telephone wire. He tells them of their canine ancestry, but they know him and shrug him off saying, "Poor damned nitwit." When of this he gets his fill Chu walks into the Plaza Theater. He never bothers to pay. New ushers there only try throwing him out the first time. He sits in the front row and spreading his arms and feet he hums with the music in the picture. He is happy. Music is on his mind. After the movie, even if he has seen it for three days straight, he is very content. Chu stands in front of the theater and tries to show people the announcements as they continuously try to scare him away. Then he walks up and down the street. He will stop at busy corners and direct traffic. When he tires of this he goes for the last time to the Canton Café. He sits down at the counter and orders coffee. He refuses anything else even if it is given him by some stranger who wants to do a good deed when he sees how thin Chu is. It is here that Chu's tired eyes shine like those of a young boy. He takes a new snipe from his pocket, and after lighting it, he smiles and shows the decaying bits of food hanging between his decaying teeth and purplish gums. Chu is happiest at the Canton Café. It is here that he sips hot coffee until the wee hours of the night when Lin Lew, with Oriental delicacy, pushes him out.

Chu dislikes having to leave, because he is happy and with music on his mind. It is at the Canton that Chu spends all the nickels that people give him. He puts them, one by one, into the fancily lighted juke box. As the records mechanically come up, begin revolving, and are touched by the needle, the music, of whatever kind it may be, is singularly Loco-Chu's. If anybody else comes close to the juke box he growls and says, "Mine. Get out. You son of a b–ch. Get out. Mine." And it is rightly Chu's music. It is all he has.

Kid Zopilote

When Pepe García came back from a summer in Los Angeles everybody began to call him Kid Zopilote.[18] He did not know why he did not like the sound of it, but in trying to keep others from calling him that he got into many fights and scrapes. Still everybody he associated with persisted in calling him Kid Zopilote. When he dated a girl with spit curls and dresses so short that they almost bared her garters, everybody more than ever called him Kid Zopilote. It annoyed him very much. But everybody kept saying, "Kid Zopilote. Kid Zopilote." When he reasoned that it was a name given him because he dated this particular girl, he began to go with another one who wore very shiny red slacks and a very high pompadour. But to his dismay he found that he was still Kid Zopilote. All the girls who were seen with him were quickly dubbed Kiddas Zopilotas. This hurt their pride. Soon even the worst girls began to shun poor Kid Zopilote. None of the girls wanted to be seen with him. When he went to the Tira-Chancla Dance Hall very few of the girls consented to dance with him. When they did, it was out of compassion. But when the piece ended the girls never invited Kid Zopilote to the table. They thanked him on the run and began talking to someone else. Anybody else. Somehow all of this made Kid Zopilote very sad. He blamed everything on his cursed nickname. He could dance as well as anybody else and even better. Still he was an outcast. He could not understand what his nickname had to do with his personality. It sounded very ugly.

When he came back from Los Angeles he had been very happy until he went out to see his friends. He had come back with an even greater desire to dance. To him everything was in rhythm. Everywhere he went, even if it was only inside the house, he snapped his fingers and swung his body. His every motion and action was, as they say, in beat. His language had changed quite a bit, too. Every time he left the house he said to his mother, "Ma, I will *returniar*[19] in a little while." When he returned he said, "Ma, I was *watchiando* a good movie, that is why I am a little bit late." And Señora García found it very hard to break him of saying things like that. But that was not the half of it. It was his clothes that she found very odd. When he opened a box he brought from Los Angeles and took from it a suit and put it on, Señora García was horrified.

"Why, Pepe, what kind of a suit is that?" asked Señora García.

"Ma, this is the *styleacho* in Los Angeles, Califo."[20]

"Well, I certainly do not like it Pepe."

"Ah, mama, but I like it. And I will tell you why. When I first got to California I was very lonely. I got a job picking fruit in no time at all and I was making very good money. But I also wanted to have a good time. So—one day I was down there in a place called Olvera Street[21] in Los Angeles and I noticed that many of the boys who were Mexicans like me had suits like this one. They were very happy and very gay. They all had girls. There were many others, but they were not having any fun. They were squares. Well, I tried to talk to them, but it seemed as though they thought they were too good for me. Then I talked to the ones that were wearing drapes and they were more friendly. But even with them I could not go too far in making friends. So I bought this suit. Soon I went down to Olvera Street again and I got invited to parties and everything. I was introduced to many girls."

"But I do not like the suit, Pepe. It does not become you. I know now that you came back from California a cursed *pachuco*. A no-good zoot suiter. I am very sorry I ever let you go in the first place. I am only thanking Jesus Christ that your father is dead so that he would not see you with the sadness that I see you now."

"Well, ma, I will tell you something else right now if that is the way you feel about it. I am not the same as I used to be. I used to think that I would never want to wear a suit like this one. But now I like it. If the squares in Tucson do not wear a suit like this one, is that my fault or is it for me to question? No. And I do not care. But if I like it and want to wear it I will. Leave me alone, ma, and let me wear what I please."

"You will not leave this house with that suit on, Pepe," said his mother, as she stood before the door, obstructing his path. "I will not have the neighbors see you in it."

"The neighbors do not buy my clothes, ma, so if they do not like my taste they can go to hell," said Kid Zopilote, as he gently moved his mother from the door and went out.

After that Señora García said nothing. Whenever Kid Zopilote went about the house with his pleated pants doing the shimmy to the radio, she merely sighed. When he clomped his thick-soled shoes in rhythm, she left the room in complete disappointment. When Kid Zopilote put on his long finger-tip coat, his plumed hat, dangled his knife on a thick watch chain, and went out of the house, Señora García cried.

Every day Kid Zopilote walked past the Chinese stores, the shoe-shine parlors, barber shops, bars, and flop houses on Meyer Street. Sometimes he spent the entire day at Kaiser's Shoeshine Parlor. This was where, through time, a few lonely zoot suiters had been attracted by the boogie woogie music of the juke box. All day they put nickel after nickel into it to snap their fingers and sway their bodies with the beat. On other days Kid Zopilote went uptown to the Pastime Penny Arcade. Here again, the zoot suiters came in hour after hour to try their luck with the pinball machines. They walked by the scales a few dozen times a day and instead of stopping to weigh, they took out a very long comb and ran it through their hair to make sure that it met in back of the head in the shape of a duck's tail. Then they went outside to lean on the window. They sat on the sill and conversed until very late at night. Here they followed the every action of the girls that passed. They shouted from one side of the street to the other when they saw a friend or enemy, their only other action being that of bringing up cigarettes to the lips, letting the smoke out through the nose, and spitting on the sidewalk through the side of the mouth, leaving big yellow-green splotches on the cement.

One morning Kid Zopilote got up very early and went to visit his uncle who was from Mexico. When he got to the house, Kid Zopilote walked in the front door and found his *tío*[22] was still asleep in street clothes. But it was very important to Kid Zopilote to find out the true implication of his nickname. So he woke his uncle. After the two started a fire, made and ate breakfast, with an inquisitive look on his face Kid Zopilote began, "*Tío*, you are a *relativo*[23] of mine because you are a brother of my mother. But I know and you know that my mother does not like for me to visit you because you are a *wino*. But today I came to ask you something very important."

"What is on your mind?" asked the uncle.

"Well, before I went to Los Angeles everybody I knew used to call me Pepe. But since I came back everybody now calls me Kid Zopilote. Why? What is the true meaning of Kid Zopilote?"

"The zopilote is a bird," said his uncle.

"*Sí—?*"

"Yes, the zopilote is a bird . . ." said his uncle, repeating himself.

"What more, *tío?*" asked Kid Zopilote.

"Well—in truth, it is a very funny bird. His appearance is like that of a buzzard. I remember the zopilotes very well. There are many in Mazatlán because the weather there is very hot. The damned zopilotes are as black as midnight. They have big beaks and they also have a lot of feathers on their ugly heads. I used to kill them with rocks. They come down to earth like giant airplanes, feeling out a landing, touching the earth. When they hit the earth they keep sliding forward until their speed is gone. Then they walk like punks walk into a bar. When the damned zopilotes eat, they only eat what has previously been eaten. Sometimes they almost choke and consequently they puke. But always there is another zopilote who comes up from behind and eats the puke of the first. Then they look for a tree. When they ease themselves on the poor tree, the tree dies. After they eat more puke and kill a few more trees, they once again start running into the wind. They get air speed. They become airborne. Then they fly away."

"So you mean that they call me Kid Zopilote because they think I eat puke?" asked Kid Zopilote as his eyes became narrow with anger. "Tell me, is that why?"

"Not necessarily, Pepe, perhaps there are other reasons," said his uncle.

"The guys can go to hell then. If they can't call me Pepe they do not have to call me anything."

"But I would not worry about it anymore, Pepe. If once they began to call you Kid Zopilote they will never stop. It is said that a zopilote can never be a peacock," said his uncle, "and you probably brought it onto yourself." So Kid Zopilote went away from the house of his uncle very angry.

One night there was a stranger at Kaiser's Shoeshine Parlor. While he was not a zoot suiter he had the appearance of one of those slick felines that can never begin to look like a human being even if he should have on a suit of English tweed and custom-made shirts. He was leaning against the wall, quietly smoking a cigarette, when Kid Zopilote arrived. As usual Kid Zopilote saluted the zoot suiters with their universal greeting, "*Esos* guys,[24] how goes it?"

"*Pos ahi nomás.*[25] Oh, just so-so," said another *pachuco.*

"Well, put in a good jitter piece," said Kid Zopilote. Before the *pachuco* could slip the nickel into the slot, the stranger slipped in a coin and the juke box began to fill Kaiser's with beat.

Kid Zopilote and the other *pachuco* were thankful. After the stranger sized up Kid Zopilote he said, "Have a cigarette, won't you?"

"Thank you," said Kid Zopilote. And from that day Kid Zopilote smoked the man's cigarettes. In time he was being charged extravagant prices for them but Kid Zopilote always managed to get the price. He walked into the Western Cleaning Company and walked out with pressing irons. He went into business establishments and always came out with something. He stole fixtures off parked automobiles. Anything. Kid Zopilote needed the cigarettes at any price.

One day the man said to him, "You know, Kid, I can no longer sell you cigarettes."

"I always pay you for them," said Kid Zopilote.

"Yes, I know you always pay for them. But from now on you can only have them when you bring your friends here. For every friend you bring me I will give a cigarette. Is that fair?"

"Fair enough," said Kid Zopilote. So in time many young *pachucos* with zoot suits began hanging around Kaiser's. Every day new boys came and asked for the stranger and the Kaiser directed them up a little stairway to the man with free cigarettes. In time he no longer gave them. He sold them. And the guys who bought them were affected in many ways. Talaro Fernández crept on the floor like a dog. Chico Sánchez went up and down Meyer Street challenging everybody.

Gastón Fuentes opened the fly of his pants and wet the sidewalk. Kid Zopilote panted like a dog and then passed out in a little back room at Kaiser's. Even Kid Zopilote was not getting the cigarettes for nothing because in no time at all he brought in all the potential customers. He had to pay for his smokes as did everybody else. In order to get the money he went to work hustling trade for Cetrina who gave him a small percentage from her every amorous transaction. In the morning when trade was not buzzing Kid Zopilote stayed in her room and listened to dance records. When he tired of that he headed uptown to the Pastime or Kaiser's. Sometimes he walked into Robert's Café for a cup of coffee. There, when any of the squares that knew Kid Zopilote from the cradle asked him why he did not go to work, he got mad.

"Me go to work? Are you crazy? I do not want to work. Besides, I have money. I sell kick smokes and I can get you fixed up for five dollars with a *vata* that is really good looking," he said.

"That is no good. You will get into a lot of trouble eventually," they said to him.

"No, I won't. Anyway, I haven't got a damned education. I haven't got no damned nothing. But I'll make out." Then Kid Zopilote got up and snapped his fingers in beat and swayed his body as he walked out.

One day Kid Zopilote was caught in a riot involving the *pachucos* and the Mexicans from the high school whose dignities were being insulted by the fact that a few illogical people were beginning to see a zoot suit on every Mexican and every Mexican in a zoot suit. It ended up with the police intervening. The Mexicans from the high school were sent home and the *pachucos* were herded off to jail. The next day they were given free haircuts. Their drapes and pleated pants were cut with scissors. They crept home along alleys, like shorn dogs with their tails between their legs, lest people should see them.

"I am glad it happened to you, Pepe," said Señora García, "I am glad." But Kid Zopilote did not say a word. His head was as shiny as a billiard ball. His zoot suit was no more. All day he stayed at home and played his guitar. It was strange that he should like it so much, but now there was nowhere he could go without people pointing at him should he as much as go past the front door.

"Pepito," said his mother, "you play so beautifully that it makes me want to cry. You have such a musical touch, Pepe, yet you have never done anything to develop it. But you do play wonderfully, Pepe."

One day as Kid Zopilote strummed his guitar, a boy looked over the fence and said to him, "*Tocas bien*. You play very well." But Kid Zopilote said nothing. This boy looked like many of the other American boys he knew that never had anything to do with him. "I play too," continued the boy, "so I hope you will not mind if I come into your yard and play with you. I will bring my guitar and perhaps we can play together. I learned from my Mexican friends in Colorado. I am attending school here."

"You can come if you wish," said Kid Zopilote. So the boy did and in time they were good friends.

One night the boy said to Kid Zopilote, "You were not meant to be a damned *pachuco*."

"Look, I like to play the guitar in your company but I do not want you or anybody else to tell me what I should be and what I should not be," said Kid Zopilote in an angry tone.

"I am sorry. We will just let it go at that," said the boy.

So, while Kid Zopilote's hair did not grow, he spent hour after hour with his friend who was thoroughly overcome with the beauty with which Kid Zopilote executed and with the feeling he gave his music. When Kid Zopilote's hair began to respond to the comb the friend took Kid Zopilote to visit friends. They went from party to party. They played at women's luncheons. They played on radio programs. Both were summoned for any event which demanded music.

"Pepe will be the finest guitar player in the whole Southwest," said Kid Zopilote's friend.

But when Kid Zopilote's hair grew long and met in the back of his head in the shape of a duck's tail, he no longer played the guitar. Anyway, most zopilotes eat puke even when better things are available a little farther away from their beaten runways and dead trees. As Kid Zopilote's uncle had said, "A zopilote can never be a peacock." So it was. Because even if he can, he does not want to.

Southside Run

One morning a new bus headed west on Broad Street on the beginning of the Southside Run. It had green windows and was painted yellow as are all the buses belonging to the Star Bus Company. Pete Echeverría, the driver, pushed in the clutch and, stepping on the accelerator, made the new motor whine. It made the pretty counter girl inside Cariogla's Italian Bakery[26] look out the window for a second. It caused the bootblacks outside Kaiser's Shoeshine Parlor to look up from the pages of *Jazz News* and follow it. The basket boys at the Rincon Market stopped their chores momentarily to gaze at it. And so did the gentlemen of leisure who spend all their time under the shade of palms at the Plazita making thousands of dollars with their mouths. The bus proceeded past the Estrella Restaurant where Pete stuck out his gloved hand to wave at the giggling waitresses standing outside. And then it came to a stop at the intersection of Broad Street and Alamosa.

Cars with two aerials, fog lights, fox tails, mudguards, balloon tires, and rebuilt motors roared by with would-be Romeos in them. They honked loud Yankee Doodle horns. Cars with sputtering motors that had once been rebuilt and stripped of all but those essential parts of a car chugged by with ex-would-be Romeos, their wives, in-laws, and kids piled high. Pete threw the bus in gear and crossed Alamosa Street toward Pike. On the corner of Pike and Broad Street the wheels ground to a stop. Two ladies with flowers in their hair, painted lips, and jaws that went up and down as the gum they chewed became rubber, got on and the doors automatically closed.

Turning south on Pike, Pete was happiest. He drove slowly past this, the oldest part of the city. Pete's eyes left the street ahead momentarily and he let them wander up the old stone steps of the Chinese Chamber of Commerce building. Past the silent offices of the Chinese Nationalist Party.[27] Past the junk yard which many years ago was the only stable when Billy the Kid rode the purple mountains west of the town. Past the Arizona Broom Company whose proprietor has a pretty daughter. Past the Chinese Evangelical Church. And past old houses whose rough-hewed stones and out-of-date architecture tell more of a city's history than volumes of painstakingly compiled lore.

For almost two blocks there are not many houses on the west side of Pike Street. It is because off Pike the land drops abruptly to form the more immediate valley of the Santa Inez River and the inner boundary of El Hoyo. Tito Fuentes rolled down this slope one night, ended up in Albertina Cresta's back yard and in the morning found himself only in his pants, with his shoes, socks, hat, billfold, shirt, and dignity gone. This does not mean that all slopes necessarily end in holes or back yards. Tito, being romantic, could have lost everything elsewhere. But to avoid scandalizing Albertina's good name he married her. Where he rolled down a slope he now lives as close to Heaven as it is possible to be while on Earth. After all, Albertina helped him recover his dignity with the aid of her small bank account. And by marrying her hasn't Tito fulfilled another Sacrament?

Past the two blocks on Pike from where the back yards of El Hoyo are most visible there is the Pike Street Garage, a grey building with blue letters clarifying the why of its existence. With cars jacked up and their motors strewn about. With bearded mechanics in greasy overalls smoking cigarettes and wondering where to begin. Immediately past the garage is the Tiradito,[28] the wishing shrine which is said to perform miracles even though there is doubt in the minds of many as to who lies beneath the cement cross and the wax-heavy candle racks. The bus came to its next stop in front of the Sunrise Grocery. School children got off saying, "G'bye, Pete." "Come back for us, Pete." Pete nodded and said he would. Meanwhile cars chugged past him as he waited for the smallest and consequently slowest of the children to get off. Then the doors of the bus closed and Pete drove on. He glanced at the big, sad, faded-red school building where dozens and dozens of children ran after one another, shrieked, hopscotched, played marbles, and wore out shoes while waiting for the bell which would call them to classes. The school building sits exactly where there was once an immense land enclosure. On it, it is said, lived many years ago a rich Chinese land baron who went from restaurant to restaurant, from dumping area to dumping area, and collected scraps for his hundred pigs or more. Even his food he gave to the pigs. And good pigs they were for when he sold one he always received for it a good price. Under the rickety shack he lived in, situated in the very center of the enclosure, he buried the money. One day he fell ill from lack of food and was unable to get up. This was a bad thing because his weak cries could not be heard above the snorts and oinks of the pigs. So when the pigs got hungry they ate his bony carcass, pigtail and all. His ancestral philosophy had never told him of a *chicano* adage which says, "It is no crime to be a pig, only to be snouty."

Off the school grounds the land drops very jaggedly because it is where the Paradise Grove Gardens and Dam used to be. On the higher land is where the early pioneers met in gala *fiestas* that lasted weeks. On this higher land rickety carnivals set up their tents. It is where Nino Aberna, an old man with a very flat nose, now without sight or teeth, was doped for boxing matches, took on all comers, and claims he was never knocked out.

Past these grounds on Pike the bus went past many houses. Some, belonging to the occupants, have pretty gardens and very clean children who never get dirty unless the gate is left open. Other houses, occupied by tenants, have junk piled high and shrieking children who continually run into the street. The bus came to a stop on 29th Street, the end of Pike, headed west one block, and turned south on San Juan. The houses on San Juan are set apart. They are constructed within the limited architecture provided by scant savings and loans which leave very little for the intent of Spanishizing them, Mexicanizing them, Colonializing them, or Puebloizing them.[29] They are simply houses with sometimes plastered but usually unplastered exteriors. With rickety wood porches which seem about to fall the instant one's foot is set on the decaying wood. Houses with sacred interiors where the photographic history of the family is perched on a little table in the living room with the pictures of friends and sometimes favorite movie stars to give them company. Houses in which family history is well recorded in scratched walls and faded spots where the jelly left by small hands was unwisely washed off with wet rags.

Farther down on San Juan the bus came to a stop at the Modern

Housing Project, a war-inspired human beehive where everybody's
private business is public topic. Where it is known by all which house
is overflowing with goodness and which never had its share. Where
everybody knows by the aroma what the family in C-2 had for breakfast. Where everybody has disinterestedly counted how many shirts
the gent in B-9 owns while his wife wears the same washable day in and
day out. Where everybody talks of how lazy the lady in D-6 is because
she throws away good clothes instead of washing them. And where
everybody knows that the less said of the loyalty of the lady in C-8 the
better.

After the bus made its stop at the corner and a few people got off,
the bus moved on. It went very slowly past the store of Fay Wing. Vice
there is rampant. Fay, however, who has been cursed at by the wives
of the individuals who patronize his store and buy his rotgut, silently
goes on making a living even if the wives complain of seeing no part
of the men's checks. Many times the drunks come out from behind
the bushes near Fay's store, where they hide from the authorities and
their wives, and they direct the traffic. It is not rare for them to go to
sleep in the middle of the street but usually they go to sleep behind
the bushes while the hot sun beats them brown. From the street, on
certain days, the panorama there gives one a Hollywood version of a
Central American revolution because of the men strewn about as if in
eternal slumber. Dead? No. Dead drunk. With dust on their faces. With
stinking pants. Torn shirts. Heavy work shoes with strings one con-
tinuous knot. When a potential customer asks Fay Wing, "You got good
sherry wine?" Fay Wing points nonchalantly to the drunks lying about
and says, "You lookee. *Tú milando.*"[30] Fay Wing also sells Bromos.

After Fay's the bus turned west on 38th Street and went past more
houses. These, for once, the houses of independent men and women
who got tired of living in the rented houses in the center of El Hoyo.
Houses here seem to grow with the family because there is always another room under construction. Houses which have flower pots and
little pails from which extend the shade-giving leaves of sweet potato
vines. Houses from which emerge yelling children who throw rocks
at everything and everybody, and mutts that chase automobiles. And
on corners, the inevitable Chinese stores. During depressions and lean

times it is these and the bean crop that keep *chicanos* alive. In the days of old when the pig-tailed ancestors of these same storekeepers carried the beginning of their businesses on their backs, *chicanos*, who are as a rule not very good business men, hid in trees with big clubs. When the honorable ancestors went by they jumped from the trees, clubbed them, and made off with the roving grocery store's merchandise. But now their descendants, through the lure of an enchanting bit of generosity, which is thrown on top of the groceries and commonly known as *pilón*, have built the stores belonging to the Fongs, Lims, Toys. All do a slow consistent business while the Modern Markets, Super Markets, De Luxe Markets uptown go into debt and out of business.

At the railroad tracks on West 38th the bus headed south on 16th Avenue. It roared past blocks of livestock yards. It went over the cement bridge built over the dry Santa Inez River. Once again there are more houses with *comadres* sitting out in the sun combing their very long tresses or the ones of their younger daughters. Houses where *compadres* get very drunk and where the police car is ofttimes sent to pacify noisy parties. But it is also where there are little palm crosses on many of the doors. It is where the humility of men before the will of God comes before envy, malice, hate, and jealousy. It is where one is most apt to see people taking flowers, with their heads bowed and kicking dust as they go, to the houses of the newly deceased. For it is then that the friendship that existed or might have existed has its greatest worth. It is then that acquaintance has its trial of virtue. Then the houses thin out into the desert.

Pete made a "U " turn and the bus returned through all the aforementioned places. On its way it picked up many of the people going to work. It picked up Teresita who is as beautiful as any woman can be at thirty but who, to support her invalid father, has had to refuse marriage offers. The bus stopped for Tomás, an old man who will die before his small brood grows up because, loving the life and the pleasures of bachelorhood, he married too late. The bus stopped for Señora Alvedre who goes to Mass daily to thank God for the goodness of her sons who built for her a little house with tile in the kitchen and a patio overflowing with flowers. For Florencia, an old wasted woman who worked hard to support her two sons. As soon as they began working, the two acquired obligations and left her scrubbing floors for people uptown, while they make the pretense of being upright and proud men. For Armidita with her pouting little lips who is in love and supports her veteran boy friend. For Alfredito, with his sparkling eyes and black curls he is forced to brush out of his face constantly. He supports his mother by shining shoes. All of these the bus picked up and took to town for a nickel.

At night, on the last trip, Pete was a tired driver practically asleep at the wheel of the shining new bus he drove toward town for a night's rest.

Maestría

Whenever a man is referred to as a *maestro* it means that he is master of whatever trade, art, or folly he practices. If he is a shoemaker, for example, he can design, cut, and finish any kind of shoe he is asked for. If he is a musician he knows composition, direction, execution, and thereby plays Viennese waltzes as well as the *bolero*. If he is a thief he steals thousands, for he would not damn his soul by taking dimes. That is *maestría*. It is applied with equal honor to a painter, tailor, barber, printer, carpenter, mechanic, bricklayer, window washer, ditchdigger, or bootblack if his ability merits it. Of course, when a man is greying and has no apparent trade or usefulness, out of courtesy people may forget he is a loafer and will call him a *maestro*. Whether he is or not is of no importance. Calling him a *maestro* hurts no one.

During the hard times of Mexico's last revolution many *maestros* left Mexico with their families with the idea of temporarily making a living north of the Rio Grande. But the revolution lasted for such a long time that when it finally came to an end the *maestros*, now with larger families, remained here in spite of it. During the hard times of the last depression they opened little establishments on West Broad Street and North Pike where they miraculously made a dollar on some days and as many as two or three on others — always putting on, because they were used to hard times, a good face. When good times returned, most of the *maestros* closed up their little establishments and went to work for the larger concerns which came back in business. Some left for the increasing number of factory jobs in California. But some, enjoying their long independence and believing that it is better to be a poor lord than a rich servant, kept their little establishments open.

Gonzalo Pereda, for example, was a *maestro* who kept a little saddle shop open on West Broad Street. Being a great conversationalist he was not against having company at all hours. Being easy with his money he was always prey for those that told him of need in their homes. And easier prey still for those that often talked him into closing up his establishment, so that they might gossip of old times over a bottle of beer. Being a good craftsman, therefore, had never helped to give the *maestro* more than enough with which to provide for his family.

But if there were men in the world who worried about their work after being through for the day, as far as the *maestro* was concerned they deserved to die young. It certainly was not so with Gonzalo Pereda. Life, he figured, was too short anyway. When he closed up in the afternoon he rid his mind completely of jobs pending and overhead unpaid. He simply hurried home to feed his stable of fighting roosters and to eat supper with his family. Even before taking off his hat he made his way to the back yard to see that his roosters had fresh water and that their cages were clean. That the *maestro* did all of this before going in to greet his family does not mean that he liked the roosters better. But the family, now grown up and with its own affairs, could wait. The roosters, dependent on his arrival for their care, could and should not.

One day when the *maestro* came home, he found a little cage in his back yard. Attached to the top of it was a tag which read, "A present from your friend Bernabé Lerda. Chihuahua, México." In the cage was a red rooster. The *maestro* stuck his finger through an opening and had to jerk it out immediately when the rooster picked at it with a bill which seemed to be made of steel. The *maestro* took a thin leather strip from his pocket, opened the cage, and tied it to the rooster's leg. Then he took the rooster out in order to examine him carefully. The *maestro* looked closely at the rooster's long thick legs, at his tail, which by its length might have belonged to a peacock, at the murder in both of his eager eyes; and the *maestro* knew that this rooster would assassinate any unfortunate fowl pitted against him.

After gazing around a bit the little rooster stretched and strutted. He flapped his wings a few times and then he crowed. The *maestro* was amazed. How could it be, he asked himself, that an animal could possess such pomp? How was it that he knew he was a better rooster than any other that had ever emerged from a hen's egg and therefore strutted about like a race horse confident of winning the Kentucky Derby? How did he know he was such a handsome example of chicken-hood that he, without doubt, could be the Valentino of any chicken yard?

Well, it was unbelievable, but it was so. And the *maestro* was sure that this rooster, being from Mexico no less, would slash his way to thirty victories once they put him in the pit. A few minutes later, when one of the *maestro*'s sons saw the rooster, both decided that he must have a worthy name: they decided to call him *Killer*.

So great a stir did Killer cause that the *maestro* forgot all about eating supper that night. While he watched admiringly, Killer took his time about eating his grain and drinking his cool water. One would have thought that the *maestro* could aliment himself by merely gazing at the conceited rooster as he strutted about. The *maestro* said, "The minute he goes into the pit the other rooster will drop dead from fright. Just look at the beautiful creature."

And so it was. The following Sunday afternoon the *maestro* burst in through the front door with Killer. Killer was still hot under the wings from having chased the other rooster and then having slashed it to ribbons. He was still kicking inside the cage as if asking for all the roosters who ever sported a gaff to take him on. "You should have seen him," said the *maestro* to his wife. "Killer is the greatest rooster that ever lived." Then he took Killer to the back yard to cool off.

During the night there was big commotion in the yard. Killer had gotten out of his cage and was attacking the other roosters through the wire fronts of their cages. Already, in a minute or so, there was blood in front of the cage belonging to a rooster named General, who had retreated to the back of his cage for safety. Killer was squaring off, with his neck feathers ruffled, at another cage, in an effort to pick out the eyes of a rooster named Diablo. "He is really cute, isn't he?" asked the *maestro*. Then he took Killer and holding him said, "Well, I guess it is only natural for him to want to fight. He had no competition this afternoon." When Killer was put in another cage, the *maestro* and his son went back to bed.

After the Killer's second fight, the following Sunday, the *maestro* once again came in through the front door with Killer. This time Killer had disposed of his adversary in less than two minutes. The *maestro* was happy. "I am convinced," he said, "that Killer is a butcher if there ever was one." And in victory the *maestro* brought Killer through the front door after the third, fourth, and fifth fight. Now, of course, Killer traveled to and from the pit in style. His was a big cage, made and de-signed to give him a lot of comfort, with letters reading, "Killer."

On the Sunday that Killer won his sixth fight the *maestro* was so happy when he brought Killer through the front door for his wife to ad-mire that tears came from his eyes as he said, "Every rooster that sees this champion can say that the Devil has taken him." And on that day Killer established himself firmly as the best rooster that had ever come to fall in the *maestro*'s possession. This Sunday, after all, had been a great one for the *maestro*, financially speaking and otherwise.

The following Sunday the *maestro* got up very early. Before his daughter left for church he had her take out the camera in order to photograph Killer. The picture that came out best would be sent away to *Hook and Gaff*, a magazine dedicated to cockfights and poultry. They photographed Killer from various angles. In the arms of the *maestro*. Perched on top of a pole. Looking into a hen roost.

But that afternoon, after the fight, the *maestro* did not storm through the front door to tell how Killer had all but peeled and removed the en-trails from the opposing rooster. The *maestro* hurried around the side of the house to the back yard with Killer in his hands. Killer, the in-vincible one, had met its match. After six battles had come his Water-loo. The reason that Killer was not dead was because the *maestro* had stopped the fight and forfeited his bet. But Killer seemed more dead than alive. His bill was open as if to force breath into his lungs. One of his wings was almost torn off. His back was deeply gashed. One of his eyes was closed. The *maestro* worked frantically to keep Killer alive. He put flour under the torn wing. He took a damp rag and wiped the blood off Killer's head. The *maestro* looked as though he had lost his best friend.

For many days the Killer did not eat. He only stood, and weakly, on his long, thick legs. The *maestro* came home many times to take care of him. He brought Killer some baby-chicken feed in order that he might eat something when he recuperated enough to open his eyes. But to no avail. The *maestro*'s gladiator still seemed close to death.

Then, of a sudden, Killer got better. He began to pick at the baby-chicken feed. And the *maestro* was overwhelmed with joy. Killer did not strut as before, or crow, or flap his wings, but he would, in time. Many things, the *maestro* often said, were fixed by time alone.

Toward the end of Killer's convalescence the *maestro* felt proud of the job he had done in rescuing the Killer from death. As a finishing touch he decided to give the rooster, who was beginning to act somewhat like the Killer of old, some little pieces of liver. These would give him more blood. So, while the *maestro*'s son opened Killer's bill, the *maestro* pushed a little piece of liver down Killer's throat. But the second piece caused Killer to gurgle, to kick momentarily, and then suddenly to die in the *maestro*'s hands. With tears in his eyes the *maestro* stroked his beloved Killer, bit his lip as he wrapped the limp body of his Spartan in a newspaper, and tenderly put it in the garbage can. Then, without supper, the *maestro* went to bed. His beloved Killer was gone.

Like Killer's plight, it might be added, is the plight of many things the *maestros* cherish. Each year they hear their sons talk English with a rapidly disappearing accent, that accent which one early accustomed only to Spanish never fails to have. Each year the *maestros* notice that their sons' Spanish loses fluency. But perhaps it is natural. The *maestros* themselves seem to forget about bulls and bullfighters, about guitars and other things so much a part of the world that years ago circumstance forced them to leave behind. They hear instead more about the difference between one baseball swing and another. Yes, perhaps it is only natural.

Ofttimes when *maestros* get together they point out the fact that each year there are less and less of their little establishments around. They proudly say that the old generation was best; that the new generation knows nothing. They point out, for example, that there are no shoemakers any more. They say that the new generation of so-called shoemakers are nothing but repairers of cheap shoes in need of half soles. They say that the musicians are but accompanists who learned to play an instrument in ten lessons and thus take money under false pretenses. Even the thieves, they tell you, are nothing but two-bit clips. The less said about other phases of *maestría*, they will add, the better.

When one of the *maestros* dies, all the other *maestros* can be counted upon to mourn him. They dust off the dark suits they seldom wear, and offer him, with their calloused hands folded in prayer, a Rosary or two. They carry his coffin to and from the church. And they help fill his grave with the earth that will cover him thereafter. Then they silently know the reason why there are not so many of the little establishments as before. Perhaps it is natural. There are not so many *maestros* any more.

Mexican Heaven

El Barrio's[31] inhabitants, with very few exceptions, are a very pious lot. On Sundays and days of obligation the Mexican that does not attend the services is rare. On the walls of all Mexican homes crucifixes and religious pictures can always be seen. However, this does not keep Mexicans from criticizing, but always in tender tones, their parish priests, usually Spaniards or Latin Americans who present the word of God with near comic eloquence.

One day, many years ago, a young priest fresh from the seminary was assigned to the parish. To all appearances he was one of those priests usually assigned to churches uptown. And in churches uptown, most Mexicans feel, the priests, not being Spaniards or Latin Americans, perform ecclesiastic ritual too methodically to suit the Mexican temperament, not to say anything about how insipidly the sermon is presented. So, when the young priest, whose name was Father Raymond, said his first Masses in his newly learned seminary Spanish, many a Mexican was halfway out of the church long before he was ready to recite the final prayers.

However, Father Raymond, who in his seminary days had often dreamed of becoming at least a bishop, resolved to do something about it. By frequenting every kind of Mexican occasion possible in order to learn the true character of his parishioners, by crying, at first, at the infamy of the hot sauce he was served when he ate Mexican food in one of their homes, and by listening to the strains of Mexican music whenever the opportunity presented itself, he soon became quite Mexican. And the Mexicans, at length, forgot his name was Father Raymond and called him, to make the transformation complete, Padre Ramón.

Thus it was that Padre Ramón often went hunting with some of the young men of the parish while other priests, on their days off, played golf. He accompanied them on one occasion to the nearby border town, at their long insistence, to see a bullfight.[32] He got into discussions of philosophy and theology with old-timers who, at least in the beginning, delighted in making him appear the loser of a friendly argument and sent him back to the rectory determined to probe into his reading so as not to be caught without resources when the same problem came up again.

After two decades, when his hairline began to recede and when he began to put on weight, Padre Ramón was considered one of the parish's permanent fixtures. Already his life was so given to his immediate duties that the thoughts of attaining ecclesiastic prominence no longer entered his mind. And as far as his parishioners were concerned, though it was said that he made sinners shiver in the confessional booth, Padre Ramón, with all due respect, was the apostle next to God.

Whenever an infant son or daughter was taken to him for baptism, the proud father always said to Padre Ramón afterwards, "Well, Padre, you will have to go to our house for a little toast. We will be expecting you." And all loved the fact that to Padre Ramón an extended invitation was a certain acceptance.

When it was time for the young Mexicans of the parish to receive catechism lessons prior to making their First Communion, it was Padre Ramón who supervised the after-school classes where, besides seeing that they gave good ear to the Our Fathers, Hail Marys, Ten Commandments, and the Act of Contrition, he saw to it that they did not raid the school desks of the regularly enrolled Catholic school students. During bad times it was he that solicited personally from business men the new overalls and white shirts with which, months later, his Mexicanitos, with grave looks on their faces, went in a group to receive the Holy Host for the first time.

When a Mexican got married it was always Padre Ramón who tied the bonds of matrimony for the couple. Following the ceremony a reception without him was incomplete, so Padre Ramón was often forced, in order that nobody would feel hurt, to suspend other duties and to go for his chocolate and cake and glass of wine. There grooms often said, "As soon as my *vieja*[33] gives me some sons I will go see you, Padre. *Ande*,[34] drink another glass to us." And, maintaining his ecclesiastic dignity, he always did.

However, the duty most trying for Padre Ramón was the administering of Extreme Unction. Many times he had to succor Mexicans that he had known personally. And in the completion of this great duty, Padre Ramón was often up at late hours. His greatest heartbreak came when he arrived too late to fulfill his mission and had to stay to comfort the newly deceased one's family.

One rainy night Padre Ramón was called to administer Extreme Unction to a dying man who lived in a lion's den near the edge of town. Now, a lion's den is an old garage or deserted house which serves as shelter for a happy-go-lucky group of individuals referred to as *winos* by the rest of the world. For food they prey on the neighbors' chickens. For love they seek out lonely but passionate divorcees. They only go to work long enough to buy a red wine costing 87 cents a gallon. And all sleep around an old stove on discarded blankets, rags, or an occasional mattress rescued from the city dump.

When Padre Ramón got to the door of the garage, he was met by an old man who said, "He really did not want us to call you, Padre, but we thought it would be best."

Padre Ramón barely heard this when from inside, amid a roar of horrendous coughing, a defiant voice angrily shouted, "If you brought a Padre, tell him to take himself far away from here."

"That is what I mean, Padre, he has been carrying on like that for days. He is defiant of all."

"What happened?" asked Padre Ramón.

"He had tuberculosis and now pneumonia has come. The doctor came and said that there was no hope." Then Padre Ramón and the old man went inside.

When the sick young man, bathed in perspiration, lying on an old mattress, wrapped up in dirty blankets, and in the company of some friends about him, saw Padre Ramón before him, he said bitterly, "Go away, Padre. I want nothing from you. Go aw—" The young man began to cough so violently that Padre Ramón could not but kneel and offer him, though he was sure it would do no good, some medicine from a bottle nearby.

"But why?" asked Padre Ramón, on realizing that the young man's life could no longer be saved. "Why do you want to deny your soul the Sacraments?"

"Padre, why?" asked the young man, looking with searching eyes at

Padre Ramón, amid coughs and violent gasps for air. "Why, if the God
which we must love and whose laws we must obey is so just, why does
He do this to me? I do not want to die. Do you understand? Why then,
does He do this to me?"

"The ways of God are often mysterious. But as He gives us life, so
He takes it from us," explained Padre Ramón. "And when He does, it
is good that we should return to Him in a state of grace."

The young man coughed violently and then shivered. Padre Ramón,
feeling that the young man's hour was near, said, "*Anda*, we must do
His will."

"But I still do not understand, Padre, why He is taking my life. I,
who have never spoken His name in vain, who never failed to be moved
by the beauty of His works. I do not understand," said the young man.
He coughed violently for a while and then said, "Never having been an
ambitionist, Padre, I never stepped all over my fellow man in order to
gain what I did not really need. Therefore, except on insignificant occa-
sions, never did I ever lie and cheat. Because I never was an *igualado*[35]
who thinks that what God did not mean for me I should take by force,
I have never coveted anybody else's possessions. I was always happy
with those things that God put within my reach."

Padre Ramón swallowed hard. The young man coughed and the
perspiration seemed to smother him. Then, with tears in his eyes, the
young man continued, "True, Padre, I do not mean to say that I have
been perfect. Often, when I was hungry, I stole chickens for my friends
and myself. But I stole them from the Mexican Consul who, in order
not to make Mexicans look bad in the eyes of the law, never reported
his loss. Also, mine have been many women. But only after making
sure that my affairs with them could pervert them no more than they
already were. And, many times have I been drunk. But never to any
great degree since I have never had much money. Then I got sick. Alas,
Padre, not even to the Virgin of Guadalupe, the patroness of all Mexicans, do I now say a prayer. And now you know, since I am going to die
so young, why I want you to go away and let me die in peace."

"But," said Padre Ramón, "perhaps your good faith in the Almighty
will be taken into consideration. Come, let us go ahead, that your soul
may be saved—"

"Yes, Padre," interrupted the young man, "many times have I heard pretty words. But how can you expect me, who was only starting to live, to want to die? What could I find in Heaven, even should I go there, that compares to what I know and cherish. To this gay Mexican music I love to hear, to these dark-eyed girls which are to my mind the sweetest creatures on the face of the earth, and—" The young man coughed and coughed. Then he lay back and took his eyes off Padre Ramón.

"Of course," said Padre Ramón, "since we have every assurance that the Kingdom of Heaven is the finest of all, I do not think it wrong to assume that it borrows some of El Barrio's finest aspects and even improves on them."

The young man coughed and then asked, "What do you mean, Padre?"

"Oh," said Padre Ramón, trying to comfort the young man now so obviously close to his hours of agony, "that if God meant for you to be one of the chosen, you may well see, on getting to the Gates of Heaven, that Saint Peter is guarding them attired in Mexican *charro* suit and a big sombrero. After presenting your worthy credentials and entering, I am sure that the first thing that will come to your ears is the music which you love so much. It will sound day and night from the melodic guitars of Mexican angels. There the beer you love will flow, God permitting, in golden rivers. And wine in deep lakes and well fermented, not made in test tubes like some of the stuff one often buys around here. As for the dark-eyed girls you adore, surely they will be just as pretty and sweet in Heaven, and you can rest assured that up there they will never grow old and fat, and never become mothers-in-law. You will be able to ride with them on flying serapes . . ."

The young man's face was now turned toward the padre.

"And there, I assure you," continued Padre Ramón, moved by his own eloquence, "every meal will be a banquet. There will be plates upon plates of hot enchiladas. There will be tasty Mexican tacos, and with much more meat than any you ever ate. The tortillas, that Mexican form of bread which we all love, will be bigger and softer. The tamales, once in a while here stuffed with veal, I am sure will be stuffed with filet mignon in Heaven. And the beans, those beloved frijoles which are the necessity of every Mexican's table, will be fried in butter and cheese. The green chili sauce will be so tasty that even though you will be crying as you eat it, you will be licking your fingers. And—"

The young man, wide-eyed now, halfway sat up and bending his head humbly before Padre Ramón, said, "Padre, if you will, would you proceed, that I too, perhaps—"

Hours later, after confessing a few sins, receiving his last Holy Host, and with a little print of the Virgin of Guadalupe in his hands which Padre Ramón had given him, the young man died. And Padre Ramón, with a heavy heart, bade farewell to the young man's friends and returned to the rectory to say a rosary for the soul he had humbly tried to prepare for the Creator.

Las comadres

Whenever two *chicanos* find that they have many things in common, they often end up baptizing each other's children and becoming *compadres*. If they work together, one *compadre* will often say to the other for all to hear, "*Compadre*, you are the best boilermaker in Arizona. Tell them who is number two." If they drink together it means they constantly seek each other's company, share the most intimate of secrets, and even cry over their beers, at least until they become co-signers. All of this automatically makes their wives *comadres*. When two *comadres* meet, no matter how much they criticize one another behind each other's back, they hug one another as though they had not seen each other for years. Then they sit down somewhere and talk over the latest *mitote*, gossip, flying over El Hoyo's back fences.

In the late 20's two *comadres*, escaping the crowded tenements on Alvarado Street, bought adjoining lots in El Hoyo and in time moved into half-finished adobe structures. One of these, Anastacia Elizondo, was a stout *comadre* with four daughters and a husband named Lazarillo[36] who worked for the railroad and who, it was known to everybody, beat her up now and then for being a lousy housekeeper. The other, Lola López, was a *comadre* who, to escape the city laundry, had converted her front room into a store where she eked out a living by selling the five cents of yellow cheese, the ten cents of beans, and the *chango*[37] coffee. She had two young sons, Tino and Kiko, as well as a husband named Nacho who constantly complained of the ailments he had incurred in a fall while building the house and therefore could not work but always came home drunk to serenade his Lola, as well as the neighbors, at daybreak.

Whenever Anastacia got one of her beatings she immediately ran next door to her *comadre* Lola with tears welling from her eyes to bubble, "*Me p-pegó*. He . . . He b-beat me, *c-comadre*. Wh-what am I t-do?"

"Oh, he will change, Anastacia. He will change," comforted Lola. "I am sure of it."

"Wh-what a m-miserable cr-creature I am," sobbed Anastacia. "I wish I were d-dead."

In the ensuing years, though the rest of the world was to experience such far reaching events as the stock market crash, the end of prohibition, a cruel depression, and the rise of Schicklgruber,[38] the human condition of El Hoyo and its inhabitants remained very much the same. True, a decade and a half had given Anastacia a slight down over her upper lip along with a few more pounds. However, her bad housekeeping habits continued, along with her usual beatings. Lola, in turn, had enlarged her store and ran it with the help of her two sons. She was still serenaded by the ever ailing Nacho at daybreak. Meanwhile, Anastacia's oldest daughter Maria Luisa and Lola's son Tino, who had scratched, bit, and kicked one another in the days when Anastacia came over after one of her beatings and who saw one another through the years with the familiarity of brother and sister, came to fall in love, an event which, once realized, was obvious and final.

Hitler's march, however, could not but have repercussions felt all the way to El Hoyo. And, long before the Japanese bombed Pearl Harbor, the ensuing trickle, then river, of money which found its way to El Hoyo via the air base, increased railroad activity, an aircraft plant, and ultimately allotment checks, was such that even the spirit of *comadreada* underwent a change. Soon *comadres* who had known each for years, on installing inside plumbing, suddenly turned their faces and put their noses in the air when they chanced on one another in the street. Other *comadres*, buying chenille bed spreads and venetian blinds for the first time, soon said of other *comadres* not yet as fortunate. "Ay, those peoples. *Esa gente*. They do not know how to live." And still other *comadres*, moving out of El Hoyo, thanks to their husbands' steady encounter with the time clock, went as far as to say, "El Hoyo. Where is that?" The sickness even afflicted a few *compadres*.

Through all of this Anastacia, considering herself a very level headed person, merely said to her *comadre* Lola, "Ay, *comadre*. What liars some women are. They have much more tongue than sense. As for me, you know how my Lazarillo has always earned his good checks, especially now that he often works double shifts. Yet never have I given to bragging."

Lola merely nodded and said nothing.

One night Lazarillo's rage was so great on finding that his food was not ready when he came home from a long shift that he blackened one of Anastacia's eyes. Immediately Anastacia ran next door to her *comadre* Lola with tears welling from her eyes. "He has tr-tried t-to k-kill me," she cried. "Ay, *comadre*. What am I t-to do?"

Lola, often tempted to tell Anastacia to correct her housekeeping habits, merely said, "Oh, he will change."

However, the following beatings Anastacia received were so violent that she decided on separation. She cashed in a few war bonds and, with her daughters in tow, moved far away from El Hoyo and her tormenting husband Lazarillo. For a long time nobody saw or heard much of Anastacia. *Mitote* had it, however, that she was now working at the air base and had dyed her hair. And, *mitote* had it that one day she was overheard saying to another *comadre* who had also moved out of El Hoyo, "Ay, how good it feels to live away from El Hoyo, away from so many low class people. I am so glad my daughters now live away from there and will never marry beneath their class." As to her *comadre* Lola, Anastacia had been known to answer when asked about her, "I am sorry, *pero yo* . . . I do not know any Lola López."

Anastacia's daughter María Luisa, however, kept on seeing Lola's Tino in spite of her mother's advice until the day Uncle Sam greeted him and gave him travel orders. Anastacia, overjoyed, sighed with relief and said, "Thank God he is gone. I am sure any daughter of mine can do better than to keep company with the son of an ex-laundry worker." But María Luisa, having given her beloved Tino the greatest proof of her love to take with him . . .

Months later . . . when it was obvious, Anastacia became indignant. She cried. She cursed. She threatened to kill herself. "But what will your father say? What of our neighbors? What of . . ."

"I don't care about the neighbors, *mamá*," replied María Luisa. "As for my father, I already told him."

"You what?" asked Anastacia, shocked.

"I phoned him and told him," said María Luisa, matter of factly. "All he asks is that I be a good wife."

Once again Anastacia cried, cursed, threatened to kill herself. But, realizing it was to no avail, the embossed invitations went out the minute Tino phoned informing María Luisa the dates of his leave.

On the morning the young couple emerged from the cathedral as man and wife, Anastacia, in white satin, white gloves, and a gigantic hat, excitedly went about her new friends, among them many Smiths and Hendersons, assuring them that her new son-in-law was of the most excellent family, scarcely noticing the presence of the *comadre* Lola and her *compadre* Nacho, both of these awed by the magnificence of the affair. At the reception, held at Anastacia's fashionable apartment rather than at Lola's house in El Hoyo as tradition dictated, it happened that María Luisa's corsets did their job so well that, to the surprise of the select guests, the bride's labor pangs began and even before she could be helped to the bedroom, nature relieved the bride of a screaming, kicking *chicano*. In the excitement the young priest who had arrived at the house for his chocolate and cake could do no more than to start to make a half hearted effort to preach about sin. But with Anastacia crying, then fainting, the guests in a state of exhilaration and disbelief, and the affair in a general state of confusion, he smiled inwardly and poured himself some whiskey from a nearby bottle. To have been heard above all the commotion he would have needed a bigger set of lungs.

Late that afternoon, the petals of María Luisa's bridal bouquet still fragrant, found Anastacia in El Hoyo, crying inconsolably on her *comadre* Lola's shoulder. "What a miserable creature I am, *comadre*. Today has been the most tragic day of my life. How I wish I were dead."

"Tragic? On the contrary," said Lola. "I think this day has been a very memorable one for both of us. We are both now mothers-in-law, grandmothers as well as *comadres*. And, because we are now more than *comadres*, I must tell you it would be best if you moved back to your house. Lazarillo is still there. I am sure he misses you though it is said you have forgotten him."

"Bad tongues, *comadre*. Bad tongues.[39] I have never forgotten my beloved Lazarillo. Ay, *comadre*. What would I ever do without you?"

That very night, under cover of darkness, Anastacia and her daughters were back in El Hoyo. But if Lazarillo had once rained blows on her, more to Anastacia's dismay, he was now indifferent. Every day Lazarillo got up, ate in silence, and went to work. Even though he often came home past midnight, Anastacia now had his food ready, not to mention the great care she took to wash his clothes, clean the house. Still Lazarillo remained indifferent.

"*Qué haré?*" asked Anastacia, crying on her *comadre*'s shoulder. "What shall I do?"

"All you can do is cook his food, prepare his clothes, and clean the house as you are doing," said Lola. "He will change."

"Alas, *comadre*," sighed Anastacia, the tears running down her cheeks. "I fear I have lost his love. How I wish I were dead."

A few weeks later, however, most of El Hoyo was awakened one night by wails, cries, and crashing furniture. For a while it seemed as though somebody was being murdered. A few *comadres* maliciously even thought of phoning the police because a good scandal would provide *mitote* for weeks. But nobody did and in a few hours all was peaceful again.

Our *comadre* Anastacia, lying in bed with a pair of black eyes and her hair dishevelled, bubbled on her pillow. As she heard her *comadre* Lola's Nacho start her serenade a few windows away, Anastacia breathed deeply of El Hoyo's cool summer air and sighed dreamily. Then she gently scratched her own Lazarillo's shoulder and asked, "Are you awake, my love?"

Los coyotes

In El Hoyo, when an individual devotes himself to arranging the immigration status of others, he is referred to as a *coyote*. Everybody knows that the immigration business, la *"migra,"* is full of opportunities for graft and outright blackmail. If an individual is a farm labor contractor he is also a *coyote*. Delivering the hungry and the desperate to known degradation and exploitation, how could he be anything but? In fact, if an individual works with a pencil . . . But why go on? *Coyotes* insist that there is *coyotada* right down the line to the pick and shovel.

Many years ago, during a depression which reduced many a *coyote* to work the streets selling his treasure maps, a massive individual named Casimiro Ancheta arrived in El Hoyo. Because of his striking appearance, Casimiro was soon able to win the hand of Agripina, a working widow whose large family refused to accept him as a stepfather and then persisted, long after a quick marriage, to insult him, to question his character, to threaten him, and to make remarks about his appetite. Casimiro smarted under the constant barrage of insults, threats, and remarks but stood his ground. After all, Casimiro said in his defense, he was a general in the Mexican army. He was waiting for the true Mexican revolution to vindicate him as soon as the traitors and torturers of Mexican liberty who now had the upper hand were overthrown. Then he would go back to Mexico to resume his command, back to his homes and lands, back to his . . . Naturally, he would take Agripina with him.

Meanwhile having little to do, it did not take Casimiro Ancheta very long to meet and become the friend of Pancho Pérez, a thin moribund appearing individual who had made his front room into an office and hung out a sign—Notary. However, since being a notary was neither remunerative nor time consuming, Pancho was also in the *reina* business, that of electing queens for the Sixteenth of September and the Fifth of May, Mexico's two most glorious national holidays.

Whenever Casimiro dropped by his friend Pancho's office, by the time he had had his numerous cups of coffee and wiped clean a couple of plates of *pan dulce*, sweet bread, the conversation ultimately led to the subject of oppression, on both sides of the border. "Damn, Pancho, how I hate the cursed *coyotes* who thrive on our beloved, long suffering race. Always they are sucking the blood of the weak and the trusting, disregarding all morality and justice. Just the other day I saw Anacleto[40] Moreno putting on the airs of a decent man when everybody knows the foul source of his wealth."

"Alas, my esteemed Casimiro, what you say is tragic but true. The world seems to only applaud insincerity and false appearances. Truth and justice are dead," said Pancho, gazing sadly at a picture of Benito Juárez framed on one wall and then at a picture of Porfirio Díaz framed on the other.[41]

"Still, Pancho, I will never allow such a sad state of affairs to defeat me. There will come a day when the forces of truth and justice will carry the day," said Casimiro, reaching for the last piece of sweet bread on the plate in front of him. "Great forces."

Whether the forces which gathered all over the world and those which rose to oppose them stood for truth and justice is a matter of geography. However, after the Imperial Navy bombed Pearl Harbor, El Hoyo's fathers and sons flocked to the colors, some drawn by posters and others ensnared by the local draft board. In addition, a war plant to make bombers was set up and an air base mushroomed in the desert to train pilots and crews. In the ensuing labor scarcity even Casimiro and Pancho found jobs standing behind a supply window checking out tools at the war plant.

Now, while Pancho Pérez might have been satisfied with the novelty of a constant paycheck and be content to check out tools for the duration of the war, such was not the case with Casimiro Ancheta. From the checkout window Casimiro could not help but notice, and not without envy, the numerous raffles, lotteries, and pools going on before his very eyes. It was then that his feet began to hurt. In fact, on hearing of shortages, rationing, hoarding, and then thinking of the logical speculation, Casimiro's feet not only hurt but the pains shot up his legs, his spine. Thus Casimiro knew the opportune moment for helping his beloved, long suffering race had arrived. He said to Pancho, "The moment has arrived, firm comrade, when we must start to fight for El Hoyo's heroes on the home front. We must organize in order to help our race to have the true representation it justly deserves. Only that way can we guarantee all our heroes a job as well as unlimited opportunities when they return from the fields of battle."

"Well said," responded Pancho. "But how?"

"By starting an organization, my esteemed, an organization we can hand over to our heroes when they return. That is my dream."

The plan set, for a whole week Casimiro and Pancho went about El Hoyo inviting every Christian wife and mother to attend the initial meeting. And, the sincerity of their plea was so touching that Pancho's office, bedrooms, kitchen, and back yard proved small for the crowd. Then Pancho, calling for everyone's attention, welcomed the assembled and introduced Casimiro Ancheta, whose brilliant idea had brought them together. The latter got up and after thanking Pancho Pérez, outlined his proposal for bringing civil light and political prestige to El Hoyo. In a long and impassioned speech ringing with the words faith, trust, unity, and strength, Casimiro, choking with emotion, beseeched the assembled wives and mothers for support. It was the only way, he assured them, of attaining political power and economic security for El Hoyo's husbands and sons fighting abroad. When Casimiro was through, the assembled wives and mothers clapped and cheered. And that very night the Alliance of Mexican-American Christian Wives and Mothers was formed, with Casimiro Ancheta and Pancho Pérez, naturally, being named president and vice president by acclamation.

In a short time, so great did the burdens of office become that Casimiro and Pancho left their jobs at the war plant to dedicate themselves body and soul to their mission. At meetings Casimiro and Pancho constantly assured the wives and mothers that that very morning special letters had been sent to General MacArthur and General Eisenhower personally, asking them to take good care of El Hoyo's fathers and sons. When an allotment check failed to arrive in time, it was always Pancho Pérez who looked into the matter. When a promotion was given or a leave was granted, Casimiro's great influence was no doubt responsible. So trusted did Casimiro and Pancho become, that contributions, dues, and assessments were unflinchingly given by the Alliance of Mexican-American Christian Wives and Mothers for everything from building a clubhouse for the returning heroes to saying masses for the unfortunate ones who remained buried in far away battlefields or returned in caskets. So great did Casimiro and Pancho come to loom in the lives of the Alliance wives and mothers that more than one found herself looking into the faces of Casimiro and Pancho with moist eyes and saying, "I will light a candle for each of you."

All of this dedication, naturally, was not without its rewards. Casimiro Ancheta, like a true general, was seen everywhere squiring manicured and perfumed *mosquitas muertas*[42] from Mexico which he promptly introduced as his nieces. Pancho Pérez, in turn, bought a fashionable house in the east side of town where *chicanos* were normally excluded and in all circumstances whispered about. And, being the guests of honor at so many testimonials, the politicians could not fail but take notice and, for fear of retribution at the polls, made sure that Casimiro and Pancho were present at all public functions, representing, naturally, the interests of the Alliance of Mexican-American Christian Wives and Mothers. Then came the bombs on Hiroshima and Nagasaki . . .

When the returning husbands and sons found out their allotment checks and money orders had been disappearing in the form of contributions, dues, quotas, and assessments, they shouted angrily, "Get out of that silly club." Others said, "Can't you see that those two are nothing but a pair of swindlers?" And still others simply said, "Those two *coyotes* really found themselves a nest of suckers." When the rumors of dissatisfaction reached Casimiro and Pancho's ears, they shrugged them off as *celitos*, jealousy. When vile insults about their ancestry were shouted at them, Casimiro and Pancho muttered, "Bolsheviks."

In no time at all the membership of the Alliance of Mexican-American Christian Wives and Mothers declined to a few dozen of the humbler and less informed wives and mothers whose luck it was to have husbands or sons still abroad or awaiting discharge. True, no longer were Casimiro and Pancho able to assess the club's hundreds of members a dollar in order to send an unfortunate gold star mother a five dollar bouquet of flowers. No longer were they able to collect fifty cents from each member in order to have a six dollar mass said for a fallen son or missing husband. But, with the membership falling off, by increasing the dues and assessments, the contributions and the quotas, and by giving dances to further the *veterano* cause, Casimiro kept meeting the payments on the many accounts he had opened for his many nieces and Pancho Pérez kept up the payments on his home.

One night Casimiro and Pancho sat in a little restaurant bewailing the proliferation of veterans clubs when they overheard a veteran say "Damn, that Casimiro and Pancho must have really cleaned up while we were away. Some wives and mothers say that they even signed over allotment checks to them, to be kept in trust. Can you imagine?" "I sure wish I could see the Alliance of Mexican-American Christian Wives and Mothers' books," said another. "I'll bet . . ."

Casimiro swallowed hard. To hear one's ancestry dishonored was one thing, but to speak of books and records . . . He lowered his head and said to his companion, "Alas, Pancho, they do not trust us. I think perhaps it would be best to disband the club."

"But we have gone too far for that," said Pancho. "I, for one, have many obligations. Anyway, haven't we been told that bingo will soon be legalized? I'll bet we can . . ."

"Didn't you hear?" asked Casimiro. "They spoke of the books. You were the one who kept them . . ."

"WE," said Pancho. "WE. Don't you forget that. Both our signatures are on everything."

Casimiro slid down in his chair. "Keep your voice down," he said. "Whisper."

That very night, into the offices of the Alliance of Mexican-American Christian Wives and Mothers, two lone figures crept through opposite doors. Both quietly made their way to the desk where the box containing the books and the records of the contributions, dues, quotas, and assessments were kept. Soon there was a scuffle, a knocking down of tables and chairs, a series of groans and grunts. A sleeping drunk was aroused and in the darkness ran into a parked patrol car, arousing a sleeping patrolman. By the time the drunk and patrolman arrived at the Alliance of Mexican-American Christian

Wives and Mothers Club House and switched on the lights, Casimiro and Pancho were sitting opposite each other, panting like mountain climbers and too tired to move a muscle. Casimiro, scratched, uncombed, and disheveled, said, "W-w-we j-j-just f-fought a p-pair of th-thieves m-m-mak-k-king off w-with our c-cash b-box and r-records."

"Y-y-yes. Th-thieves," added Pancho Pérez.

The following day the newspapers carried a full account of the affair as well as pictures. Casimiro, resembling a well fed convict, and Pancho, resembling an assassin, were written up as two heroes who had almost foiled a pair of robbers' plans. When the *americanos* read the papers and saw the pictures, they said with slight smiles, "Mexican business."

Chicanos reading the papers muttered, "*Cabrones.*"[43] In their wrath some swore to . . . Others vowed to . . .

In any case, for a long time nobody saw hide or hair of Casimiro Ancheta and Pancho Pérez. Rumor had it that they had skipped the country, that they were hiding, that they were dead. Alas, passions cool and . . .

Months later, Casimiro sat in Pancho's office having his usual coffee and *pan dulce*. In a few hours his beloved Agripina would be home from work and this being her pay day, Casimiro had decided on supper at La Golondrina Restaurant and a Mexican movie. "Alas," sighed Casimiro. "Agripina is the love of my life." Pancho, in turn, was bemoaning the great number of queen candidates for the approaching Sixteenth of September. "To have so many queens robs the patriotic festivities of their significance," said Pancho. "I maintain that there should be but one queen."

In time the conversation turned to the subject of oppression and specially to a *coyote* named Carlos Vega who had cashed checks for wetbacks during the war, had reaped a fortune, and was now the business agent for the laborer's local. Carlos had naturally joined forces with another *coyote* named Julio Palafox, an ex-bootlegger who now had a very thriving "*migra*" office uptown. Caught between these two coyotes a victim . . . Thus Carlos and Julio had become the darlings of incumbent as well as aspiring politicians. Lately they were engaged in forming the League of Mexican-American Clubs for Political Progress. "If they suc-

ceed in uniting the clubs, do you realize the killing they will make?"
asked Casimiro. "God help our race from ever uniting under two such
immoral, criminal scoundrels."

"Alas," sighed Pancho. "I don't get mad because they do it. It's just
that . . . they don't invite."

The Migrant

It was still dark when the food truck arrived at Williams Farms, Camp Three, causing the dogs in the vicinity to start a round of barking. The driver maneuvered the truck into a clearing between two rows of shacks and parked. He turned off the motor and lights, honked a couple of times, and then got out to remove the sides of the truck to display his merchandise and wait for customers.

Very slowly the women of the camp emerged from their shacks, many in housecoats, some already in work clothes, to buy the over-ripe fruit, vegetables, and assorted cans as well as the fading baloney, cheese, and day-old bread. Teófilo Vargas, who had been lying awake most of the night, fully dressed on some boards which served as his bed, walked out of his shack, took his place among the customers, and bought a loaf of bread and some slices of baloney, his ration for the day. He treated himself to a large cup of coffee and then walked back to his shack.

Seated on a wooden crate, Teófilo slowly drank his coffee. Meanwhile, the barking of dogs gradually became distant, isolated. In the slowly receding darkness the cries of demanding infants and the shouts of waking children began to compete with radios suddenly turned on at full blast. Momentarily Teófilo thought of his own children, his daughter Adriana, his son . . . At the moment Teófilo thought of his son, he was jolted back to reality. The grief he had brought on his own family was his fault, nobody else's. Teófilo swallowed hard and closed his eyes with the determination of one who would shut out his past, present, and future. At dawn, his food supply carefully put away, Teófilo padlocked his shack and walked to a nearby ravine and eased himself. Then, with the sun coming over the horizon, he slowly walked to the fields to get a sack in order to start up and down the rows of cotton.

The first hours went by quickly. To begin with, the sun was not,

as yet, oppressive. A pleasantly cool breeze was blowing, perhaps an-
nouncing the end of the summer. Because it was Saturday and many
of the local pickers were not brought out from Clayton, the fields were
not crowded. In addition, the cotton was easy to pick. At the rate he was
going, Teófilo estimated that he would pick no less than 400 pounds
during the day. He only hoped the picking would last into the afternoon since the ranchers always called it a day if they saw there were
not enough hands to make the picking worthwhile. Then he would go
to Clayton and send the money he had earned during the week to his
wife. It was not much, but he knew Natalia would put it to good use.
Perhaps he might treat himself to a meal in town.

At noon, however, the cotton picking was called off. The notice ran
by word of mouth through the fields. "*Se acabó.*" "*No más pisca.*"[44]
Gradually the fields emptied as the pickers worked their way toward
the scales. There the bags were weighed and emptied. The pickers
were paid off. The tired men and women, through for the rest of the
week, shook the dust from their clothes. The locals got into their cars
and drove toward the highway. The migrants returned to their shacks,
Teófilo Vargas among them. This week he had not earned as much as
he had hoped, but he had worked while the picking was available. That
was the important thing. In camp Teófilo bought a bottle of soda and
walked toward his shack to eat a baloney sandwich.

Some time later, the lunch pause over, the men came out of their
shacks to raise the hoods of their cars and trucks in order to work
on dirty, neglected, often abused motors. Salesmen, their cars and
station wagons full of blankets, T-shirts, slips, socks, silk stockings,
and general merchandise, were making the rounds. The women came
out to hang clothes in the hot sun. Still other migrants, their children
hastily scrubbed and dressed, emerged from stuffy shacks and piled
into cars and trucks in order to drive to Clayton. Teófilo knew that if
he was going to buy a money order to send his family, he also had to
go. But, he didn't want to get to town too early. Town, on Saturday,
meant places to spend your money. Town meant cheap restaurants and
cheap clothes at high prices. It meant enticements to have your picture taken by sidewalk photographers. It also meant enticements to
buy dark glasses, watches, rings. More than that, town meant bars for

drinking and dancing, leading to whoring and gambling. And the next day, the Sunday hangover. Teófilo, for the moment resting in the scant shade of the wood and tar paper shack, intended to hold on to his hard earned money and spend as little of it as possible. There were rumors that the cotton picking machines were on their way to Williams Farms. When they got there, it meant that he, along with others, would have to move on.

But then, Teófilo mused, his entire life had consisted of moving on. With his parents Teófilo had moved from the Texas valley to Oklahoma, the Dakotas, Kansas, Illinois, and Michigan to the cotton, beet, carrot, and berry fields. He had slept on the flat, hard boards of the family truck, in tents, shacks, barracks-like housing, and under the stars. He had survived sand storms, dust storms, rain storms, and heat waves. At last, when his parents, exhausted and worn, finally bought a house with the GI insurance paid them when his brother was killed at Bastogne,[45] they settled down. Teófilo might have settled down with them, but the lack of opportunities and the postwar let-down forced him to the fields again, to Oklahoma, Kansas, the Dakotas, wherever. And he always returned to the valley not much better off than when he left. At twenty-two Teófilo decided to change his luck and, with some friends, he struck out for California, from where everybody returned to Texas rich. In order to avoid the low wages in the Imperial Valley, Teófilo and his friends went North. In the Central Valley Teófilo and his friends moved from crop to crop, worked from dawn to dusk, ate unevenly, and slept in barns, cars, shacks, and bus stations. For all their trouble, California's riches eluded them.

Then came Natalia, a city girl Teófilo met at a Sunday matinee when the old car he and two companions were driving back to Texas broke down near Central City in Arizona. Natalia, whose family had left the migrant trails during the early 40s, found Teófilo handsome and unpretentious. She told him she would be at the matinee again the following Sunday.

Teófilo, in turn, was in love. In order to see Natalia again, he decided not to go on to Texas. The next day he bid his friends good-bye and rented a room in downtown Central City. For the next few weeks, as his chance meeting of Natalia flowered into a courtship, Teófilo picked cotton in the nearby fields. And in February, Natalia's love assured, Teófilo departed for California.

Very carefully Teófilo sought to avoid the mistakes of the previous year when, in a vain effort to outguess the weather and the contractors, he crossed and recrossed the state. This time his travels took him directly to Ventura, then Salinas, and ultimately Delano. In the orange groves, lettuce fields, and grape vineyards he worked like a man driven. By being careful with his expenses and reducing his pleasures to an occasional movie, he mailed every possible dollar to Natalia for safekeeping. He returned to Central City in mid-September to march Natalia to the altar in a rented tuxedo, to ride around town in a decorated car, and to dance at the home of his new in-laws at the reception. The fields of California, for the time being, were relegated to the back of his mind. Teófilo still picked cotton during the first months of his marriage, but now he arrived at the cotton fields with an ample lunch, and after picking the quota he set for himself, he boarded the bus back to town and went home for a shower and a hot supper. Teófilo's life underwent other changes. At Natalia's insistence he got dental checkups and bi-weekly haircuts, along with a new wardrobe for evenings and Sundays. But the most dramatic change came when three months after their marriage, a doctor informed Natalia that she was pregnant. Teófilo was jubilant. "One thing for sure," said Teófilo, planning ahead. "My son is going to school. He will never be a farm worker."

"What if we have a girl?" asked Natalia.

"All the more she will go to school," said Teófilo. "No daughter of mine will even go close to the fields."

When the cotton season came to an end, rather than take the bus to California, Teófilo, through the intercession of his father-in-law, got a job at the ice plant. His job consisted of swinging ice chutes on to the railroad cars as they passed through Arizona on the way to eastern markets. The work, though hard at first, soon became routine. The pay, though not much, was steady. The fields of California receded farther and farther into Teófilo's memory.

And, far away from the blazing sun in distant fields, the uncertainties of the elements, the hasty rush between crops to find ranches taken over by *braceros*[46] and "illegals," plus the allied discomforts and indignities suffered by farm workers, Teófilo prospered. He bought a new car, not one of the battered hulks the used car lots sold to desperate field hands. He started buying, on time, a lot on which to build a house. And months later, when Natalia gave birth to a daughter later christened Adriana, Teófilo paid the doctor and the hospital fee on the spot.

Meanwhile Teófilo's manners, namely his tendency to use a tortilla as a fork and his often careless use of the wash basin, began to improve. When he forgot and noticed Natalia gazing at him, Teófilo replied: "O.K. O.K. So once a farm worker, always a farm worker."

"Many of us are ex-farm workers," Natalia reminded him.

Late in the afternoon Teófilo was awakened when someone started banging on the door of his shack. Teófilo got up and opened the door. It turned out to be the camp gorilla, dressed in a brown pin-striped suit, patent leather shoes, and smelling like a barber shop. He was collecting the agreed on dollar-a-day rent. "You owe me for today and you might as well pay me for tomorrow," said the gorilla. "I won't be back until Monday." Teófilo reached into his pocket and paid the gorilla two dollars. When the gorilla walked out, Teófilo, aware that it was getting late and that he must get to Clayton in order to buy a money order, changed his pants and put on a clean shirt. Then he padlocked the door of his shack and walked out of camp.

Luck, somehow, was with Teófilo. As he walked up the road toward the highway, a family in a pickup stopped. Teófilo ran up. "*Van a Clayton?*" he asked. They gave him the sign to jump in back. Some fifteen minutes later Teófilo was dropped off in Clayton and he set about the crowded main street to look for the store where, he had been told, money orders were sold. Asking directions, he located it. At the store, not only did Teófilo buy the money order but also a stamped envelope which he addressed at a wall counter. On walking out of the store, Teófilo dropped the envelope into the first mail box he saw. As he walked away from it, he breathed easier.

Afterwards, while he might have followed the crowds shopping in many stores, eating in restaurants, lining up outside the movie theaters, or walking into one of the noisy cantinas, Teófilo's only stop was at a market where he bought a can of beans, a small can of sausages, and two oranges. With the bread and baloney he had in his shack, Teófilo had enough food to last him through Monday. Teófilo walked out of the store and at the first intersection he left the crowded main street, turned a corner, and headed toward the highway. He hoped to get back to camp before dark.

One block away, as Teófilo waited for a light to change at a street corner, a car abruptly forced him back onto the sidewalk. Teófilo, shaken, cursed to himself and then saw the car stop and back up toward him. Immediately Teófilo recognized Ismael Sifuentes, who leaned over to greet him with a rousing "*Quiubo, cabrón.*"[47] Before Teófilo could answer, Ismael asked, "Where you headed?"

"Well, I . . ."

"Get in," ordered Ismael. Ismael was well known among field workers in southern Arizona and California. He was especially well known for never being available when needed. Years before, on a Christmas night when a kerosene stove on which tamales were being cooked blew up, killed his daughter and disfigured his wife, he had been drinking with his friends. Thereafter all knew and spoke of how the bones of his daughter's face had been bared by the blast and his wife's face and arms were a purple mass of flesh. She had tried to rescue the daughter from the flames. "I would gladly burn in hell right now if I could change places with my wife and my daughter," Ismael often lamented. Meanwhile he was either getting drunk or gambling.

Teófilo hesitantly got into the car.

"Where you headed?" asked Ismael a second time.

"Back to Williams Farms, Camp Three."

"Good. I'm not far from you. I'll take you back," said Ismael. Then he introduced the two farm workers in the car with him. "Meet Tomás García, the fugitive," said Ismael. "He fled his wife and *chavos*[48] in Texas because they were better off on welfare."

"It is just that . . ." started Tomás.

"Don't apologize," laughed Ismael. "The world is full of fugitives." Ismael then turned to the other farm worker. "Meet Carrot Hands," said Ismael, laughing uproariously.

"I'm Joe Pérez," said the other. Teófilo indeed saw that the man's hands were the color and texture of carrots, the result of pesticides. Pérez and Teófilo shook hands as Ismael drove off.

However, instead of heading toward the highway, Ismael drove around a few streets and into a clearing reserved for the customers of the Los Chingones Bar[49] and stopped. "*Vénganse,*"[50] he said, getting out of the car. Teófilo hesitated, got out of the car and was thinking of taking his two cans and oranges and walking away when Ismael put his arm around him and said, "We'll have two, maybe three beers and then we're off to the camp. O.K.?"

"But you see, I . . ."

"Don't say no, *cabrón,*" said Ismael, leading his friends through the door of the Los Chingones Bar. "You're with me. Besides, I'm going to pay."

At that hour, though the juke box was playing "Mary Ann" at full blast, the bar was empty except for a few farm workers. Teófilo followed Ismael and his two friends to a table, wondering how soon they would leave. Too many times two or three drinks turned into a drunk, a drunk into a . . . Teófilo slid into a booth, followed by Ismael and his friends. The waitress came up to take their first order.

Little by little, pickers Teófilo had not seen in years began to greet him. Some merely nodded on recognizing him, while others walked over to the table to exchange greetings. "*Quiubo,*" one said. "I haven't seen you in years. Heard you married a city girl and you learned to use flush toilets."

"Yeah, I was away from the fields for a couple of years," said Teófilo. "I'm back though. I couldn't stay away."

"Once a picker, *mano,*[51] always a picker. See you later."

"*Adiós.*"

"*Adiós.*"

The beer in front of them, Ismael toasted to the health of his friends and the bottles went to their lips. After drinking, Teófilo thought: "Once a picker, always a picker." Still . . .

For almost two years Teófilo lost contact with the fields when, during the Korean conflict, an aircraft company moved into Central City. Among the hundreds who sought and received employment, Teófilo, not having any particular skill, was assigned to a department which cleaned the oil and grease from engine cowlings. Hard work? Perhaps. But to Teófilo it was certainly preferable to farm labor. As Teófilo steam hosed and scrubbed cowlings, he became aware that the electricians, mechanics, and sheet metal workers earned more than the scrubbers. What was more, they did not have to wear rubber boots, rubber pants, and rubber jackets to work. Teófilo even thought about night school, then he remembered that he had never had much luck with numbers.

Yet, even scrubbing cowlings had its rewards. On Saturdays and Sundays Teófilo worked on his family's future home. And, with the help of some of his coworkers, the house went up "from the foundations." Teófilo, Natalia, and Adriana moved in when it was partially finished. "My parents were in their late forties when they bought a house after my brother was killed," he said to Natalia. "You and I are luckier."

Meanwhile Natalia gave birth to another child, this time a boy. When she suggested that they christen the boy Teófilo and call him Teo for short, Teófilo reluctantly agreed. "Well, even if he has my name, with his broad forehead he is going to be smart," said Teófilo. Then he added: "He is going to school so he can be somebody even if I have to steam hose and scrub the cowling of all the planes in the air force. I don't want him to pick crops, wrestle ice blocks, or scrub cowlings. No way. Not my son." And while Teófilo might have gone on scrubbing cowlings the rest of his life, the necessity to do so ended with the Peace of Panmunjon.[52]

When the aircraft company handed out the final paychecks and the pink slips, Teófilo sought employment at the ice plant, without success. During his absence diesels had been replacing steam engines. And the diesels, cutting the number of stops on the way to the eastern produce markets, were causing labor cut-backs at the ice plants. Dozens of men waited on corners for spot work, often in vain. Others left Central City, leaving behind possessions, dreams. Teófilo, still drawing his unemployment, began to take the contractors' busses to the cotton fields. Perhaps it was so. Perhaps once a picker, always a picker.

Some time later, while Ismael was away from the table, a camp follower everyone knew as Rana[53] spotted Teófilo. Rana walked over. Teófilo swallowed hard and felt trapped. *"Buenas, compa,"*[54] said Rana, "you gonna buy me a beer?"

Teófilo hesitantly nodded. He had heard of Rana's tactics which included the adept use of the stiletto.

"*Mesera*," shouted Rana, calling for a waitress. A moment later she came up. "Bring me a cold one," said Rana. "My friend here is gonna pay."

As the waitress headed for the bar, Rana turned to Teófilo. "You were away from the fields for some time, weren't you?"

"Yes," said Teófilo. "But I was out in California earlier this year. I was up North."

"Well, a man can't fight his destiny," said Rana.

When the waitress returned with Rana's beer, Rana took the bottle as Teófilo paid the waitress. "Thanks, *amigo*," said Rana. "If you need something, a woman, some grass, just call me." Then he moved on.

A short time later Ismael returned to the table. "What the hell did that goddamn Rana want?"

"The usual," said Teófilo. "A beer."

"Well, he better not come back," said Ismael defiantly. "If he does I'll kick his goddamn ass. He's poison."

Teófilo, in turn, was thinking about his destiny.

The men and women who chopped cotton were picked up at designated corners in the Central City barrio. After a twenty-mile ride, they were delivered to various cotton farms. After nine hours of work with half an hour off for lunch, they were paid what was left after the lunch, transportation, and cheap wine was subtracted. Then they were driven back to Central City and dropped off at the corners where they had been picked up.

Teófilo, riding out daily with the unemployed, the desperate, and the hungry, suffered the blistering rays of the sun as he chopped along. He always wondered, as he worked along, if he was taking salt tablets in the right number. Many times he had seen others fall from heat prostration, dragged to the edge of the fields, and revived. On more than one occasion an ambulance was summoned, uselessly. As Teófilo chopped, he knew that he could be earning six or seven times as much if he were in California.

At night, when Teófilo sat with his wife and two children, he thought of how in one or two seasons he might be able to earn enough to pay for some lumber he bought in order to finish the house as well as for some furniture Natalia and he had purchased when the checks from the air-

craft company had been coming in. He secretly harbored the wish that
the war might have lasted longer.

In the fall, when the cotton picking season started, Teófilo's earnings increased. Four hundred pounds a day was his daily goal, and on
good days he picked even more. As he sat around with the incoming migrants during the lunch break, Teófilo asked about California. "Don't
bother," he was told. "The *braceros* and the illegals have it all." "Keep
out of California unless you want to put yourself in the hands of the *coyote* contractors who will suck your blood." "We're going back to Texas
and I swear we'll never go back to California."

In spite of the warnings, Teófilo felt that for him, for Natalia, and
for his two children, California was the answer. "If I go for just two seasons," he explained to Natalia, "I can pay off the materials I bought for
the house. We can pay off the furniture."

"I hope something turns up here so you won't go. But if you go, we'll
go with you," said Natalia.

"That's out," Teófilo said. "I've seen too many families start on the
road and never get off. In a couple of years the kids will be in school and
I don't want their education to be interrupted like mine was. In Texas
we used to leave for the fields by the end of March and come back in
November. That's why I never learned anything. I don't want that for
these kids. I want them to be smart so they never have to pick anything.
So if anybody goes, I go."

Hours later the Los Chingones Bar was jammed; the *chingones* were
noisy. They bragged about their feats in the fields. "I've picked as many
as 800 pounds in one day," said one. "That must have been twenty years
ago," countered another. After feats in cotton came feats in celery, lettuce, melons. Then came the boasts of earnings. "I earned over two
hundred dollars a week for five weeks," said one. "That's nothing!" The
defiant *chingones* had their day. "I stopped the whole field because of
that goddamned foreman." "We kicked the chicken dealer's ass when
we found out he was putting the finger on the illegals he was robbing."
And so forth.

Ismael, not to be outdone by the other *chingones*, banged on the
table in order to be noticed. "Where is the waitress?" he demanded,
looking about. "I ordered beer and some shots of tequila almost half

an hour ago." When the waitress arrived with the drinks, Ismael paid, then lifted his shot glass for a toast. "*¡Viva México, cabrones!*" he said. His companions raised their glasses, then all drank. "Someday I'm going there," added Ismael, putting down his glass and reaching for the lemon. Teófilo put down his shot glass, bit into the lemon, and then sat back, dejectedly looking at the bottles and glasses in front of him. Ismael looked at Teófilo and asked, "What's the matter? *¿Qué pasa?* Come on, Teófilo. Get with it. Screw sadness, forever." On finishing, Ismael looked around for the waitress in order to call for another round.

Suddenly, some chairs, tables, and glasses were upset and all faces turned toward the commotion. It was none other than Rana and a field worker swinging wildly at one another. After a few more swings, both rolled on the floor, neither landing a decisive blow. Not one man from among those who immediately crowded around to watch the spectacle dared to stop the two contestants. The only encouragement given was for more violence. "Kill each other." "Let's see blood, *chingones.*" Those who knew Rana taunted him. "Is that you on the barroom floor, Rana?" "*¿Qué pasa?*" "What, no knife?"

Rana, bleeding from a scratched cheek, momentarily wrested himself from his adversary, jumped to his feet, and grabbed a nearby chair. Before he could hit his adversary with it, however, the bartender came from the bar and intervened. "Cut it," he said. "*Córtenla.*" Then, directing his voice at Rana, he shouted, "Out. You are the one who is always causing trouble around here."

Rana defiantly threw the chair aside and slowly walked out the back door. The waitress and the bartender straightened the chair and tables. Then, obviously for the benefit of the audience, the bartender snarled, "If they want to kill each other, let them do it outside."

The short commotion over, Ismael turned to his friends. "Call that a fight?" he asked. "Hell, I've seen *cabrones* rush out of bars holding their intestines in with both hands. Those were fights." He drained his glass. Then, looking about for the waitress and spotting her nearby, he shouted, "*Mesera! Mesera!*"

The waitress came over, removed the empty bottles, and took Ismael's order. Teófilo, in turn, was getting drowsy. In spite of the loud music coming from the juke box, the noise of the happy *chingones*, Teófilo fleetingly thought of his family and wondered what he was doing in a bar.

When the waitress returned with Ismael's order, Ismael looked down the cleft of her blouse, then said, "I've got it good for you, my dark one."

"I'm not your dark one and save whatever you've got for your wife," the waitress snapped. "I understand she was quite pretty until . . . You owe me a dollar and ten."

Carrot Hands laughed, as did Tomás García. Humiliated, Ismael scowled and countered, "Okay, *cabrones*. Pay. Pay up. I'm broke." Carrot Hands looked hopelessly at Teófilo, then at Tomás García. Teófilo hesitantly went to his pocket for the fourth or fifth time. The waitress took the money and moved away to attend to others.

Ismael drank, then said, "I don't know what satisfaction everybody gets from reminding me of my daughter's death and my wife's accident. You'd think I set fire to the shack." He took a deep breath and then wiped the tears from his eyes. "After we drink this one we are going," Ismael informed his companions. Then he put the bottle to his lips and didn't lower it until it was empty. "Come on," he said, slamming the bottle on the table. "Let's get out of this goddamn dump."

As Ismael drove out of the parking lot a while later, Teófilo breathed deeply of the fresh air and settled back. He figured that he still had about four dollars and some change in his pocket. It made him wish he had never caught sight of Ismael in the first place, even though the reverse had been the case. He felt around in the back seat and located his two cans and his oranges, his Sunday meal. In any case, he knew he would soon be back in his shack in order to get some sleep. As the car sped up the highway, Teófilo dozed off, the events of the past year coming back to haunt him.

Teófilo made every effort to warn Natalia of the hardships migrant families were subject to. He told her of the foul shacks migrant families were forced to occupy, of discrimination at roadside restaurants where migrants were refused service, and of gas stations whose facilities were closed to them. Still Natalia insisted and in the end . . .

When Teófilo and his family arrived in northern California, contract workers and wetbacks were everywhere displacing domestic migrants, keeping wages down, and enriching the contractors and *coyotes* who thrived in all situations. With surplus hands available, periods of work decreased, and an ever increasing number of domestic migrants fled the fields or found themselves broke and hungry and living in squatter camps, under bridges or the stars, and at the mercy of the elements.

At least in the beginning, Natalia hid her displeasure and tried to make the best of a bad situation. Accompanying Teófilo, after all, had been her idea. To improve their situation, she even did a stint in a packing shed, with disastrous results. The young woman she, along with others, entrusted her infants to, suffered an epileptic seizure, and Natalia returned from her job to find Adriana and Teo dirty, hungry, and crying at the top of their lungs. As Natalia tearfully cleaned them, clothed them, and fed them, she swore never to let them out of her sight again.

On Saturdays Natalia dressed her two children as nicely as circumstances allowed and then all four got into the car and headed for the nearest town. At the stores Natalia looked, mostly, and then bought only the indispensable. At the market Natalia compared prices, examined and weighed every purchase, and stocked her shelves and ice box when the quarters they were occupying made it possible, and then she cooked an ample supper.

On Sunday morning, church. "We must be thankful," she said.

"For what?" asked Teófilo. "The way things have turned out, I should have come alone. Where I'm working there's talk of a strike. If it comes, we'll have to move, or starve."

"Oh, things will change," said Natalia. "Meanwhile we must keep our faith."

A few weeks later, things did change. They got worse.

Teófilo, Natalia, and the two children were on a farm in northern California. Teófilo was working in an orchard while Natalia tried to make a home of a one room shack. They had been lured there by a contractor who had praised the farmer, the housing, and the working conditions. But the shacks were very dirty and within a week Teo had developed diarrhea. Anxiously Natalia boiled the bottles, hoping to control the situation. As the days wore on and the situation did not improve, Natalia became alarmed.

In desperation Teófilo and Natalia took Teo to a doctor in town who, after making sure that he would be paid for the consultation, quickly examined Teo and made his diagnosis. "Nothing to worry about, *amigos,*" he said, scribbling out a prescription. "The boy is going to be fine."

In spite of the prescription, Teo's condition persisted. And Natalia in desperation turned to Teófilo. "We cannot live like this, Teófilo. We just cannot. And you ought to have more pride than to permit it. Teo is sick, and if we do not get him away from here, we will lose him. You understand? We will lose him." Teófilo saw that Natalia had reached the end of her patience.

That night Teófilo and Natalia piled their belongings into the car and, with their two children, started home. Two days later they drove into Central City and the reassuring walls of their as yet unfinished house. Teo was feverish. But, in spite of doctors, the hospital, and prayers, he passed away. "I'm sorry," said Teófilo to a sobbing, bitter Natalia after the funeral. "I'm sorry." However, an inconsolable Natalia was not listening.

A week later, Natalia found a job in a store. Teófilo, frustrated and bitter, took the bus out of town. He would write as soon as he earned some money.

Some time later, Teófilo woke up when Ismael's car hit a deep rut. "Damn these roads," shouted Ismael. Teófilo sat up as Ismael brought the car to a stop. Teófilo rubbed his eyes and, looking out the windows, failed to recognize the surroundings.

"But this is not . . ." he began.

Ismael quickly reassured him that as soon as they ate a bowl of *menudo*[55] he would drive him to Williams Farms. "You are with me, *cabrón,*" said Ismael, getting out of the car. "Your woman is not going to beat you up if that is what you are worried about. Come on." Meanwhile, Tomás García, without taking his leave, walked away, leaving Carrot Hands in the company of Teófilo and Ismael.

The three then waited in a long line of field workers in front of a large shed where the *menudo* was being ladled into thin bowls from large boiling cans. Teófilo paid for his own and Ismael's, hoping it would be the last time he would reach into his pocket. Carrot Hands paid for his own. Then they sat down on some makeshift benches to eat the hot *menudo* and some cold corn tortillas. Eating the *menudo* without the benefit of spoons, the customers slurped the *menudo* directly out of the bowls.

As the hot *menudo* went down his throat, Teófilo wondered what his wife and daughter, far away, had for supper. He comforted himself with the assurance that Natalia would somehow provide. And right then and there, with the hot *menudo* singeing his palate, Teófilo decided to leave Ismael and head for Williams Farms, Camp Three, wherever it was, even if he had to do so on foot. Ismael, he reasoned, never knew when to stop.

No sooner had Ismael's head been partially cleared by the *menudo* than he announced to Teófilo and Carrot Hands that he must look into a little game. "We won't stay long," said Ismael. "Then I'll drive you both back to your camps and I'll tuck you in for the night, *cabrones*. Besides, if you go on the road now, you'd probably get beat up, robbed, maybe raped." Ismael laughed loudly at his own statement.

Teófilo winced and trembled as a man chained to an inescapable fate. "But you see . . . I have no money, Ismael, I . . ."

"We're just going to look, that's all," said Ismael, walking ahead. "We won't be long."

A few yards away, Ismael came to a shack and knocked on the door. The door opened slightly and a suspicious face peered out at Ismael, Teófilo, and Carrot Hands. "These two are with me," said Ismael. The door opened and the three walked in. At a makeshift table dice were being rolled by the light of a lone light bulb. Around the table were six or seven players, their anxious faces awaiting the stop of the thumping rolling dice. The shack reeked with the smell of human perspiration and smoke.

The immediate situation soon became obvious. One farm worker, a thin, toothless individual everybody called Wilo, was on a winning streak. He kept rolling, passing, and calling for new points and making them. Ismael took some money out of his pocket and began to bet with the lucky player. At the end of a series of passes, the dice changed hands. Ismael showed Teófilo a fistful of crumpled bills. "We are in luck," he whispered to Teófilo. "Get on this skeleton when he gets the dice again. He will be our salvation, unless he drops dead."

Teófilo, now down to two dollars and some change after having paid for the *menudo*, hesitantly decided to play just one dollar, only one. If he lost . . .

When Wilo got the dice again, he made another string of passes while calling for new points. Teófilo nervously bet with him. And, much to his surprise, Teófilo began to pick up bets. He was nervously counting dollar bills and putting them in his pocket when Wilo lost the dice.

When the dice came to Teófilo, he declined them. Ismael, in turn, rolled a nine and lost the dice in four rolls. "Cursed luck," he muttered.

When Wilo got the dice again, Teófilo, betting with him, doubled the size of his bets. Then, feeling Wilo's streak couldn't last, brought the size of his bets down. Wilo's streak cooled. The dice changed hands and came to Ismael. He put down three dollars and muttered, "my luck has got to change. It's just got to." He rolled an eight and doubled his bet while calling for a new point. Covered, he came up with a four. Two rolls later the dice passed from his hands.

As it was late, a wine merchant came in. Ismael, desperate, shouted to Teófilo for five dollars, bought two pints of cheap port, and covered a bet in front of him. He lost. "*¡Chingue a su madre!*"[56] he roared. Looking about for Carrot Hands and failing to spot him, Ismael shouted to Teófilo for another five. Teófilo hesitated. "*Ora, cabrón,*"[57] he said. "I'll give 'em back. Come on." Teófilo hesitantly gave Ismael another five from his winnings, now decreasing rapidly, hoping . . .

At that moment three whores came through the door, bringing into the crowded shack the smell of sweet perfume. The Mexican queen, a young girl with a flowered dress, found her way to Teófilo's side. Ismael, in turn, embraced both the blonde and the mulatta who completed the trio. "Now my luck is going to change," he said. "Teófilo, another five. This little game is about over." Teófilo complied.

Ismael drank heavily of the wine, kissed the girls, and then eyed the dice awaiting him. He put down the five dollars, rolled, and disgustingly looked, when the dice stopped, at a pair of snake eyes. Once more Ismael looked toward Teófilo. The other hands looked at Teófilo too.

They knew he had won twenty, perhaps thirty dollars in addition to what he had given Ismael.

Teófilo, in turn, eyed the girl. He would use her, he decided, as a pretext to leave the game. Once outside the door he would pay her and disappear. Surely he'd find Williams Farms, Camp Three, Ismael or no Ismael. He drank deeply of the wine to fortify himself, then put his arm around the girl and started for the door.

At the door, however, one of the pickers who had been losing stepped in front of Teófilo. "*¿A'ónde vas?*"[58] he asked.

Teófilo felt the picker's hot breath. "I am leaving," he said.

"You're not going anywhere with all that money," the picker said.

"Hell I'm not. I won it fair and square."

The picker pulled out a knife. Teófilo stepped back.

"Why can't he go with me?" the girl asked. "Why not, *hijo de la* . . . ?"[59]

"He can go with you, but later," the loser snarled.

Nervously Teófilo returned to the game. He drank deeply of a bottle of *mezcal* somebody put in his hands. When the dice came to Teófilo, Ismael said, "Come on, Teófilo. This is it." Teófilo rolled a six. As Teófilo picked up the dice, he was presented with the butt of marijuana by a picker who said softly, "Drag on it. It will calm you down."

Teófilo took a deep drag, passed the butt on, and failed to come up with the needed six. Thereafter, the bets Teófilo covered, he lost. In addition, Ismael took another five from him and put them into the game. Teófilo saw his winnings disappear. The girl at his side remarked, "You and your friend are *salaos*[60] tonight." Then she moved next to a picker with more luck.

Teófilo, his money almost gone, his mind reeling from the beer, tequila, *vino*, marijuana and the smell of perspiration, smoke, and cheap perfume, said to Ismael, "I must go. I'm sick. I . . ."

"Wait for me in the car," said Ismael, still harboring illusions with a few crumpled dollars. "I'll take you back to your camp in just a few minutes."

Teófilo staggered out and headed in the direction of Ismael's car. He had not gone far when he bent over and emptied the entire contents of his stomach. Then to complete the job, he opened his fly and relieved his kidneys. Straightening up, he breathed deeply of the night air and momentarily felt better. As he looked about, however, he failed to recognize Ismael's car. He decided, his head and temples aching, to find an empty shack.

At the first shack which Teófilo stumbled into he was rebuffed: a man and a woman cursed his unexpected entrance. Teófilo hastily exited. As he crept into a second shack thinking it was empty, a youngster began to cry, a mother to shriek. Once more, Teófilo stumbled out into the darkness. Unexpectedly a dog attacked him and gashed his leg before Teófilo was able to kick him away. At last, on the third attempt, Teófilo pushed open the door of a tiny shack, slammed the door shut, and fell to the dirt floor in a heap, his thoughts, his dreams, his fears in disarray. Then silence . . .

Gazing at the cotton field before him, Teófilo was aghast. Never had he seen such giant cotton balls, ripe for picking. What was more, he was alone. He had no competition from locals, "braceros," "ilegales," or other migrants. Teófilo ran toward the waiting field, his sack ready, when, all of a sudden, he heard the roar of the mechanical pickers. They came into view, dozens of them. Quickly picking all the cotton in their path and leaving the field bare.

Then the mechanical pickers headed for the tomatoes, grapes, lemons, lettuce, and . . .

Hours later, Teófilo came to when he heard some rapping on the door. Teófilo momentarily raised his head to listen. His head spun; his temples seemed about to burst. Looking about, he wondered where he was. Soon there was more rapping on the door. "Wake up, sinner," a voice said. "Wake up and hear the voice of God."

Teófilo once again raised his head. The voice faded. Teófilo then rolled over on his back. Even though he was perspiring, he shivered uncontrollably. He managed to raise his head, prop himself up on one elbow, and struggle to his feet. He stumbled toward the door, fighting to keep his balance. He opened the door and surveyed the quiet shacks nearby. Then his memory cleared. He remembered he still had some money left when he had stumbled out of the dice game. He felt for his pocket. It had been turned inside out and it now flopped outside his torn pants legs. Ismael, he thought. Ismael? He had lent at least three times to Ismael, perhaps four. That he knew. That he remembered.

Since the camp seemed empty, it was probably because it was still too early in the morning. Teófilo closed the door and fell to the ground to get some more sleep. This time, to keep from shivering, he curled up into a ball.

Hours later, Teófilo woke up again. This time he woke up to the noise of children running outside his shack. He was thirsty, so much so that his mouth and lips felt like sand paper. Teófilo got up once more, steadied himself to keep from falling, and went outside and down a row of shacks to find some water to drink. When he found the water tank, he put his mouth to the spigot and turned the handle. The tank was empty.

Desperate, thirsty, and hungry, Teófilo walked about the camp, wondering where he was. In front of a shack he saw a young girl. "What camp is this?" he asked.

The young girl looked at Teófilo momentarily, then shrugged her shoulders.

"Do you know what time it is?" he asked. This time the young girl ran off.

At that moment the door of a nearby shack opened and an older woman came out. "*Perdón, señora,*" said Teófilo. "Could you please tell me what time it is?"

"Almost six in the afternoon," the woman said. "Can't you see the sun?"

"Yes, yes," said Teófilo. "You see, I'm looking for Williams Farms, Camp Three . . ."

"Well, this is Acme Farms. Williams Farms, Camp Three, is over there a few miles," she said, pointing west.

Teófilo, his step unsteady, his head aching, and his throat parched, stumbled toward the setting sun. He had to get to Williams Farms, Camp Three, by Monday.

Doña Clara

Whenever a Mexican arrives in Tucson and asks the first *chicano* he sees where one might get a room, he is always sent to Doña Clara in El Hoyo. If he is on his way to California for the fruit season and stays only overnight, Doña Clara gives him a room for the night and instead of charging him, sends him off the next morning with best wishes and a *burro*, some beans wrapped up in a tortilla. If the new arrival plans to remain, she advises him beforehand not to try sneaking in women, not to leave the bath faucets dripping, and to pay the rent in advance whenever possible.

Every morning Doña Clara puts a rag over her hair and changes linen, sweeps floors, empties ashtrays, hangs up clothes for her untidy tenants, and orders Don Chon, her helper. He grumblingly scrubs the bathrooms, does carpentry work where it is needed, and cuts wood for the furnace during the winter. By six o'clock, Doña Clara has hurried uptown to pay this or that pending bill, has visited an occasional sick *comadre*,[61] has gone to the market for groceries, and has prepared her working daughter's supper. At night, she sits in the front room with Ernestina, her daughter, Don Chon, and any of the tenants who want to enjoy a game of *capote*, a Mexican card game. When she is not there, it means that she and Ernestina have gone uptown to the Mexican theater, where Doña Clara, in spite of her own past trials, cries like a child.

Having so many duties, however, does not mean that Doña Clara shirks her moral obligations. On the contrary, every Sunday she puts on her best clothes and hurries to an early mass with Ernestina. When it is over she reverently pays her respects, by lighting a candle and saying an additional prayer to the images of those saints to whom her soul and the souls of her family she has entrusted. Then she gets back to her housekeeping. It is on Sunday afternoon that Doña Clara often serves chicken with *mole* sauce or prepares enchiladas for the benefit of the less financially able of her tenants. After the meal is consumed, the tenants retired, and Ernestina called for, Doña Clara is left alone with the dirty dishes. Late that night as the last of her tenants stumble in, from her room which is close to the front door, she says in a low voice, "Be sure and lock the door."

However, not always has Doña Clara been the Doña Clara her tenants know. Not always has she been the one who lends them money when they need it or the one that shouts indignantly to those taking advantages of her goodness, "Either you pay your rent, loafers, or you will find your suitcases packed and on the sidewalk." Neither has she always been the Doña Clara her neighbors know, the one who humbly assists the wakes of those called to their eternal reward, the one who stands in line in front of the Tolteca Theater with her attractive daughter, and the one whose appearance slowly becomes more Indian with the years.

Many years ago, long before El Hoyo became as crowded as it is today, Doña Clara, then quite young and attractive, moved into a single room, not far from where she lives today, with her husband Fernando. Both had just come from Mexico and as yet Fernando Aragón was trying to overcome the difficulty of a new language and a new country. In order to subsist, Clarita, as she was known then, began taking in washing while Fernando traversed the city in search of employment. While some jobs were available to him, Fernando found most below his dignity. "I would rather die of hunger," he would say, "than work like an animal for twelve dollars a week. But don't worry about a thing, Clarita. Someday we will be rich. I guarantee it, Clarita. I guarantee it."

However, five years later, except for a son whom they christened Armando, Fernando and Clarita's situation was virtually unchanged. True, Fernando was no longer out of work. He had become a photographer's agent and spent most of his commission with friends. In their company, it did not become unusual for him to disappear for entire weekends. And to justify his actions to Clarita, he would say, "One must cultivate his friendships. After all, knowing people will someday change our situation. Why, just the other day I was talking to a man with capital who promised me . . . ."

Fernando was so intent on cultivating friendships that whenever the liquor went to his head, he got into the habit of borrowing money on the sparse furniture Clarita had bought. It forced Clarita to work even more in order to pay the notes off before they came to take the furniture away. And as if this was not enough, Fernando soon surprised Clarita by buying an automobile. He parked it in front of the door and summoning Clarita out, he said, "Look, Clarita, it is ours. This car will make me rich. Soon everything will change. I guarantee it."

In no time at all, however, the automobile that was to make Fernando and Clarita rich only succeeded in keeping Fernando away for longer periods of time than before. And if Clarita had once worked to pay the rent, buy the food, and make good Fernando's notes, she now also worked to meet the payments on the car. Many months later, when she paid the last installment, Fernando said to her, "Ah, Clarita, I don't know what I would do without you. But you can be sure that things are definitely going to change. I guarantee it."

If being an easy spender had made Fernando Aragón the first voice among his cronies, owning a car made him much more. It meant that whenever a celebration was to be held, he drove the officials about to make the arrangements. Fernando Aragón could always be counted on to furnish the car in which to carry the queen, the ladies in waiting, and dignitaries. And when the celebration ended, he, being a gentleman of importance in such matters, saw to it that every official was taken home, even though it be in some nearby city such as Nogales, Douglas, or Casa Grande. And as usual, Fernando said to Clarita on returning, "I have already told you that one cannot expect to get anywhere if he is a hermit."

As the social obligations, though unprofitable, to which Fernando now dedicated his time constantly brought him in contact with so many so-called "ladies of position" with whom he began to have affairs, it led him ultimately to look with disdain upon Clarita. Often he would say to her, "I do not understand it. I do not see how you can look so badly in your clothes. I am convinced that you have no taste at all. *Nada de gusto.* For example, Señora Fuentes looks much better than you do." So one day, after a small quarrel over money, Fernando disappeared. Two weeks later a loan company truck was sent to pick up Clarita's stove and chairs. Clarita, however, only waited vainly as days became weeks and weeks became months. And three months later, still waiting for Fernando, she was blessed with a daughter, Ernestina.

When the Great Depression came along, Clarita, besides taking in mountains of washing, working in kitchens uptown, and doing housework a few nights a week, was at length able to get enough money together with which to rent an empty house. There, between the chore of keeping rooms, in addition to her other tasks, she found time enough in which to teach her two children the rudiments of reading and writing Spanish.

When Armando and Ernestina started school, for the sake of not seeing them go to school looking like urchins, Doña Clara opened credit at the San Dimas[62] Outfitting Company. There she bought Armando his tennis shoes, eight- and eleven-cent socks, overalls, and shirts. For Ernestina, she bought organdy and other odds and ends of yardage and, buying a sewing machine, also on credit, personally made Ernestina's dresses.

As time went on, things began to get even better. Armando got a newspaper route and brought home, besides his earnings, milk and pastries. Ernestina helped willingly by lending her mother a hand with the sweeping, cooking, and making of beds. And Clarita, now beginning to be known as Doña Clara, by saving on groceries, by mending and remending her own and her children's clothes, and by saving every spare nickel, undertook to buy the house during a period when only bootleggers and Bank Night winners were thought to have money.

When Armando at length finished high school and found a job, Doña Clara dedicated herself solely to her family and to renting rooms. Having less to do, she put on weight and began, now and then, to give herself the luxury of an occasional visit to the beauty shop. By scrimping and saving for an entire year, she was able to visit, with Armando and Ernestina, relatives she had not seen for twenty years. She went for a hurried consultation, when she was periodically talked into it by some acquaintance, to the card readers who foretold, as always, the trip, the stranger, and the change of fortune.

Being able to pay all of this naturally incurred further obligations. It meant that whenever solicitors from the various Mexican organizations came around, she was expected to contribute heartily to their causes. It meant that if a *comadre* was evicted, Doña Clara could and should be expected to take her, the rest of the family, the furniture, and the pets until another house could be located. It meant that often her tenants, too, taking advantage of her generosity, delayed in paying the rent. However, neither this nor what we shall soon learn, changed her noble spirit.

A few months before the war, sensing that it would be quite unpatriotic to be drafted, Armando joined the Army. True, his absence caused Doña Clara to lie awake nights, reading and rereading his letters, as well as entrusting his safety to one saint and then another. It led her to leave the running of the house to her daughter during the summer of '41 while she went to Texas to visit Armando at camp. At length, however, Doña Clara became somewhat used to the idea. The Army, she reasoned, would not be a bad experience for her son. Besides, on completing his enlistment he would be home again and her house would once again be complete. But, such was not the case, since Armando, to Doña Clara's great sorrow, died at Pearl Harbor.

While this might have destroyed completely the morale of any other mother, especially one like Doña Clara, who had placed all her hopes and aspirations on her son, it did not do so to Doña Clara. While it led her, at first, to cry until her eyes were red and sore and to spend entire days in her room without seeing anybody save Ernestina, Doña Clara at last shook off as best she could her deep grief, and if she cried, she did so inwardly.

Then, with only black dresses as the outward sign of her tragic loss, she began to be the Doña Clara of old. She was the comforter who sought to remedy other hearts' trials with words, and when these did not suffice, in a handshake she left a few crumpled dollar bills. The refuge of all those she lovingly refers to as her "*paisanitos,*"[63] trying to make a living following the harvest, getting lumps in the preliminaries for twenty dollars a night.[64] And others, students of little means, hungry bohemians, dreamers, and all those that walking in the front door of her house are thankful to find, often quite far from home, *un rinconcito mexicano*, a little Mexican corner.

Life Is But a Tango

Whenever Simón Esperanti[65] went for a stroll in downtown Manhattan, he did so with an air of distinction. He wore silk shirts, a conservative hat, and very neatly tailored suits. He was Argentine national boxing champion in one of the heavier weights. Therefore Simón felt that he was an ambassador without portfolio representing the land of tango and filet mignon.

Every morning Simón got up at five o'clock and ran through Central Park. After breakfasting on juices, cereal, four eggs, and a small steak, he headed for the Acme gym where he worked out with the heavy bag, punched the small one, skipped rope, and bullied his sparring partner.

For the first few weeks after his arrival, Paulino, his new manager, went to the gym and said to him in Spanish, "Yes, Simón, you are headed for big things in this country." Simón only nodded in approval and kept on with his workout. Simón was itching for fights, and plenty of them. He planned to take home one of the world championships or else change his name to *atorrante*,[66] in other words, bum.

After leaving the gym Simón ate dinner. It consisted of vegetables, milk, and another steak. The afternoons Simón spent peacefully. Sometimes he saw a Spanish picture. Other times he spent the entire afternoon in his thirty-five dollar a week apartment, listening to his collection of tangos by Carlos Gardel and Hugo del Carril.

For supper Simón ate a gigantic three dollar steak with potatoes and drank a cup of coffee—the latter being his only vice. After conversing of his pugilistic possibilities at the Café Antillas with his friends, some gesticulating Cubans and some beer-loving Mexicans he had met soon after his arrival, he went back to his room, wrote a letter home or listened to his records, and then went to bed.

When Paulino told Simón the name of his first foe and the site of the bout, Simón scowled and said, "I came to fight contenders. And here you match me with an unknown *atorrante*. I will murder him."

Paulino bit his cigar and said, "I know, *che*,[67] I know. But you have to go up the ladder."

Simón came back, "I know. But I did not come all the way from my beloved Buenos Aires to fight for nickels. I have already spent part of two thousand dollars I had earned in my own country. I want money fights. It is your business to get them for me."

"I will, *che*, but you have to beat a couple of prelim boys first, you will get your chance. Then, just think, Simón, when you go back to Argentina they will declare a national holiday for you. A national holiday for Simón Esperanti, the conquering gaucho."

"Don't recite poetry, Paulino. Get me fights," said Simón.

"I will," said Paulino. "But right now concentrate on the fight. You will fight Kurasinski at about seven o'clock. We will have to take the bus at four in the afternoon to get to the arena in time."

"To think of it. Me, Simón Esperanti, fighting Kurasinskis. By the way, Paulino, be sure that the next fight is somewhere in the State of New York, will you?"

"All right, *che*. All right," said Paulino, biting his cigar.

The following week, as Simón sat in his corner waiting for the bell, he glared across the ring at Kurasinski. At the bell Simón rushed him, took a left in the face, and all but tore Kurasinski apart with a furious body attack. In less than two minutes of the first round Kurasinski lay flat on his back, out. After the fight Simón said to Paulino, "I told you I would murder him. From now on I want no more *atorrantes*. I want to fight contenders."

In his second fight Simón had no trouble disposing of a has-been named Trucker Tribolet in less than twenty seconds of the second round. He got a small write-up in the American papers which spoke of a promising future. He got a big write-up in the Spanish papers. These spoke of him as another Luis Firpo.

Paulino rushed into the gym one morning and said to Simón, "*Che*, I have a fight for you with Spoiler Thomas. You have to win. After all, you must uphold the honor of the Argentine. This one will be in St. Marcus Arena. We get closer to the Garden all the time."

"What round do you want me to lay the *atorrante* on your lap?" asked Simón.

"I leave that up to you," said Paulino, biting his cigar.

So Simón trained as he had never trained before. He shook the gymnasium rafters when he hit the heavy bag. He actually tore the punching bag off its stand. He did everything but eat his sparring partners alive.

Two weeks later, as Simón sat in his corner waiting for the bell, he glared across the ring at his opponent. Curling up his mouth, Simón showed Spoiler the fiercest gaucho snarl he could muster. But Spoiler only spat through the corner of his mouth and sat back.

When the bell rang Simón charged Spoiler. Spoiler sidestepped and Simón went into the ropes. The crowd laughed. Simón, not believing it, faced Spoiler Thomas again. Spoiler dropped his hands, turned his back, and walked away. Simón snarled and charged. Spoiler turned around suddenly and jabbed Simón twice with his left. The crowd was hysterical. Simón threw a left and a right, but wild. Spoiler landed another two lefts. Simón found himself, for the first time in his life, clinching. In the clinch Spoiler Thomas stuck his thumb in Simón's eye. Spoiler Thomas elbowed, cuffed, laced. Spoiler spat on Simón's hairy chest. The referee broke it up. Simón threw a flurry of wild haymakers. But Spoiler only danced away, sticking lefts in Simón's face as he went back. The bell sounded and Simón went back to his corner.

"Oh, you got him. You got him," said Paulino, biting his cigar, "only keep your left up and box him. Box him."

"Box him? Do you know what you are saying, *atorrante*?" asked Simón, trying to catch his breath and talk through his battered mouth.

The bell sounded and Simón moved out cautiously. Spoiler sidestepped Simón and caught him with a left hook. Simón gritted his teeth and snarled. He cocked his right and charged into a left thrown by Spoiler Thomas. Then came a crashing right by Spoiler. Simón hit the canvas, bounced, and then lay still.

For many days Simón Esperanti did not leave his apartment. All day he listened to his collection of tangos, the saddest ones he could find. The American papers wrote of another promising prospect ruined by the Spoiler. The Spanish papers said nothing. The gesticulating Cubans discussed Havana and the beer-loving Mexicans discussed bull-fighting.

At length Simón put himself in higher spirits by blaming Paulino for his defeat. "You told me to box him," he said.

"Well, we have to start from the bottom again. That's all," said Paulino, biting his cigar.

For a few weeks Simón trained diligently in the hope of fighting again. But Paulino was unable to get him any fights. Not even preliminaries. Soon Simón's money was gone. He left his thirty-five dollar a week apartment and moved into a ten-dollar a week room. Paulino advanced his gladiator three dollars daily for food and the rent. Soon, however, Paulino decided that it was too much. "You eat too much," said Paulino, biting his cigar. "Get a smaller room."

Simón, having no alternative but to accept whatever Paulino had to offer, found a five-dollar a week room and borrowed money to supplement his two-dollar a day food allowance. When he sat at the Café Antillas with his friends, the gesticulating Cubans and the beer-loving Mexicans, he said, "Life is but a tango, *amigos*. Sad. And sometimes, bitter. When I left my beloved Buenos Aires I had two thousand dollars. Now I have nothing. I had eight suits and I have sold all but the one I have on. I used to wear silk shirts and now I buy leftovers on Delancey Street. Yes, *amigos*, life is but a tango. Sad. And sometimes, bitter."

Simón kept on training and hoping to fight again until one day Paulino said to him, "I don't mind paying your rent. But I can only give you a dollar a day for your food. You eat too much."

Simón was outraged. He reminded Paulino that it was he who had told him to box Spoiler Thomas and had all but been killed in doing it. "If all you can give me is five dollars a week for rent and one dollar a day for food, you can tear up my contract. I will get another manager."

"Listen," said Paulino, biting his cigar, "if and when you fight, you fight for me. You owe me more than three hundred dollars. That is how much I have advanced you."

The next day Simón ate veal cutlets for the first time in his life. He was drinking his third cup of coffee when he noticed that a young Puerto Rican lady was looking into the juke box. Simón got up and suggested a new tango. She approved of his selection. Simón introduced himself as the best tango dancer in the Argentine. "And if you want, I will gladly teach you," added Simón. Thereafter Simón went to the young lady's house every day to teach her the intricacies of the tango. When Paulino refused him another nickel, Simón said, "Fine." So the Puerto Rican young lady began working extra hours, paid for Simón's room, and bought him steaks. He, in turn, taught her the tango.

One night, as Simón sat in the Café Antillas with his gesticulating Cuban and beer-loving Mexican friends, Paulino, whom Simón had not seen for months, ran in and said, "*Che*, where have you been? I have a fight for you."

"Stay out of my sight, *atorrante*. I am conversing with my friends," said Simón. He glared at Paulino. Paulino bit his cigar and ran out.

Facing his friends Simón said, with a smile on his face, "After all, *amigos*, life is but a tango. And one must dance it away."

Doña Clara's Nephew

When Cuco Alonzo, Doña Clara's nephew, first came from Mexico during the war, Doña Clara felt quite sorry for him. In the first place, it was obvious that Cuco's two worn and shiny suits were not made of English gabardine. His shirts were frayed at the collar and cuffs. His shoes, run down at the heels and semi-soleless, were mostly cardboard. The only thing that Cuco said in his own defense was, "Things have been tough for me as of late, *tía.*"[68] Thus it was that Cuco was allowed to sleep with Don Chon in the basement and was allowed to eat his three meals at his aunt's table without charge. After breakfast, Cuco went into the living room and, with the radio on full blast, he read the Mexican newspapers to find out how the *matadores de toros*[69] were doing. When lunch was over he said to Doña Clara, "Well, *tía,* I will see you later. I am going to look for a job." But, he always managed not to find one and returned to receive his aunt's sympathies, the choice piece of steak, and an occasional dollar with which to soothe his broken spirit.

After a few weeks, however, Doña Clara decided that either Cuco was not looking hard enough for a job or else was just not having any luck. Phoning up a contractor friend and explaining her nephew's plight, Doña Clara surprised Cuco when he returned that afternoon by informing him that she had found him employment.

"What am I to do, *tía?*" he asked.

"Oh, carry hods, mix cement, and easy things like that," she said.

After the first day's work, Cuco came home and about midnight Doña Clara woke up when she heard some ugly groans coming from the basement. Putting on her robe and going downstairs, she found her nephew in agony.

"What is the matter, Cuco?" she asked. An anxious look came over her face.

"Ay, *tía,*" Cuco groaned. "Surely I will die. I will die."

"*Anda,*" she said. "It cannot be as bad as all that." So, Doña Clara patiently massaged her nephew's aching back. After a few days, either by getting used to the work or by learning how to hide, Cuco began to take his work in stride and to moan less and less each night.

Two weeks later, Cuco received his first check and he immediately handed it over to Doña Clara who refused it on the condition that he buy himself some clothes and save the rest in case he should go back to Mexico. However, it was agreed that he would pay his board in the future, and he could, according to Doña Clara, sleep in the basement rent free as long as he wished. Thus it came to be that Cuco began to buy himself shirts by the dozen, some striped suits, seventeen-dollar shoes, and to be accepted among the uptown *plebes*, the boys uptown.

In a few months it was quite obvious, to Doña Clara especially, that Cuco had sold parrots for a living while in Mexico. At length she realized why her nephew had arrived in such a pitiful state. After all, Mexico's better wardrobes are never sold in Tepito, Mexico City's Hell's Kitchen. When one deals in parrots in Mexico, it means that one does everything he can except work. Cuco, for example, had scalped bull ring tickets, had bought and sold pawn tickets, had been a guide for tourists, and those moments when one deems it more important to eat than to go to hell, he had been a satisfier of whims and sins. By hanging around gymnasiums he learned who was being overtrained or who was placing bets on himself prior to boxing matches, and Cuco sold the information. By loitering in cafés, bars, and barber shops, he had managed to give his body anything it asked for. Except work.

While a parrot salesman usually lives high, oftentimes adverse changes of fortune drive him to the drastic, to pawn his clothes, to eat tripe tacos, and finally to Tepito, Mexico City's skid row. And the same happened to Cuco when the government functionary he was working for was caught providing himself with a side salary from the sale of so-called "scarcities." Only then did Cuco remember that he had a dear *tía* in the United States. And borrowing money, to be paid back with heavy interest, he packed his suitcase and headed North[70] to the land of blondes, baseball, and Coca-Cola.

Cuco, being a parrot salesman at heart, could not but look forward to the day when he would carry hods, help unload trucks, and mix cement no longer. Thus it was after finishing his day's work, he made the rounds of all the uptown bars, cafés, barber shops, and pool halls. It was on one of these rounds that one afternoon he chanced into Garza's Barber Shop for a haircut.

Garza asked him, "Massage?"

And Cuco, thinking it impolite to refuse, grunted and Garza gave him a massage.

Garza asked him, "Shampoo?"

Cuco, not understanding English too well, grunted again. Only when he paid the bill did he realize that he had grunted a few times too often.

One day Doña Clara noticed that Cuco's manner began to change. He began to come home, dress early, and disappear nightly without waiting around for supper. Soon, for no apparent reason, he asked for a private room. And now, instead of buying shirts and seventeen-dollar shoes, Cuco got so much in the habit of borrowing money from Doña Clara and some of the tenants until all began to refer to him as Mr. Lend-Me-Five and avoided him. Doña Clara, at length, said to him, "It must be quite a parasite you are courting. For she is certainly sucking your blood."

One day Cuco said to Doña Clara, "*Tía*, I feel that you are charging me too much for my room and board."

Doña Clara lost her temper and said, "*Malagradecido*. Thankless one. In the first place I am sick and tired of getting up at five in the morning to serve you breakfast and fix your lunch. From now on, since you think that I am charging you too much, you can eat out just like all the others. And if you feel that your room is too high, you can find a cheaper one elsewhere."

"I did not mean for you to get mad, *tía*," said Cuco. "I am sorry."

"I do not want you to be sorry. From now on, eat out. And furthermore, do not leave all your socks and shirts thrown around all over the room. Never in my life did I imagine that I had such an irresponsible nephew."

"I am sorry, *tía*," said Cuco.

One night, after having frequented the bars uptown as of custom, Cuco got quite drunk and not using good judgment he said to some of his friends, "You can come up and sleep at my aunt's place."

"Don't you think she will get mad?" asked one of the friends.

"No, I am her favorite nephew. Besides, aren't you boys all good *mexicanos*?" asked Cuco.

"Of course we are," they said.

"So you have nothing to worry about. So is my *tía*," said Cuco.

But so noisy and unmannerly did Cuco's friends turn out to be that the next morning, in spite of a big headache, Cuco was rudely awakened by his aunt. "Cuco," she shouted. "Wake up!"

"*¿Qué pasó?* What is the matter?" Cuco asked.

"I want you to know that your friends and your suitcase are on the sidewalk," said Doña Clara.

"But *tía*, I—I," started Cuco.

"*Tía* nothing," she said. "Get dressed and find a room elsewhere."

"But *tía*, I promise you that it will not happen again," said Cuco.

"Of that I am sure," said Doña Clara. "Hurry up. Your friends are waiting for you outside. Let's see if they will help you out."

A few days later, fearing that the worst might overtake her nephew, Doña Clara phoned his employer to find out Cuco's whereabouts. It turned out, however, that Cuco had not been to work for a week. Frantically, Doña Clara and Ernestina went uptown and with Don Chon's help made a search of all the bars and restaurants which they knew Cuco frequented, only to receive the same answer, "Sorry, he has not been around here for a few days now." So Doña Clara came to the conclusion that perhaps Cuco had gone back to Mexico and she began to feel sorry that she had treated him so harshly.

About a week later, however, since news travels fast in El Hoyo, Doña Clara found out that Cuco had married a girl uptown and had moved in with his in-laws, and taken a job as a pest exterminator.

El Tiradito

M any years ago off Main Street, a man was stabbed to death and a wooden cross was put at the head of his shallow grave by the Mexicans that buried him. By the time their children, grandchildren, and great grandchildren were born, time had succeeded in losing the dead man's true identity. And today his resting place is known to all as the wishing shrine of El Tiradito, the Fallen One.

While there are many stories concerning the identity of the man buried there, none are very convincing. Some seem to get lost in the wide and varied entanglements of unwritten southwestern lore. Others appear to be snatches and remnants of stories heard at childhood and retold at old age. Still others, no matter their source, are no less fantastic than the Arabian Nights.[71] And of all, though there are countless others which are just as probable, we will tell one.

Juan Can

It is highly improbable that any Mexican living in Tucson today ever knew Juan Can[72] personally. This being the case, his personality and his exploits are recounted in such a way as to make him a man of charms few women could resist and men were, without an exception, jealous of. Coming at an early age from Sonora in Mexico into what was then Arizona Territory, a wilderness of sand, mesquite, and lawlessness, he was, before finally becoming the proprietor of Tucson's largest drinking establishment, a stagecoach driver, prospector, Indian fighter, and ore buyer.

As the Tecolote's[73] proprietor, Juan Can's life might have been uneventful. He could have married one of the many women that he knew in order to raise fat children and then pass away to be buried in the city's new cemetery. But such was not the case. Juan Can fell in love with Teresita Ríos, a young lady whose ancestry, beauty, and bounty far surpassed those of any *señorita* for hundreds of miles around. While Teresita Ríos finally fell victim, though perhaps reluctantly, to our *caballero*'s charms, it did not take Juan Can very long to find out that plebeians had no right to such high aspirations as were his. Don Joaquín Ríos, Teresita's father, whose ancestors had been granted vast lands by the King of Spain many decades before, saw to that. So, when Juan Can humbly took off his sombrero in Don Joaquín's presence in order to ask for Teresita's hand in marriage, he was indignantly ordered away from his loved one's tapestried and sworded home to the smoke and noise of the Tecolote.

For many days and nights Juan Can brooded. Then, because he knew that the humblest of men in his land often became *generales*, *presidentes*, and *matadores*, he shook off the despair that was his and vowed that one day he would be so fabulously rich that nothing would be beyond his reach. Teresita Ríos was an angel escaped from Heaven as far as our *caballero* was concerned, and he vowed he would make her his very own. He would acquire so much land, gold, and power that buy her he would, if it be necessary.

So, in almost no time at all the Tecolote began to change. It grew ten or twelve times its original size. Performers from the coast were brought in to put on shows formerly given by disorderly clients. At its bar men lost their minds and their souls. At its gaming tables men lost their fortunes and their honor. And the stature of our *caballero* grew in a few years to such heights that his silk shirts, his pearled six-guns, his imported cigars, and his pearled neck-pins were the pinnacle of every poor boy's aspirations. In his safe were the deeds for the ranches, farms, and other properties which kept falling into his hands. All of this drove Don Joaquín Ríos and others to spend sleepless nights, to wish that lightning would strike Juan Can, whose initial sin had been to fall in love.

One day Don Joaquín Ríos met with others, and behind closed doors it was resolved that the power of Juan Can would be curbed. Of course, Juan was not to be killed. All the assassins in Arizona Territory were his friends. Juan was not to be driven out. He had committed no crime. Besides, the soldiers were his staunch friends and often borrowed money from him. So, it was natural that they decided to ruin Juan Can at the gaming table, where, it was known to all, his luck was so great that his acres increased with each turning card and his herds doubled with the galloping of the dice. For this it was decided to import from Mexico the renowned gambler Pasquinas, whose stinking nose and foaming mouth had vandalized some of the most precious jewels of womanhood won from others at the card tables of Europe and Latin America.

A few weeks later a carnival came to Tucson. It set up its patched tents off Main Street. In the main tent there were clowns, acrobats, and horsemen. In the small sideshow there were the usual fire-eaters, con-tortionists, and man-fashioned freaks. At night, when Tucson's popu-lation lost itself in the spectacle, Juan Can, with the adorable Teresita Ríos at his arm, laughed at the antics of the performers in the show and then cast doubtful glances at the freaks in the sideshow. As he was leaving the grounds to escort Teresita home, a voice whispered to him, "Come back, Juan, there is heavy betting in the back of the bearded lady's tent. Heavy betting."

Juan Can came back. And unknown to him he sat across the table from Pasquinas, disguised as a clown and backed monetarily by jeal-ous scavengers out to peel the feathers off the peacockish Juan Can. Up to midnight steady hands and sharp eyes kept the game quite even, though the stakes increased with each reshuffling of the cards. Sud-denly the clown sitting opposite Juan began to shake slightly as he dealt. His breath began to smell. Saliva appeared on the corners of his mouth. Noticing this, Juan's eyes opened wide and his heart beat faster at the sudden realization that he was matching nerves, wits, and cards with the one and only Pasquinas. To withdraw, however, was out of the question.

In a few hours the noise and music of the circus were gone and only a few players were left. Pasquinas's stinking breath filled the tent. Juan Can, though tired and red eyed, was wiping his forehead. A smile was on his lips. He felt that he had won so much, in spite of his gasping for clean air, that it was enough with which to buy Arizona Territory to give to Teresita Ríos for a wedding present.

But, before dawn, a lone figure crept stealthily to the back of the bearded lady's tent. It stopped behind the silhouette of the player's slender form. A knife glistened in the lonely moonlight. It was thrust through the tent into Juan Can's back, who, with wondering eyes and an open mouth, fell forward on top of the money he had won, no longer to mind the stench of Pasquinas's breath.

After Juan Can was buried, Teresita Ríos daily lit a candle at the grave of her loved one. Years later, when she went to unite herself in death with the one whom she was never able to have while on earth, Juan Can's grave did not suffer the indignity of loneliness. From then on, since Mexicans are very pious, men and women started paying homage to the will of God by lighting candles nightly over Juan Can's grave. Some lit them in the hope that Juan would be finally cleansed of all his earthly sins and admitted into Heaven. Others lit them for personal reasons pertaining to love affairs and desires, for it is believed that the grateful souls of the departed often repay even the humble gesture of lighting a candle a hundredfold.

Now, many generations later, time has succeeded in flattening the mound of earth over Juan Can's body, if it is his that lies there. The wooden cross has been replaced by a durable one of cement. Instead of an occasional candle flickering itself away on some rock, many candles burn on tallow-laden candle racks. And while there is doubt in many a Mexican's mind as to who is buried there, the faithful ones who have been lighting candles there for generations are convinced of one thing, that El Tiradito, the Fallen One, whoever he may be, grants wishes to those blessed with sublime faith.

The Pioneer

üero means blond and *chulo*, in the presence of ladies, means handsome. Güero Chulo was neither, but that is what everybody called him because Maximiliano Torres Carbajalando[74] was too long and complicated for people to remember. He was born in a little lazy Mexican town. He grew up running errands for a restaurant. And lived insulting aristocracy. "How I hate this damned *fifi* aristocracy," he would say, "that would melt if it went out in the sun." One day, he sneaked under a barbed wire at the border into this country without aristocracy and after a few days found himself in Tucson's El Hoyo.

Soon, however, he found out that not all Mexican aristocracy was to be found south of the border. Here, he found that Mexican aristocracy was not even Mexican at all. It was Spanish American, smoked cigars, and spoke Spanish only sparingly. "How the hell is it that they cannot talk Spanish," he asked, "when their feet are dark, the sun never hits them, and the damned feet are still dark?" So the Güero Chulo used to get so mad that he even insulted the forefathers of the Spanish Americans. "They say that they have been here since the days of the Conquistadores and are now Spanish Americans. They probably came with the snakes," he said. "*Pues*, well, I came under the fence and I am better than all of those damned self-styled pioneers," he finished. "And I will prove it."

At first, the Güero Chulo did not know what to do. Because he could not lower his dignity to work in the restaurant, he stayed out of work until people got tired of feeding him and then became a "geologist" and went to work digging cesspools. He became a "landscape artist" and mowed lawns. It was sad for the proud Güero Chulo to injure his dignity in this manner, but a living is a living. Sometimes, out of sadness, he bought a bottle of bootleg whiskey and got drunk in his room at the Imperial Hotel.

One day, as he sat in a little public park, he heard two old-timers tell tales of the buried treasures in the Cerro del Gato[75] Mountains. He had gazed at these mountains from his little room at the hotel but had never imagined any treasures being buried there. So, every night, after working as a geologist or landscape artist, he wandered up and down the purple mountains, hoping that the long-dead Texan who had buried the treasures would appear and direct him to their location. For months he walked nightly in the lonely mountains. Sometimes he tripped and fell over a sleeping steer. But El Tejano, the Texan, never appeared.

One morning as the Güero Chulo came out of the mountains, he saw a car coming through the desert toward him. Promptly, he hid behind a mesquite bush. Soon the car came to a stop and two men got out. "I guess this spot is good enough, eh, Joe?"

"Yeah," answered the other. "I think so. Let's take out the shovels and plant the stuff here." So the two men dug a hole large enough to bury a horse. Then they began unloading small wooden crates from the rear of the automobile. They covered the crates well and then drove away. Then Güero Chulo came out from behind the mesquite bush and after following the car with his eyes as far as he could, he ran to the spot, got on his knees, and frantically began digging with his hands. And it turned out to be imported cognac. So the Güero Chulo became a dealer in bootleg liquor. He became the scourge of the mountains. When any bootlegger planted his liquid fortune anywhere in the Cerro del Gato Mountains, the Güero Chulo came out of nowhere like a vulture, and left but an empty grave. His conceit grew with his ability. After every theft, he left a little card at the bottom of the grave inscribed with the following message—"*Muchas gracias del Agradecido. Many thanks from the grateful one.*"

One moonlight night he hid behind a bush and saw that a bigger than usual crate was being buried. This was the way Güero Chulo liked it! The bigger, the better. When the two men drove away and Güero Chulo got to the crate, which seemed only partly buried, the lid flew open and a thug said, as he pointed a shotgun at Güero Chulo, "Here, wise guy, take some of this." And the Güero Chulo caught two barrels of buckshot. He ran and ran. And long before he was able to sit, Prohibition came to an end.

Sadly, he returned to geology and landscaping. But somehow, the

Güero Chulo was not happy. It seemed to him that he was not being treated as the glorious name of Maximiliano Torres Carbajalando deserved. "I must make contacts," he thought. But nobody wanted any contact with him. "Well, I never wanted a damned thing from these damned self-styled pioneers," he said. "Well, I came under the fence and I am better than all of these damned self-styled pioneers," he finished. "And I will prove it!"

When World War II was declared, and everybody capitalized, the Güero Chulo was not outdone. He became a warworker and as a sideline cashed, for a small fee, the checks of the migrant railroad workers.

One day, one of them said to him, "*Qué ladrón.* What a thief."

And the Güero Chulo did not answer. He was Spanish American, smoked cigars, and spoke Spanish only sparingly. Truly a pioneer, he.

Something Useful, Even Tailoring

One hot summer day Gonzalo Pereda, the tailor, was growing impatient. Every now and then he looked up from the coat he was working on and glanced at a little alarm clock nearby. He wondered what could possibly be detaining his son, Luis. Luis was supposed to have been there at one. Now it was almost three and there was no sign of him yet. True, it was summer, reasoned Gonzalo, resuming his work. So why not let Luis have his fun? After all, he was only fifteen. But Luis had been having his fun, and as a matter of principle, if it was understood that he was to be at the shop on Tuesday and Thursday afternoons throughout the summer, it was his duty to be there.

At last, a few minutes past three, Luis Pereda rushed into the shop, breathing heavily and wiping the perspiration from his forehead.

"What happened to you, Luis?" asked Gonzalo. "You were supposed to be here at one. It is now past three."

"Papa, you see . . . We played . . ." he said, trying to catch his breath. "The game didn't end until half an hour ago. Then I rushed home to wash up and change my clothes and here I am. I'm sorry."

"Well, at least you're here. That's something. Sit down for a while and catch your breath. Then I want you to get a razor blade and unsew the cuffs on those blue pants up on the rack. They are going to call for them by five o'clock."

Luis sat quietly for a while and then got up to get the blue pants his father had pointed out, picked up a razor blade, and went to work.

For a long time both father and son worked silently. At length Gonzalo looked toward his son. "How did it go today, Luis?" he asked.

Luis swallowed hard. "We lost," he said sheepishly.

"Bad?"

"Yes. We were beaten bad, *papá*," he said, a tone of sadness in his voice.

The bitter truth was that Luis and his teammates had been massacred. The torture of having lost a ball game 21 to 1 was still too much to bear. It was then that Gonzalo saw his son Luis wipe a tear which threatened to run down his face.

"What's the matter, Luis?"

"Nothing papa. Nothing," said Luis, fighting hard to regain his composure. He was through unsewing the first cuff and was about to start on the other one.

"Defeats are part of life, Luis. Don't feel bad."

But Luis did feel bad. He had tried hard that day, as though his very life depended on it. Playing centerfield he had made four good catches out of the many screaming drives the opposing team made to the outfield. True, he had gone hitless. But he had scored his team's only run as a result of a walk and an eventual balk. Now his father tried to make him feel better by telling him that defeats were part of life. Rot. It was his father's excuse for making him learn tailoring, Luis reasoned. And how he hated it. Baseball was to be his life or nothing. Didn't his father realize that there were players like Billy Herman and Dizzy Dean who made thousands and thousands of dollars in one season? No, he probably didn't.

Only a year ago, when the Cubs and White Sox were in town to play an exhibition game during spring training, Luis had been fortunate enough to spot Gabby Hartnett getting out of a cab. Luis had run over to him and, before he was besieged by a screaming mob of future big leaguers, Luis was able to shake the great player's gnarled right hand. A warm sensation swept him. As he went around the back of the park to await his opportunity to jump the fence and make a dash for the bleachers, Luis felt as though he were walking on air. Later, watching the game amid the noise, excitement, and suspense, Luis knew where his golden future lay.

Now, as he watched his father about to shape some lapels with the aid of a sponge, pad, and heavy iron, he wondered if he had ever had any dreams beyond the hot, stuffy tailor shop with its sewing machine, cutting table, tape measures, scissors, spools of thread, and racks bulging with coats and pants which, once ready, nobody ever seemed to call for.

Gonzalo ran the steaming iron across the pad protecting the lapel he was shaping. He glanced momentarily at Luis, now picking the cut threads out of the second cuff. It was easy to tell, from the look on his face, that his mind was still on the lost ball game. Well, mused Gonzalo, what else can I do for him? When he was born I wanted the world for him. At eight I had Professor Julio Torres give him piano lessons. When the professor told me he was progressing admirably, I dreamed that perhaps someday he might be a concert pianist. But in two years he rebelled. "Spank me, *papá*," Luis had said, crying bitter tears. "Spank me, but don't make me study the piano. I hate it." When he decided it was the violin he wanted, I bought one for him, thinking perhaps . . . But the enthusiasm didn't last very long and the violin is now gathering dust at home. Now it's baseball which dominates his existence. So, what else can I do for him? Gonzalo took the iron off the sleeve board, removed the pad, and prepared the other lapel for the same process.

But then, I had my dreams, too, thought Gonzalo. How well I remember the anxieties I gave my two older sisters when, in their endeavor to keep me off the streets, they apprenticed me to the local maestro in Santa Rosalía that I might learn tailoring. Close to four years I spent there, under the whip and poisoned tongue of that bilious individual. Then one day I saw the youthful Rodolfo Gaona perform in the local arena. "He is the richest man in the world," I heard somebody say. And from that moment on I knew I had to be a *matador de toros* or die trying. What hungers and what horrendous beatings the animals and the ranch guards gave me, sending me back to tailoring to dream some more. When the revolution came I guess it was natural that I should almost immediately find myself riding with General Demetrio Macías. More hungers and privations. Then, still spurred on by the exuberance of youth, came the night we assaulted Quintanares and my horse was shot from under me, shattering my wrist along with all my dreams. Gonzalo then recalled the words of Louis Stein, the little tailor who had given him his first job when he found himself friendless and hungry in El Paso. "No matter their dreams, Gonzalo, when you have sons, teach them something useful, even tailoring."

Gonzalo put down the iron and took the coat off the sleeve board.

He was about to hang up the coat when he noticed Luis, now through with his assigned task, looking at him. "What do you say to going for some cold drinks for us, Luis?" asked Gonzalo, reaching into his pocket for some change.

"Good idea," said Luis, his face lighting up. "Good idea."

Trouble in Petate

Pepe was a very fortunate man. He owned a little red rooster who crowed very late. By that time the sun was so high in the sky that only a fool would have thought of doing anything else but turn over and sleep until late in the afternoon. This does not mean that Pepe was lazy. But is it not wise for a man to take care of his ribs? Is he not using good judgment in practicing that most self-preserving of all the arts, the art of leisure? Of course. So Pepe did.

Late in the afternoons Pepe opened one eye, yawned, and then opened the other. Putting his two hands under his head for pillows he stared at the roof of his little house to look at the rays of the sun as they came in through the cracks and openings. Then he gazed about the room at the good amounts of wild fruit he picked up in the hilly jungle above his little patch. He gazed at Pulgas,[76] his dog, sleeping at his feet. Pepe considered his good fortune and decided that he was content. For Pepe to have had more would have been reason for him to grow old before his time. Oftentimes Pepe felt very sorry for people who owned too many horses, too many cows, too many chickens, and too many worries. So it pleased Pepe to own no horses which constantly ran away and stood in danger of being stolen. He owned Orejas,[77] a grey little donkey who slept even longer than Pepe himself. He owned no cows for which he would have been forced to build a barn or shelter. He owned Enamorada,[78] as was his goat's name, who preferred running into the hilly jungle to meet her suitors by moonlight. Neither did Pepe own too many chickens. He had four or five cacklers with bare necks, but these were enough to give him the eggs he ate. Therefore, Pepe did not have too many worries.

After getting up, Pepe rolled up his grass sleeping mat, put it in a corner, and went outside to stretch in the sun. Because his white clothes kept the mosquitoes away from his body during the night and kept his body cool beneath the torrid tropical sun during the day, Pepe never bothered to take them off except to wash them by beating them against the rocks near the brook. But this was only before a celebration or before going to church in the little village of Feria.[79] After breakfasting on wild fruit, Pepe inspected his little crop and sighed happily at the prospect of a good harvest. Pepe felt sure that when he sold this crop he would have enough money to order a rifle from Petate City.[80]

Afterward Pepe took his long machete from where it hung inside his house and whacked off the head of a stray chicken he had caught a few days before. Pepe well realized that it would have been foolish for him to eat his own chickens; after all, they furnished him with eggs. There is also that verse which implies that there is no tastier meat than that of the neighbor. So Pepe peeled, cleaned, and proceeded to cook his supper over a little fire. Since Pepe had good taste, he was not one to eat the chicken by itself. He boiled a few ears of corn he had taken from an overburdened stalk on the way home from Feria a few nights before. Not to mention the tomatoes, bananas, and limes which, being wild and belonging no nobody, Pepe would never have to account to Padre Ramón for when he went to confession. After supper Pepe relaxed in front of his house to watch his little red rooster as he chased the cackling chickens. To milk dreamy-eyed Enamorada. And to watch the sun as it fell behind the far mountains.

At night Pepe sometimes mounted Orejas, his donkey, and took the little road to Feria with the intention of drinking a few harmless thimbles of *chispa*.[81] And the trip never turned out long or dismal. Because most people did their traveling in the cool of the night, Pepe always joined a group along the road. In the group there was always a troubadour or at least a would-be troubadour who would sing the songs Pepe loved to hear. More often than not one in the group would offer, on acquaintance, his bottle, and Pepe, being obliging, always took a little drink so that the one that offered it would not feel insulted.

Feria is not a big village. It is no more than a church, *ayuntamiento* or municipal hall, school building, *chispa* station, and houses with bars in the windows. This does not make of these houses jails. The Feria jail is in back of the *ayuntamiento*. Pepe knew this well, and for a reason. Once, during a little celebration, he had been unjustly forced to sleep there for disturbing the peace. But that had been long ago.

The other intention of Pepe's trips to Feria was a village maiden named Dalia. Dalia lived in a little house near the edge of the village with her father and mother. Whenever the thimbles of *chispa* went to Pepe's head, he rode, as best he could, past Dalia's house on Orejas. Stopping in front of her window, Pepe let his eyes wander up and down each of the window's bars. Turning his face away disinterestedly he would hear from behind the bars, "*Buenas noches.* Good evening, Pepe." And it made Pepe tremble. Yet, he did not know if he trembled with fear or joy.

When Pepe looked toward the window and saw Dalia, it usually made him fall off Orejas, almost. He found he could do nothing with his hands. It made his eyeballs want to explore his head even while his eyelids opened wider. His head always went limp and rested on one of his shoulders while butterflies went up and down his back.

After Dalia closed the homemade curtains that fell between her and the bars in the window, Pepe regained his senses and rode back to the *chispa* station for one more thimble. After drinking it he imagined that the curtains were in his little house and that when they fell, they fell only to keep out the light of the moon. Then Pepe mounted Orejas and took the road back to his little patch to go to sleep with Pulgas, his dog. But he did so very happily.

2

By the time Pepe got to the village on Domingo de Resurrección, Easter Sunday, the sun was high in the sky. Already the girls were adorning the fronts of their little houses with paper decorations. Little stands which would sell *chispa* were taking shape in front of some of the houses. In front of other houses tables were being arranged so that one could eat a *perrucho*[82] of meat and sauce in comfort. There were other little stands going up which would sell firecrackers and *egganios*.[83] *Egganios* were of vital importance. When a young man loves a young girl, all he has to do to prove it is break an *egganio* over her head. He has to make sure, of course, that the *egganio* is filled with confetti and not with the egg's original yolk and white.

In the afternoon Padre Ramón said a mass of importance at which Pepe managed to get many good views of Dalia who attended with her mother and father. In fact Pepe paid so much attention to Dalia that if somebody had asked him what the sermon had been about, Pepe would have said that Padre Ramón had been selling rosaries from the pulpit. Then there was a procession in which all took part. And it not only took place inside the church but all over the village as well.

After the procession was over, firecrackers began to go off. The little stands began to do business. The young men and women met in the clearing in front of the church and danced the kipop in native Peta-teño costumes. Padre Ramón, who took a profound interest in each of his subject's spiritual well-being and knew each by name, went from one little stand to the next tasting the *chispa* that was being served. He sat at the little tables to sample the *perruchos* and sucked his fingers in approval of the delicious but very hot sauce.

Pepe, as usual, was drinking too much *chispa*. By the time the sun went down and the dancing of the kipop was taking place inside each little house, Pepe had passed out, had been revived, and was on the way to passing out again. The *perrucho* sauce was all over his white clothes. The *chispa* wanted to fly out his mouth every time he opened it to talk. But all the villagers expected this deportment of Pepe.

When the *chispa* went to Pepe's head, he decided to hire three troubadours to serenade Dalia. When they got to her window he ordered them to play a soft and dreamy kipop. They played. But Dalia did not look out the window. Pepe had the troubadours play a loud kipop. They did. Still Dalia did not open the curtains to acknowledge the serenade. Pepe was surprised at her attitude. He sent the troubadours away and sadly sat down under her window.

Soon Pepe heard someone crying softly inside. Pepe got up, looked through the window, and saw Dalia crying.

"Dalia," he called.

She turned around and Pepe realized that she had been crying for a long time.

"What is the matter, Dalia?" he asked.

"I am the most unfortunate woman in the world," she sobbed.

"Why?" asked Pepe.

"They are going to marry me off to Don Teodoro," she said.

"What?" asked Pepe, falling back, his head clearing quickly.

"Yes, they are going to marry me off to Don Teodoro."

"Don't they know that you are mine?" asked Pepe.

"Yes, but they will marry me off to Don Teodoro anyway. They will not let me marry you because everybody in the village says you are a man of many vices," she said.

"But I have only the popular vices," said Pepe.

"I know. But what am I to do? I do not want to marry a man as old as the moon and as fat as a pig," she said.

"Leave it to me," said Pepe. "I will fix Don Teodoro. Just because he is the *presidente municipal* does not mean that he will take the lady of Pepe."

"Oh, Pepe," said Dalia, her face brightening up, "you are wonderful."

That night when the villagers gathered in the square, under a stand, to hear a speech by Don Teodoro, Feria's first authority, Pepe was in the crowd. Don Teodoro talked of his wonderful administration. He spoke of his two gendarmes who kept law and order. Then he spoke of his future by telling the listeners that he had been granted the hand of Dalia, the daughter of the village blacksmith. All the people clapped and cheered. Pepe gritted his teeth and threw an *egganio* at Don Teodoro. Pepe was so mad that he threw another *egganio*. But when the *egganios* landed all were surprised to see that Pepe had thrown eggs at the first authority, at Don Teodoro, the *presidente municipal*.

Immediately the two village gendarmes jumped on top of Pepe. They tried to hold him but he fought like a lion. And why not? Was he not fighting the henchmen of a pig who wanted to take his Dalia from him? After a fierce struggle they dragged Pepe to the *ayuntamiento*, but no matter how hard the two gendarmes tried they could not subdue Pepe. Don Teodoro shouted, as he held up his staff, the staff of authority, "*Quieto, perro*. Quiet, dog. Isn't the first authority talking?" But Pepe did not quiet down. Padre Ramón, who had been nearby, walked into the *ayuntamiento* to find that Pepe had almost subdued the two gendarmes. On seeing Padre Ramón walk in, Pepe quickly stood still.

"What goes on here?" asked Padre Ramón.

"This dog," said Don Teodoro, "has shown his disrespect. He has not kept quiet when I have thrust in his face the staff of authority. Look at him. Who can quiet a dog like that?"

Pepe got so mad at being called a dog that he broke away from the two gendarmes, jumped on top of Don Teodoro, grabbed the staff, and broke it over the outraged *presidente*'s head. The *presidente* sat down and wept. He said something about resigning the next day. Then Pepe said, "Come on, Padre Ramón, let us go to the church so that you can tell me what a bad thing I've done."

Once inside the rectory Padre Ramón said, "Pepe, how do you expect to reach Heaven when you do things like that?"

"Padre, I did nothing wrong. I was only ridiculing him so that he would not insist on marrying my Dalia."

"Perhaps, Pepe, but you should not ridicule the law. Don't you know that the authority vested in the *presidente municipal* is what keeps our fair village so peaceful?"

"Yes, Padre Ramón, but a pig like that should not be *presidente municipal* in the first place. Anyway, I take orders from only one authority, and that is you, Padre Ramón. After all, by right the power of the church is much greater than that of a dozen fat municipal *presidentes*."

"Thank you," said Padre Ramón. Padre Ramón realized that Pepe merited a little wine. After the good padre, the guardian of Pepe's soul, poured Pepe some wine, he told him that he must repent. Pepe repented. The padre, seeing Pepe repent, rewarded him with more wine. Then he poured himself some wine.

"I still insist that the church is the first and only authority and that you should be *presidente municipal*," said Pepe. And even if Padre Ramón agreed, he told Pepe that he must never ridicule the *presidente municipal* again. After Pepe and Padre Ramón drank their fill, Pepe said, "Padre, if you are too sick tomorrow, I will say mass for you."

"Pepe," said Padre Ramón with a stern look on his face, "you are impossible. I truthfully wonder if you will ever go to Heaven with such thoughts as that one. You better mount Orejas and go back to your little house."

"Very well, Padre Ramón, but call me if you need me." Pepe got up and went out the door. He mounted Orejas and went back to his little patch. True, he was sad. Padre Ramón said that he wondered if he would ever get to Heaven.

But what more Heaven was there, Pepe asked himself as he rode, than being well fed, well rested, well drunk, and well loved?

3

One afternoon when Pepe returned from the jungle, he found a stranger on his little patch. He had seen many strangers before, but none of them had ever looked like this one. This stranger was very tall, very bearded of face, wore dark glasses, and was very quick in his movements.

The stranger had two overburdened little donkeys. From one donkey's back he took a little telescope with three very long legs which he set on the ground and then he began to look through it. After that he walked about and jumped up and down in certain places. For a moment Pepe thought that the stranger was crazy. Perhaps he had had too much *chispa*.

While the stranger took a box from the other donkey's back and took from it many curious-looking objects, Pepe decided to walk around in back of him in order not to arouse him as he proceeded to inspect Pepe's patch. The stranger was so busy putting his ear to the ground, taking a little notebook from his shirt pocket and smiling as he wrote figures in it, that he did not bother to look around at all. Pulgas, at last, decided that the stranger had gone unmolested long enough. He sprang on the stranger's trouser leg only to be rudely shaken off. At that moment the stranger noticed Pepe and said, "Good afternoon, *señor*."

So surprised at being called a señor was Pepe that he looked around for a third intruder.

"Do you want to sell this land?" asked the stranger.

"No," said Pepe. "When my father died he told me never to sell it."

"Well," said the stranger, "I have been examining it and I find it very bad."

"It may be bad but I live off it," said Pepe.

"Do you call this living?" asked the stranger.

"Of course. Me and my dog and my donkey and my goat and my chickens are very happy here," said Pepe.

"You say that because it is the only place you know. Have you ever been elsewhere?" asked the stranger.

"Oh, I have been to Feria," said Pepe.

"Feria! That hole? My friend, you have never been anywhere. Have you ever been in Petate City, or at least Petatillo?"[84] asked the stranger.

"No," said Pepe.

"I feel very sorry for you then. You have never lived. You have never seen the wonders of the world. I feel very sorry for you," said the stranger.

"What wonders?" asked Pepe.

So the stranger began to tell Pepe of the wonderful things in the city. He told him of houses built on top of one another. He told him of big and broad streets. He told him of seeing the army of Petate as it marched each morning through the streets of Petate City. Then he told him of the beautiful women. "Of course, they are far prettier than these fat country creatures around here who know nothing of dressing themselves—"

"I have a girl in Feria who knows how to cook, sew, and will give me healthy sons," Pepe interrupted angrily.

"Well," said the stranger, "I have looked at these fat country girls. In Petate City, or Petatillo even, the ugliest there I would not trade for the best one around here."

Taking a picture from one of his pockets, the stranger showed it to Pepe and said, "That is the kind of women we have in the city. My friend, you have never lived. You know nothing. You must go to the city so that you can become a man. So that you can become wise to the ways of the world. So that you will wear clothes of style and not those rags you have on. Look at yourself." Pepe looked down at his clothes and bare feet ashamed.

The stranger said, "Think of it. Petate City with its beautiful build-ings, its music, its lovely ladies. Truthfully, my friend, you are wasting your life away around here." Pepe took another look at the stranger's picture.

"And you say all are as beautiful as this one?" asked Pepe.

"Of course. Most are much more to look at than this one. I only carry her picture because I feel sorry for her. Just like I feel sorry for a good-looking young man like you who throws his life away here in the jungle when he could be dancing his life away in Petate City. After all, life is a kipop and one must dance it away,"[85] said the stranger.

Still Pepe could not think of selling his little patch.

Then the stranger said, "Well, at least, will you let me stay here tonight?" Pepe, being good of heart, said he could.

That night the stranger set up his tent near Pepe's house and Pepe, asking God to forgive him, killed one of his chickens in order to have something good to compart with the stranger. He felt very badly when he removed that part of the chicken which showed that it would have laid many more eggs. But he forgot about it when the stranger, who ate most of it, began to tell Pepe of the wonders of Petate City.

"Yes, I certainly feel sorry for you if you have never seen the Bay of Petate by moonlight, walking arm in arm with one of the many pretty girls in Petate City. That is living. Then you can take her to a little place where they will serve you drinks. A troubadour will play love songs which will win for you the girl's heart." Pepe sighed.

"And there you will be, with a girl like that in your arms," said the stranger, showing Pepe the picture again.

Then the stranger took a flask from his pocket and gave it to Pepe. Pepe took a drink. His eyes almost fell out of his head. "This is much better than *chispa* or even better than Padre Ramón's wine," said Pepe, taking another drink.

"Of course," said the stranger, "take another one."

"Tell me more of Petate City, will you?" asked Pepe.

So the stranger took a deep breath and again told Pepe of the won-derful things that were in the big city. He told him of the tall buildings. Of streets. Of armies. Then he told Pepe of the beautiful women. "They are far prettier than these fat country creatures around here who know nothing of dressing themselves in order to make themselves look desirable." Pepe sighed.

"Perhaps you don't want to hear more. Perhaps you are satisfied with this life. If so, I cannot blame you. It is all you know."

"Please tell me more," said Pepe.

"There is not much more to tell. You must see it with your eyes in order to feel a part of its grandeur," said the stranger.

"Is it really that wonderful?" asked Pepe.

"Yes, even more wonderful than the words of a poet could describe. And if you will sign this paper," said the stranger, taking a paper from his pocket, "the wonders I have spoken of will be yours."

"I know nothing of legal papers," said Pepe.

"But you know something about money," said the stranger.

"I have a few *lanillas*[86] once in a while when I sell my crop," answered Pepe.

"Well," said the stranger, "I will give you a thousand *lanillas* for your little patch." Pepe swallowed hard. He did not know that so much money existed.

"All right then, two thousand," the stranger said. He took the money from his pocket and put it in front of Pepe's eyes. Pepe almost choked and asked for the flask again.

The next morning Pepe got up very early, since in thinking of the money he now possessed he had been unable to sleep, mounted Orejas, and taking Pulgas with him, departed.

4

Pepe was in such a hurry to get to the big city that when he went through the village of Feria he did not slow down long enough to bless himself, as had been his custom, when he went by the church. He did not stop long enough to drink a thimble of *chispa*. Riding past Dalia's house he put his nose in the air when he noticed that she was standing by the door.

"Pepe," Dalia called. But Pepe went by as proudly as a peacock passing the cage of a buzzard.

"Pepe," she called again. But Pepe only spurred Orejas faster.

"Pepe, are you mad at me?" asked Dalia, running up from behind. "Answer me, Pepe, *Pepito mío*,[87] are you mad at me?" she asked, grabbing Pepe by the sleeve. Pepe became angry at the liberty she was taking and tried to free his sleeve.

"Pepe, what is the matter?" she asked.

Pepe sneered and said through the side of his mouth, "Keep away from me, you country wench." Dalia instantly released his sleeve and Pepe spurred Orejas forward, leaving Dalia sitting in the middle of the road, crying as only a woman can.

Before Pepe could get to Petate City he had to take a train from Petatillo, a city of lesser importance. Pepe's mind was so much farther ahead of Orejas that he scarcely noticed the pretty terrain he was going through. To both sides of the road spread the jungle, with its wild fruits, with its every sort of animal, with its flowers and beauty indescribable. Little monkeys swung from one tree to another along the road in an effort to show for Pepe, but he did not notice them. Multi-colored birds of every description flew past Pepe, who did not turn his head as they swooped by to flitter back into the jungle. After all, why should Pepe turn his head? Didn't he have two thousand *lanillas* in his belt?

Late in the afternoon, when Pepe made out the spires of the Petatillo churches at a distance, he reined Orejas and scanned the road up and down. Then he spurred Orejas into the jungle and dismounted. After tying Orejas to a stout tree he walked back to the road. Orejas began to bray. Pepe stopped. Orejas was braying and stamping the ground. Orejas was screeching and whining like only a donkey who loved his master could. Pepe swallowed hard. He retraced his steps into the jungle and faced his companion. When Orejas saw that Pepe had come back, he stopped braying. Tears came to Pepe's eyes.

"Orejas, *Orejitas mío*," said Pepe, "I am sorry. I am very sorry." Pepe began to cry. "I cannot take you with me. I wish I could. But I cannot." Pepe embraced Orejas. Orejas nudged his nose into Pepe's shirt and licked Pepe's stomach. "Honest, Orejas, *Orejitas* of my life, if I took you to the city the people would laugh at you. They would laugh at me. They would laugh at both of us. So I leave you. If you stay here like a good donkey, perhaps some traveler will pass by and take you to his house."

Then Pepe kissed Orejas, turned his face, and hurried away. Orejas began to bray, began to screech, began to strain the rope that held him. But to no avail. Pepe had abandoned him.

Near Petatillo the jungle began to thin out into individually fenced little patches. Many farmers hurried their little donkeys along the road and Pepe thought he saw the image of Orejas in each. Little dirty-faced kids, with somber eyes, with fat bellies exposed, watched him hurry by and Pepe felt that they were judging him for the injustice he had committed against Orejas. Even Pulgas put his tail between his legs.

At night, when Pepe finally got to Petatillo, he stopped at a little hotel, locked himself in a room with only Pulgas to keep him company, and frantically counted his money over and over again.

The next day he would take the train to Petate City.

5

When the little train started for Petate City, Pepe stuck his head out the window to admire the well-kept fields and to wave at country folk whose only contact with the rest of the world was the passing of the train. As Pepe gazed out the window, a thin individual in a dirty white suit, a stickpin in his tie, cufflinks which he did his best to keep visible, and a briefcase, tapped him on the shoulder and asked, pointing to the seat in front of Pepe, "Is this seat occupied?"

Pepe took Pulgas off the seat and said, "No. No, it isn't."

"Are you going to Petate City?" asked the individual, sitting down in front of Pepe.

"Yes. Yes, I am," answered Pepe.

"Permit me to introduce myself then, so that we can make the trip interesting. My name is Octavio Claveles Villar[r]ica y Tostada.[88] I am going all the way to Petate City."

"Mine is Pepe," said Pepe.

"Glad to make your acquaintance," said the individual. Then he went on, "Do you live in Petate City?"

"No," answered Pepe, "I am going there for the first time."

"You mean you have never been to Petate City?"

"That is right," answered Pepe.

"Then say no more," said the individual, "because I can tell right off that you are a man in quest of worlds to conquer. I wager that you are in search of adventure. You are most likely in search of the love of angel-faced women. Ah, in Petate City you will find them. You are not a bad-looking fellow. I am sure that Petate City will be to your liking. I have been all over the world myself. I have lived. I went to Espánica[89] to visit the tombs of my ancestors. Ah, Espánica, how I long for it! Petate City is fine. I do not mean to run it down. But Espánica, ah! Nothing is as beautiful as Espánica. I was born in Petate City. But, of course, I have nothing but *sangre azul*, the bluest of blood, in my veins. I have the royal blood of the house of Villar[r]ica y Tostada. I could tell all that I am an Espánico. But no, I say that I am a Petatiero and I am proud of it. Even if I have royal blood and a coat of arms. That is the way I am."

Pepe was so nervous at having such a grandiose person sit next to him that when the fruit salesman went by he summoned him and picked three apples for the individual and one for himself. Pepe was reaching into his shirt for some money. But the individual held his hand and said, "Oh, no, no, let me pay for this." So the royal individual paid for the four apples after dickering with the salesman as to their price. Then he said, "It is robbery. It is a case of assault by these barefoot bandits who would rob one of his last *lanilla* for a measly apple." Ashamed, Pepe put his bare feet under the seat.

"But that is the way I am," continued the royal individual. "After all, one must spend his money in order to enjoy life." Octavio Claveles Villar[r]ica y Tostada bit into an apple. "Robbery. Banditry," he finished.

It made Pepe very happy to make friends so quickly with a man of the world. No doubt this acquaintance would lead to greater things. Perhaps if he confided in the stranger he could learn more. But before Pepe could do so, the individual, who had been eyeing Pepe up and down, said, "You know, I am not one that confides in everybody. But I will tell you a secret. I am a man that can tell an intelligent man right away, so I will tell you that I suffer greatly. That is the reason that I travel around making true friends like you."

"Why do you suffer?" asked Pepe.

"Well, you see, it is a long story. But to make it short, I used to make money very easily. I used to make tons of money. *Lanillas* and more *lanillas*. But ever since El Supremo has been in power I can no longer make any more because the government is very jealous of the Villar[r]ica y Tostada family. Now I am but a lowly merchant," said the individual. He reached, with tears in his eyes, for his briefcase, and opening it he asked Pepe, "Do you want to buy white socks?"

Pepe felt very sorry for him, so he bought two pairs. When the individual explained his need a little bit further, Pepe brought two more pairs. After the individual took a few of Pepe's *lanillas*, he said to him, "Because in you I have found a true friend, because you are truly a comrade, I will now do something for you. And very cheap."

"What?" asked Pepe.

"Well, when you get to Petate City you will certainly need a letter of introduction. You will want to meet lovely ladies, and you can't go about it in any other way but to have a letter of introduction. That way when you meet a girl all you have to do is present her parents with the letter and you will be immediately accepted." So the benevolent individual wrote a letter which stated that Pepe was a well-read man from the interior. That he was unmarried. That his was untold and fabulous wealth. That he was of aristocratic ancestry and was glad to make acquaintances of the same.

All of this made Pepe very happy. He had never dreamed that he would meet such a kind-hearted individual. By the time the lights of Petate City were in sight, Octavio Claveles Villar[r]ica y Tostada was wearing Pepe's clothes. Pepe had on Villar[r]ica y Tostada's white suit, shoes, including the stickpin and cufflinks. His was the briefcase. And he was only about one hundred and fifty *lanillas* poorer.

6

The following morning, after having located a comfortable room in the center of Petate City and after locking Pulgas in it, Pepe went out to admire the buildings and to look for city girls. But as Pepe made his way up and down the streets, looking up at the five- and six-story buildings, searching in vain for the hordes of pretty girls he expected to meet, he kept running into very dignified-looking gentlemen who only sneered as they passed him by. Most of them wore white suits, hats, mustaches, and carried briefcases. Pepe decided that the next time he would not leave his room without his briefcase.

That afternoon, after having walked Petate's main streets, Pepe walked into a restaurant to rest his tired feet. Sitting down at a table near the door in order to notice the passers-by, Pepe ordered a bottle of *chispa*. Pepe loosened his shoes, wiped the perspiration off his forehead, and was in the process of making himself comfortable when he could not help but overhear a conversation going on behind him.

The speakers were obviously men of money. One spoke of how, if one invested twenty thousand *lanillas* into this business or that, he could double the amount within six months. The other two made the same kind of claims on the doubling, tripling, and quadrupling of *lanillas*.

The speakers were well informed politically, because they spoke of rights and freedoms, of treaties and compromises, of trade and commerce. In doing so they mentioned many fancy terms which Pepe had never heard anything about. But it was natural. After all, was he not from the country? Pepe ordered another bottle of *chispa*.

The speakers were men of the world indeed. Soon they began to talk of women. They began to describe, limb by limb, the women they had conquered. They began to explain the tactics they had used for this one and that one. They began to tell of how women naturally fell to their charms. Pepe, wanting to learn, turned around.

One of the gentlemen, who had his leg crossed and was doing most of the talking, had no socks on. But when Pepe looked him over he noticed that he did have plenty of lard in his hair. Perhaps it was the custom.

Pepe noticed that the other two also had plenty of lard in their hair. While Pepe was not able to notice whether they had socks on or not, he took it for granted that they did not. It was funny to Pepe that men of money, of learning, of charms no woman could resist, should wear no socks. But Pepe was learning all the time.

As Pepe drank he almost choked when he heard the proprietor say to them, "You have been in here all day and have consumed only one lemonade each. Get out! I have to make a living."

The three gentlemen became irritated. One of them told the proprietor that nobody could talk like that to the relative of a general. The other threatened suit and warned that his uncle was a cousin of a friend who had a relative in the Chamber of Deputies. The third likewise defied the proprietor and told him that nobody could insult the sole heir to one of Petate's greatest fortunes.

The proprietor, paying no attention to their claims, thundered back, "Get out! You heard me the first time." As the three men put on their hats, picked up their briefcases, and started walking out, the proprietor said, "Go in the shade, Butterflies, so you won't get sunburned."

Pepe slid down into the chair and sipped quickly the last of the bottle. The proprietor, apologetically, came to him and said, "I am sorry for this tragic scene, my good man. But it is people like that who try my patience." Pepe swallowed hard and agreed. After paying his bill he got up and left.

Late that afternoon, as Pepe was admiring the beautiful ladies who rode in fine coaches pulled by as many as six horses on Petate Square, he noticed that a parade was forming. Some of the officers of the Petate Police Force were petting their beautiful horses and giving them lumps of sugar. Other officers were carefully adjusting cinches while the horses reared their heads backwards and forwards. After all, any well-fed horse has a lot of spirit. Other officers carefully adjusted the gold braid on their uniforms while others lit cigarettes, stuck them in fancy holders, and puffed away.

Bugles blew, the officers mounted, and the parade began. Pepe had never seen such a beautiful sight. The parade was led by a fat officer with many medals on his chest. Behind him came some mounted officers with silk flags. Then came the body of officers, a good two hundred strong, on their prancing mounts. Behind the officers came the band.

When the fat drummer bringing up the rear went by, Pepe thought he had seen the last of the parade. But as he crossed the street to get another view of the beautiful horses on which the officers were mounted, he noticed another group. Pepe wondered if it was a mob. But it turned out to be the enlisted corps of the Petate Police Force. The men marched along perfectly, but all of their tunics were faded and some lacked buttons. Their breeches were dirty and patched. The leggings were very carelessly wrapped around their bowed legs. Their shoes were worn, unpolished, and run down at the heels. Pepe resolved that if he ever joined the Petate Police Force he would do so only on the condition that he be made an officer.

At twilight, when most people in Petate City come out of their houses, Pepe was on his way back to his room when some girls passed him by on the opposite side of the street. Pepe, being shy, swallowed hard and pretended that he had not seen them. But the girls ran around the block, crossed the street, and waited for Pepe to pass them by on the corner. When Pepe walked by, one of them said, "My, but he sure looked better from far." Pepe smiled momentarily at the remark and hurried to his room to look in the mirror.

The next day as Pepe walked about he saw a sign above a door which read, "WE CURL HAIR." Pepe walked in.

"Good day, *monsieur*," said an attendant as Pepe entered the reception room. After a short consultation Pepe was led to a chair, where the attendant said to him, "Well, *monsieur*, do you want to look like a deputy, a lawyer, or just like a simple bank clerk?"

"What is the difference?" asked Pepe.

"The difference, *monsieur*, is only in the price. I suggest that you look like a simple bank clerk. The women will love you. I guarantee it, *monsieur*."

So Pepe had his hair curled. Then the attendant told him that having his hair curled would not be enough. He told him of a six-month lemon treatment which guaranteed a beard, or at least a mustache.

After being subjected to some tortures which, the attendant guaranteed, would give him posture, would make him inches taller, and would make him a gentleman loved by all the ladies, Pepe said to the attendant, "If those that saw me only knew—"

"Oh, *monsieur*, we guarantee utmost secrecy," interrupted the attendant. "After all, the best people come here. If word got out that everybody from El Supremo to his last deputy comes here, we would have to close up. The aristocracy comes here. So do those who would be aristocracy. Why should you feel ashamed? It is the custom, *monsieur*."

Then the attendant told Pepe that he must buy an odd-looking in-

strument which would thin his nose. The instrument came complete
with a book of instructions on how to put it on before going to bed. So
Pepe bought it because everybody owned one.

When Pepe went out the door, perfumed, curled, stretched, pow-
dered, and pounded, he did not feel ashamed. He walked back to his
room in the shade so as not to get sunburned. It was custom.

7

Pepe was walking along a dark street one night when he accidentally
stumbled and fell face first into the center of a group of girls who had
brought their living room chairs out to the sidewalk and were enjoying
the night air.

"How stupid," said one of them.

"Are you blind?" asked another.

Pepe felt so ashamed of himself that he started to get up when he
noticed the ankles of the girl in front of him. He admired how well her
long skirt hung. When Pepe admired her waist he felt that he was getting up too fast. After admiring the designs on the border of her low-cut
blouse, he swallowed hard. Then he looked at her round face, her picaresque almond eyes, and her fragile chin. True, she did not look like
any of the fashionable ladies that rode in coaches on Petate Square, but
Pepe felt that she had other very admirable qualities.

"I beg your pardon, young lady," he said. He thought of studying
the designs on the border of her low-cut blouse again when he realized
that there were too many girls around. Again Pepe swallowed hard. He
felt a chill go through his body. Turning around he said, "Excuse me,
young ladies, excuse me." Then he hurried off, wiping the perspiration
from his forehead as he went.

The next day after touching his slight mustache with a dark pencil,
Pepe bade Pulgas good-bye and returned to the scene of his accident. In
a short time all the girls along the street were at their windows watching Pepe parade up and down. When Pepe realized it, he headed past
the spot of his accident once more and noticed that the young lady he
was seeking had finally come to the window of her house. The same
chill went through Pepe's body as he glanced at her provocative eyes

for the second time. She winked and closed the curtains, as is custom the first time, and Pepe hurried away. He had made a conquest.

Not long after, Pepe presented his letter of introduction and was allowed to visit Filomena Farsantina, as was the young lady's name. He discovered, from the conversation of her five sisters, that he was courting a member of Petate City's foremost aristocrats. True, the sisters often said, they did not have much money. But it was only because of El Supremo's jealousy of the Farsantina family.[90]

But the biggest aristocrat of all was Teófila, Filomena's mother. She was a robust woman of fifty with a slight mustache who spoke of having had governesses in her youth. She spoke of having had suitors by the score. She spoke of how the walls of the Petate Cathedral had been adorned with orchids and its floors had been carpeted with silk for her wedding. Since a few years after her wedding, however, she had spent much time alone because Tomás, her husband, had suddenly decided to go to sea. Because Tomás, though absent, was a good provider, Teófila spent more *lanillas* with the *modistas*[91] than with the butcher and made grand entrances at the last mass.

Every time Pepe visited Filomena he was given a reception. There were, besides Filomena's sisters and mother, never less than half a dozen visitors. Pepe was always introduced to them as a well-to-do man from the interior. And in the course of the evening Teófila always said, "Yes, he is another suitor of my little Teófila. Like all my daughters, she has so many. But I do not let just anybody court her. I would not allow it as I have never allowed just anybody to court my other daughters. After all, my daughters cannot marry just anybody." Pepe trembled every time he heard this, but he felt that it was only fair. Teófila had to look out for her daughters.

At length Pepe was allowed the honor of visiting Filomena without an audience. But even though Pepe hired an instructor to teach him poems, even though Pepe hired a gentleman to teach him behavior, even though Pepe hired a troubadour to teach him songs, he still found himself at a loss with Filomena. When both sat together, Pepe's mind stopped working. Pepe found that he got chills on the hottest of nights which made him curl up into knots. But all of this did not alter Pepe's intentions in the least. Love, he had heard, overcame all obstacles.

One night, after leaving Filomena's house, Pepe went into a little restaurant for something to eat. When the waiter gave him the menu Pepe was astonished. The waiter resembled him so much that it was unbelievable. After looking each other over, Pepe began to scan the menu and the waiter hurried into the kitchen.

While Pepe ate, wondering how it was that the waiter should resemble him so much, the waiter sat down in front of him and after staring at Pepe for a long time, he said, "I bet you are from the interior."

"Y-yes. I am," said Pepe.

"I am from the interior too," said the waiter.

Pepe nodded.

"Ah yes," said the waiter, "and sometimes I wish I had never come to the city."

"Why did you come?" asked Pepe.

"Well, once I owned a little patch of land. I was very happy there. I had a few chickens, a goat, a dog, a donkey—"

Pepe almost choked.

"Well," continued the waiter, "and I was very happy. But it so happened that my little patch was surrounded by the lands belonging to General Tragatierras.[92] One day he came to me and said, 'Do you want to sell your land?' and I said that I would not think of it. Why should I? I was happy there. But the general was a very, very persuasive man. He offered me one hundred *lanillas* for my land. Still I said no. One night, as I came from the nearby village, I decided to shorten my way by going through his land. I was caught. They took me before a jury. I was called a thief, trespasser, vagabond, vandal. I was terrified. I was shaking so much when I faced the judge that he said I was guilty and my nervousness proved it. While I was in jail General Tragatierras came to me and told me that my little patch was bare and desolate. He told me that thieves had made off with my chickens, goat, dog, and donkey. He said that he would pay my way out of jail and would give me fifty *lanillas* for signing a piece of paper which gave him my land. I signed it and took the money. Five minutes later I was free. I came to Petate City. Now I wish I were still in that jail. Then I would sign no paper. My little patch, bare and desolate, would have been better than this."

"Then what happened?" asked Pepe.

"I met a girl and soon all my *lanillas* were spent. I went through hardships. Now you have me here, waiting on tables," said the waiter.

"I am very sorry, friend," said Pepe.

"You should go back," said the waiter.

"But I cannot," said Pepe.

"You must," said the waiter. "You must go back while it is still possible. Don't you think I would go back if I could?"

"I cannot leave. I am in love," said Pepe. Then the waiter put his head down on the table and began to cry.

"What is the matter with that?" asked Pepe.

"Friend," said the waiter, looking up with tears in his eyes, "must I have to tell you that in this cruel world there is no such thing as love? Take me, for example. I fell in love when I first got to the city and the girl left me for a man with money. That is the way of all women. Now I am alone. I repeat to you. All women are tigresses who rob you of your money and then abandon you. I hate them. I wish they were all dead." Then the waiter put his head down on the table and cried some more.

Pepe tried to console him. He patted the waiter on the back and said, "Love will come yet, friend. I am sure of it. And it will be a true love like the love I enjoy." But the waiter cried on.

"No," said the waiter, looking up again, "all women are bad. And if you are smart, you will leave them alone and go back to where you came from."

That night, as Pepe lay in bed, he shuddered when he thought of his resemblance to the waiter. But nothing would happen to him. Besides, his Filomena was different.

8

For the next two months Pepe dedicated himself to winning Filomena's hand. At least once a week Pepe hired a group of *kipopieros*[93] to serenade her. He took her bonbons which she quickly devoured. At length Pepe felt that nothing was better than courtship until he noticed that it was rapidly consuming his money. Of his original two thousand *lanillas* he had one thousand left.

Still, whenever Pepe went very determinedly to ask for Filomena's hand in marriage, he found that he suddenly became tongue-tied. Always at that moment Teófila walked into the room and began talking of all Filomena's former suitors. "But my daughter cannot marry just anybody. You well understand that, don't you, Pepe? She has had many suitors, just as I had in my youth. But she must marry a man that will give her everything she is accustomed to." And Pepe agreed. "She must also get married in the Petate Cathedral just as I did. Pepe, you would not believe it. But when I was married, the church was overflowing with flowers. The floors were carpeted in silk. Oh how beautiful I looked," she said, putting her two fat hands together and sighing. Pepe sighed with her.

The next day Pepe bought a ring, a beautiful white wedding dress as custom dictates, and started for Filomena's house, determined to ask for her hand in marriage. On the way he laid plans for a grand church wedding. He stopped long enough to buy a huge box of candy for Teófila, his future mother-in-law.

Accompanied by six *kipopieros* he arrived at Filomena's house and ordered the musicians to play a dreamy kipop which spoke of love. After the *kipopieros* finished, Pepe sent them away and knocked on the door. One of Filomena's sisters came to the door and asked with a sneer, "What do you want?"

"Me, I, well, I, me and Fil—," stammered Pepe.

"We don't want you to bother Filomena any longer," she said, slamming the door in Pepe's face.

Pepe frantically knocked on the door. Again Filomena's sister opened it. "Now what?" she asked.

"Me, I—" started Pepe.

"Well, what?" asked Filomena's sister.

"This wedding dress, this ring, I—" said Pepe.

"Well," said Filomena's sister, "if you must know I will tell you. She is going to marry the butcher's son."

"But how can that be?" asked Pepe.

"I don't know," she said. "But the butcher's son won the national lottery this morning. Perhaps that will explain it."

Again she slammed the door. Pepe walked away.

Back in his hotel room Pepe cried like a child. Patting his dog Pulgas he said, "*Pulguitas*, you are my only friend." Pulgas waved his tail.

"Yes, *Pulgas mío*, since we got to Petate City I have not taken you out for even a walk because I have been too proud. But I well realize that you are the only friend I have. From now on you will go everywhere with me. You must forgive that I have kept you locked up all this time." Then Pepe fell forward on the bed and cried some more. Pulgas wagged his tail and licked the salt from his master's ears.

9

The next day Pepe got up very late and said to Pulgas, "Today we will spend our last day in the city. This afternoon we will tour the city and then tomorrow we will go back to where we came from, where we belong. I am also going to buy a rifle so that we can hunt. With the few *lanillas* we still have left perhaps the stranger will sell us a little bit of our patch back." Pulgas wagged his tail, whined with joy, and jumped from the bed to the floor to the chair and back to the bed as though he were crazy.

That afternoon Pepe and Pulgas wandered into a very strange part of Petate City. In this part of the city the houses were dirty. The streets were narrow and dusty. Dogs scratched and licked their ringworms on the sidewalk. Dirty children screamed and shouted in the streets. Thin men, with their hats pulled well over their eyes to keep out the afternoon sun, passed him. Ill-kept women with lifeless eyes peered out from behind barred windows. Pepe realized that he was walking through the other side of Petate City.

That night Pepe stopped for a drink at a *chispa* station whose front door was so low that one had to duck in order to go in. Inside there were sour-faced individuals sitting about. In one corner the woman proprietor put splinters under a pot where the meat used in the *churros* was cooked.

While the *churros* in the village of Feria had always been made of goat meat and had been spiced with tasty sauce, the *churros* here were being made of dogs and cats. But after Pepe drank thimble after thimble of *chispa*, he began to eat *churro* after *churro*. The woman pro-

prietor, at length, realized that Pepe had had too much *chispa*, and with
the cardboard that she fanned the fire under the pot she fanned Pepe
and said to him, "Please, young man, leave. Please go away. Do not fall
here."

As Pepe wobbled out of the *chispa* station, wondering which direction to take in order to get back to his room, he sensed that somebody
was following him. Pulgas, quickly turning around, began barking at
the shadows. For two blocks nothing happened. But on the third, an
assailant with a club jumped from behind some bushes and whacked
Pepe over the head. Pulgas bit the assailant's leg. The assailant kicked
poor Pulgas halfway across the street. Pepe, recovering from the blow,
grabbed the assailant's arm to keep him from inflicting further dam-
age. On closer inspection Pepe saw that the man was a policeman. "I
am not a thief," cried Pepe.

The policeman tore himself away from Pepe and threw another blow
at him with his club. "But I told you. I am not a thief," repeated Pepe,
grabbing at the policeman's uniform. Pulgas, having recovered, came
up from behind and bit into the seat of the policeman's pants. The
policeman hit Pulgas with his club with such force that Pulgas smashed
into the ground, lifeless. Pepe released his hold on the policeman and
bent down to look at the lifeless form of his only companion.

The policeman, bending down over Pulgas too, said, "I did not mean
to hurt your little dog."

"But you did," said Pepe as he patted Pulgas in an effort to revive
him.

"I am sorry," said the policeman.

"I guess you are sorry you tried to kill me. I told you I was not a
thief," said Pepe.

"I have no doubt that you are more honest than I," said the policeman. "You see, I am nothing but a poor corporal on the police force. I
have to give the sergeant a cut or else I will lose my job. That does not
mean that the sergeant is crooked. But he has to give the lieutenant a
cut or else he will lose his job. That does not mean that the lieutenant
is crooked. But the poor lieutenant, in turn, has to give the captain a
cut or else he will lose his job, and—"

"My little dog is coming back to life," interrupted Pepe.

This made the policeman so happy that he proceeded to club Pepe into unconsciousness. As Pepe lay lifeless the policeman went through his pockets and his eyes lit up when he came upon Pepe's money. He patted the still dizzy Pulgas and disappeared.

The next day, when the sun was high in the sky, Pepe woke up and felt the lumps on his head. Pulgas wagged his tail on seeing that his master was not dead. Pepe made up his mind to fear the law instead of thieves. One can fight back with a thief.

Pepe went back to his room and cried at his misfortune. Realizing that he now had no money, he decided to sell the wedding dress he had bought the day before, as well as the ring. If these two costly articles had not helped him acquire a wife, perhaps they would at least help him get out of Petate City.

Pepe took the wedding dress and ring to the establishments where he bought them and was informed that his money could not be returned. Pepe took them to a house of loans.

"How much do you want for them?" asked the man behind the counter.

"Two hundred and fifty *lanillas* for both," said Pepe.

"Are you crazy?" asked the man.

"Well, that is what I paid for them," said Pepe.

"Well, I will give you twenty-five," said the man.

"I would rather throw them away," said Pepe.

"Throw them away," said the man. "I doubt if anyone will bother to pick them up."

Pepe returned the dress to the box, put the ring back in his pocket, and hurried out. As he went up the street, a policeman blew his whistle and another policeman appeared. Pepe ran across the street. Still another policeman appeared. Pulgas barked to defy them. But the policeman took both Pepe and Pulgas to jail.

Facing the judge, Pepe trembled like a condemned man.

"What is this tramp in here for?" asked the judge.

"Burglary," said the policeman who had brought him in.

Before Pepe could say anything the judge shouted, "Take him away. And throw that dog into the street."

Pepe sat in a dirty, toiletless cell, weeping at his sad plight, when he heard the guard unlock the door. "Here you have a companion," said the guard, leading in another prisoner.

"Take your filthy hands off me," said the new prisoner, spitting at the guard.

"Watch how you talk to me," said the guard, "or I will see that you get solitary."

"Go on, get the hell out of here," said the new prisoner, "or else I will get mad. Go on, get out."

The guard got out of the cell and locked the door.

"What is the matter with you?" asked the new prisoner, looking at Pepe.

"The shame of it," said Pepe, with tears streaming from his eyes.

"My good friend, I think it is more of a shame to be on the outside nowadays," said the new prisoner.

"I do not understand," said Pepe, as he saw the new prisoner making himself comfortable on the dirty sleeping mat which served as bed.

"I used to live on the outside," said the new prisoner. "When my sentence is over, I go out and do something wrong and they throw me back in. At least here I have a place to eat and sleep. That is something that not many men can boast of nowadays. At least, not honest men."

"Do you mean to say that there are more honest men in prison than out?" asked Pepe.

"Exactly," said the new prisoner.

Pepe thought about the new prisoner's words for a while and then turned around to face him. But already the new prisoner was asleep. Pepe, not being able to think of anything else, bit his nails for a while, then, following the new prisoner's example, went to sleep also.

Later that day Pepe and his companion woke up at the rattling of cans and pans. A guard came to the door of the cell and shouted at the top of his voice, "Prisoners, to the bar." Pepe and his companion went to the bars of the cell and an attendant pushed through the bottom of the door two tin plates with greasy gut and rice piled high. Pepe's cell companion sat down to enjoy his meal. Pepe suddenly felt lumps in his throat.

"Go on, eat, friend," said Pepe's companion, "you will feel very hungry if you don't."

Pepe held his nose with one hand and ate with the other.

"How long will they keep me here?" asked Pepe as he ate.

"Oh, you will find out soon enough," said Pepe's new companion.

After eating, Pepe found out that his new companion's name was Cornelio and that he was from Boquilla,[94] a little village across the bay from Petate City. "I was a tavern keeper," said Cornelio. "But I lost all my trade when my customers were killed off."

"How did that happen?" asked Pepe.

"Well, it just so happens that El Supremo[95] was to make a tour of Petate. The mayor of Boquilla, wanting to keep his post and wanting to make El Supremo happy, wrote him a letter and said to him that there were many drunks and bums. There were also cripples, lepers, and otherwise diseased and that it would be a sad thing if he should encounter such things on his tour. Who could tell? Perhaps some foreign ambassador, dignitary, or general might be on tour with him."

"Well, what happened?" asked Pepe.

"Well, El Supremo wrote back and told the mayor that he could do whatever he thought necessary. Furthermore, he informed the mayor that he would have a host of foreign ambassadors, dignitaries, and generals with him on tour. And above all, that Petate, being a great nation, had a face to maintain. So the mayor gave a big feast right in the center of Boquilla for all the unfortunate individuals. After letting them eat and drink their fill, the mayor's henchmen told them that a great show was in store for them across the bay. So the poor unfortunates got into some boats. Halfway across the bay two gunboats shot holes in the boats and all drowned like rats," finished Cornelio, lowering his head.

"Then what happened?" asked Pepe.

"Well, the mayor wrote back and informed El Supremo that the matter had been taken care of. I was so sad that I came to make my life in Petate City. But after looking it over I prefer spending the rest of my life in jail. I am an honest man. As I told you before, there are more honest men in jail than out. If you stay here long enough you will see that it is true."

"Perhaps you are right," said Pepe.

"Of course I am," said Cornelio. "The only way one can live on the outside and eat enough is to become one of El Supremo's men. Then he can rob those who can neither read nor write and do it legally."

10

At dawn the next day, Pepe and Cornelio awoke at the sound of gunfire. They looked out of their cell window into a large courtyard where a firing squad was shooting some solemn-faced men, one at a time, against a wall.

"Those are political prisoners of El Supremo," said Cornelio. More men were lined up and shot. "It is the only way he can stay in power. But don't think this is so bad. Sometimes people are shot for less," said Cornelio.

"How is that?" asked Pepe.

"Well, if El Supremo's name is mentioned in some tavern or other establishment, the police do not go and investigate. They simply throw open the doors of the place and fire into it with sawed-off shotguns. It is the only way El Supremo can stay in power."

"Is El Supremo really that bad?" asked Pepe.

"Last year, to give you another example, some people gathered to hear a speech in one of the public parks. Immediately El Supremo's men broke up the crowd by shooting their machine guns into it. They hit women in the legs. They wounded children. But it is the only way El Supremo can stay in power."

At length Pepe asked Cornelio again, "How long do you think they will keep me here?"

"Oh, it is up to you," said Cornelio.

"Up to me?"

"Yes, it is according to how long it takes them to convince you that you should join the army. That is El Supremo's conscription system. If you do not want to stay in jail all you have to do is join. Then you and El Supremo's generals can go out and put down rebellion."

"What rebellion?" asked Pepe.

"Oh," said Cornelio, "they always think one up. It is usually a tribe of defenseless Indians. Then the army comes back to Petate City and they make statues of the generals."

"I would never join," said Pepe.

"But be sure, when you go, that you never fire a gun while you are near a general."

"Why?" asked Pepe.

"Any of El Supremo's generals would die of fright," said Cornelio.

"Still, I would never join," repeated Pepe.

"I rather think you will," said Cornelio.

A few hours later Pepe's stomach began to ache. It began to make very funny noises.

"It is the food we ate last night," said Pepe.

"The food is not so bad," said Cornelio. "You must remember that most people on the outside do not make enough *lanillas* to buy any food at all."

That night Pepe felt bugs crawling over his body as he lay on his hard sleeping mat. They bit him everywhere.

"Is it like this all the time?" Pepe asked the next morning, as he scratched himself violently.

"Oh, you will get used to them," said Cornelio.

But Pepe could not bear the thought of having every bug in the Petate City jail get fat on his blood, so he called the guard and asked, "When are they going to let me out? I am innocent."

"They will let you out when you are ready to join the army," said a fat guard.

"I am ready," said Pepe. As they led him out he looked back toward Cornelio and asked, "Why don't you go with me?"

"No, thanks," said Cornelio. "I like it here."

La suerte del pobre

Hace muchos años, en un pueblo cuyo nombre no recuerdo, vivía un amigo llamado Pedro al cual todos le festejaban sus fuerzas y su aguante en el trabajo.[96] Siendo así, no faltaba quien le disparara la bebida y le dijera, "Pedro, como tú no hay dos. A todo esto quisiera que te encarg[ue]s de . . ." y así al fin llegó el día que Pedro no tenía las fuerzas de antes. Y, con su escasez de fuerzas también le llegó la escasez de amigos y de los que halagaban con el objeto de explotarlo.

Un día el rico del pueblo se encontró con Pedro y le dijo, "Pedro, quiero que vayas a buscar mi suerte y que le digas que siempre me trate como me ha tratado hasta ahora."

Pedro, encontrándose hambriento y necesitado, accedió a los deseos de quien lo había explotado gran parte de su vida y partió. Pedro, como siempre de costumbre, a buscar la suerte ajena.

El camino a su suerte fue placentero, pues verdes árboles habían a lo largo del camino. A la hora de comer, Pedro simplemente comió fruta de los mismos árboles que le cedían sombra. Lo mismo con el agua, pues un pequeño río le dio para beber a Pedro en abundancia. Al fin llegó Pedro a un imponente castillo. Acercándose, lo cruzaron por armas y después de que le bajaron el puente levadizo, Pedro entró al castillo para ser conducido al cuarto del trono. En el trono estaba sentada la suerte del rico, una princesa bien cuidada, vestida en sedas y encajes, rodeada de sirvientes cumpliéndole todos sus caprichos.

Pedro, sombrero en mano, bajó su mirada y apenas contestó: "Pues, es que vengo por parte del rico. Y, él sólo pide a vuestra merced que siempre lo trate como está hoy."

La suerte del rico sonrió y le dijo a Pedro, "Pues, vete tranquilo y dile al rico que siempre lo trataré como me ha tratado a mí."

Pedro regresó a su pueblo y después de comunicarse con el rico fue a gastar las pocas monedas que éste le cedió. Allí en la cantina Pedro decidió ir a buscar su propia suerte, para ver si aunque sea antes de morir . . .

Pues bien, Pedro salió en busca de su suerte. Pero, si el camino hacia la suerte del rico había sido placentero . . . , el camino pronto lo condujo por un desierto, con el sol escupiendo brasas. Por poco le picó a Pedro una víbora cuando se sentó a descansar. Cuando Pedro, desesperado y hambriento, iba a desnudar un triste árbol de su escasa fruta, se espinó. ¿Agua? ni que hubiera sacado de las piedras. De noche, Pedro se encontró en altas montañas, en las cuales hacía tal frío que Pedro temió dormirse. En el oscuro camino sufrió Pedro rasguños de ramas. En fin . . .

Al otro día Pedro, perdido, hambriento, desgarrado, llegó a una choza, ésta aparentemente abandonada. Pedro, desesperado, corrió hacia ella. Tocando la puerta, se le apareció una pobre mujer desgreñada, harapienta, casi un esqueleto de flaca. "¿Bueno?" preguntó la desgraciada.

"Pues, yo me llamo Pedro y ando en busca de mi suerte. Es que . . ."

"Pues, aquí me tienes, grandísimo pendejo," le dijo a Pedro su suerte, la cual entonces lo mató a escobazos.

Oral informant: Atilana H. Minjares. Told to Mario R. Suárez. An English translation of the story follows.

A Poor Man's Fate

Many years ago in a town, whose name I can't remember, there lived a friend named Pedro whose brute strength and endurance in work everyone celebrated. Therefore, it never failed that someone would treat him to a drink and say, "Pedro, there is no one else like you. By the way, I'd like to entrust you with . . . ," until finally the day came that Pedro no longer had the strength he used to. And, with his lack of strength came a scarcity of friends and of those who used to flatter him to better take advantage of him.

One day the town's rich man came across Pedro and told him, "Pedro, I want you to go look for my fate and tell it to treat me the way it has treated me up to now."

Pedro, finding himself famished and needy, consented to the wishes of the man who had exploited him a large part of his life, and left on his errand. Pedro, as was always his custom, set out to look for someone else's destiny.

The path to his destiny was pleasant since green trees lined the road. At mealtime, Pedro simply ate fruit from the same trees that provided him shade. The same could be said for the water, given that a small river gave Pedro enough to drink in abundance. In the end Pedro came across a majestic castle. Upon nearing it, he was searched for arms, and once the drawing bridge was lowered, Pedro entered the castle to be led into the king's room. There he found the rich man's fate sitting on the throne, a well-kept princess dressed in silks and laces, surrounded by servants who fulfilled her every whim.

Pedro, with his hat in hand, lowered his eyes and barely answered: "Well, I hereby come on the rich man's behalf. And, his only wish from Your Grace is that you treat him always as you have up to now."

The rich man's fate smiled and told Pedro, "Well, go reassured and tell the rich man that I will always treat him as he has treated me."

Pedro returned to his village and after informing the rich man of his fate, he went to spend the few coins the wealthy man paid him. There in the bar Pedro decided to go in search of his own fate to see if at least before dying . . .

Therefore, Pedro set out in search of his destiny. But, if the path to find the rich man's fate had been pleasant, this road soon led him through a desert with the sun spewing red-hot coals. A snake almost bit Pedro when he sat down to rest. When Pedro, feeling desperate and hungry, was about to strip a sad tree of its scarce fruit, he got pricked by thorns. Water anywhere? Most unlikely, unless he squeezed it out of rocks. That night Pedro found himself in the high mountains where it was so cold he feared falling asleep. In the dark path Pedro suffered scratches from spiny branches. After all . . .

The next day Pedro, realizing he was lost, famished, and with ragged clothes, spotted a hut, which seemed abandoned. Pedro, full of desperation, ran toward it. Knocking on the door, a poor, disheveled and ragged-looking woman appeared, looking like a skeleton for her frailness. "Well?" the unfortunate woman asked.

"Well, my name is Pedro and I am in search of my fate. It's that . . ."

"Well, here I am, you damn nitwit," his own fate told Pedro, and she then attacked him, killing him with a broom.

Translation Francisco A. Lomelí

Discussion and Analysis

Context and Backdrop

The origins and background of Chicano literature before 1965 can lead to some uncertainties and difference of opinion as to its antecedents, and whether it is more Mexican or American. The year 1848 is generally accepted as the point of its inception if sociopolitical factors are taken into consideration, factors that mark the beginnings of a people referred to as Mexican American—or, in many quarters after 1960s, Chicanos. These people were direct descendants of Spanish subjects, usually mestizos, who entered the region as early as the sixteenth century—for example, Alvar Núñez Cabeza de Vaca, Marcos de Niza, and Francisco de Coronado. A literary tradition developed as they abandoned their explorations in favor of colonization and settlement, thereby establishing a society with norms and mores that extended colonial Hispanic culture into what eventually became the American Southwest. Oral tradition, a rich reservoir of fanciful or imaginative expression, has often provided the building blocks of fiction, as Raymund Paredes has noted:

> Legends and *corridos* (ballads) have been especially fruitful sources of fictional themes. Legends are perhaps the most "literary" of folk narratives, since they are often infused with a sense of realism and evince such qualities as plot, characterization, dialogue, and figurative language. The *corrido* has these features and is, in a sense, a legend set to music. The *corrido*'s great attraction to the fictionalist lies in the proven appeal of its stories; no other type of folklore treats more vividly events that have stirred the imagination of the Mexican people.[1]

Different forms of folklore were then transformed into conventional written forms, particularly in the nineteenth century when a proliferation of newspapers collected a variety of writings from the time. From these documents we can infer the sentiments, attitudes, perspectives, and concerns of persons of Mexican descent reeling from the conquest by Anglo America after 1848.[2] The leap from an oral culture to a written tradition was already taking place, suggesting a newfound sophistication.

Such a perspective challenges and counters the notion that Chicanos remained illiterate or that they had failed to cultivate artistic renderings. In the twentieth century an exodus from Mexico took place, first because of the Mexican Revolution and later under the Bracero program (1942–1964), injecting a new vitality into Chicano culture in the Southwest. Out of the need to capture a growing expression, writings developed into a body of publishing ventures such as newspapers (e.g., *La Opinión* in Los Angeles), publishing houses (e.g., Editorial Quiroga in San Antonio, Texas), magazines (*New Mexico Magazine* in Albuquerque, New Mexico), journals (*La Revista Católica* in Las Vegas, New Mexico), and other venues. Writers such as Mario Suárez prove that a Chicano literary tradition had always existed—though modest in magnitude and more often regional in focus—despite remaining marginalized, unacknowledged, or simply forgotten. Far from being an isolated case, however, Suárez figures as an important link to the continuity of an expression of culture, while displaying a spirit unwilling to be silenced. Others had already contributed in some way to the long-standing tradition, rooted in, but not exclusive to, the Southwest: Fray Angelico Chávez, Nina Otero-Warren, and Fabiola Cabeza de Vaca in New Mexico, Josefina Niggli in North Carolina, María Cristina Mena Chambers in New York, Jovita González and Américo Paredes in Texas, Luis Pérez, Julio G. Arce, and Daniel Venegas in California, along with Mario Suárez in Arizona. The latter, then, is a watershed figure and a key precursor or initiator of contemporary Chicano literature before it was fashionable or accepted as a legitimate form of expression. Critic Raymund Paredes has pointed out with precision the following distinction: "Suárez was the first truly Chicano writer. He was comfortable with the term itself, as many are not still, recognizing its symbolic importance and understanding its slight suggestion of self-deprecation. In Suárez's fiction, the Chicano is a truncated variety of Mexican in a cultural sense, but no less a dignified and individualized human being."[3] In fact, Suárez is given credit for first using, contextualizing, and defining the term "Chicano" in 1947 in his short story "El Hoyo," and in various stories thereafter. The term gained prominence as a label of identity in the 1960s once the Chicano movement exploded onto the national scene. It is clear he identifies comfortably with the term. He does not indulge in mocking it like Daniel Venegas in *Las aventuras de don Chipote o cuando los pericos mamen* (1928); on the contrary, he qualifies its meaning through numerous examples that help explain a burgeoning identity for Mexican Americans. While intimating a "new" kind of embattled minority in search of their niche in a changing post–World War II United States, his definition serves to suggest an emerging consciousness, a perception based on knowing who one is vis-à-vis a social background of general neglect.

Mario Suárez stands out as a pioneer for embracing this invisible community with compassion, sensitivity, and particularly empathy, from which he created a viable literary project. Among his attributes, he had the foresight to create a Chicano imaginary, a unique literary space in which characters were not idealized or stereotyped. His aesthetic approach involved direct recreation, what we might term a humdrum realism that neither inflated nor devalued the persons described. Some critics[4] have unfairly labeled his depictions as only "quaint," owing to a straightforward and unpretentious realism dominated by an objectivity sprinkled with intimacy. Without a doubt, Suárez's forte was character development. He created a distinct and unprecedented gallery of Chicano and other social types and personalities defined by circumstances, character traits, psychological makeup, or language: pachucos, migrants (Mexicans, Asians, Spaniards), perplexed or assertive women, rogues, womanizers, drunks, *coyotes* (smugglers of undocumented border crossers), dreamers, machos, priests, and outcasts. He sought neither to embellish nor give in to hyperbole; neither does he needlessly ridicule, denigrate, or minimize them. On the contrary, his main objective entailed respectfully capturing flesh-and-blood personages marked by notable or conspicuous traits (i.e., "characters" in the sense of inimitably eccentric—usually humorous—qualities, features, or behavioral patterns), thanks to a *costumbrista* (local color) lens focused on quotidian life in a Chicano barrio. The best, the worst, and everything in between coexists in this ambience. He attempted to accurately represent this group of inner-city dwellers via indagations of the internal or descriptions of external features, including minute details of lifestyle, "making it comprehensible on more than a superficial level."[5] Local color clearly flourishes in his stories, not by degrading his characters' particular frailties, but by humanizing them. They seem not only real but approachable and likable, or at least intriguing, even curious. The characters, rather than being stilted papier-mâché entities, here breathe, joke around, raise hell, struggle, philosophize, grapple with their surroundings, and live in their own little world, meanwhile acting naturally and comfortably in their milieu. The characters and plots in Suárez's short stories seem to derive from situations and spaces in real life,[6] within a multicultural society comprising Anglos, Mexicans, Asians, Spaniards, and others. The reader often feels like an insider instead of a cultural voyeur because the distance between narrator and characters is minimal. The anthropological and sociological content, then, does not extend into exoticism or fetishness, effectively avoiding the Oscar Lewis syndrome found in *The Children of Sánchez: Autobiography of a Mexican Family* (1961). Suárez offers a counterpoint to the subculture of poverty theory by leaving out moralistic judgments, opting instead for a subculture of folklore and common people within their group cultural dynamics; that is, he accepts the characters for what they are instead of what they might be. Victimization is not depicted from a sociological perspective, but it can appear in situations of differing power relations between characters. The vantage point of controlled affection used by the narrators allows for these simple characters to acquire and unveil a complexity of individualized dimensions—including their imperfections—in which ethnicity and race are descriptive rather than prescriptive.

The publication of *Chicano Sketches* is long overdue. Universally recognized in the Chicano short story field for his trailblazing efforts, Suárez has been a pillar in its development and evolution. He has also served as a model through his hybrid writing style, mixing elements from both Mexican and American literary traditions. Along with Mexican writers such as Mariano Azuela and his *Los de abajo* (1915; *The Underdogs*), Suárez was drawn to creating down-to-earth portrayals of country folk who indulge in popular language and had a zeal for justice and a sense of purpose. Juan Rulfo's *Pedro Páramo* (1955) caught his attention for the inherent mystery and ambiguity in the narrative, aside from the internal portrayals of characters and a deep sense of Mexicanness. Spanish writer José Ortega y Gasset, in *La rebelión de las masas* (1930; *Revolt of the Masses*), taught him to better comprehend the pitfalls of contemporary constructions of mass culture. But Suárez's writings were also greatly conditioned and molded by his readings of American writers such as John Steinbeck, Ernest Hemingway (*Death in the Afternoon*, 1932, and *The Snows of Kilimanjaro*, 1938), Thornton Wilder (*The Bridge of San Luis Rey*, 1927), and Frenchman François Voltaire's *Candide* (1759). Steinbeck's *Tortilla Flat* (1935) and *Grapes of Wrath* (1939) left an indelible mark on his psyche, writing style, and general literary agenda. Like Steinbeck, he focuses many of his works on the poor, the downtrodden, and the dispossessed, except that Suárez seems to allow his characters greater free will. Part of the Chicano writer's fascination with Steinbeck is grounded in the latter's portrayal of a spectrum of Mexican figures, from "primitivists" to the charming *paisanos* of *Tortilla Flat* who live a relatively simple and naive existence while remaining free of contamination from a highly materialistic society. Steinbeck and Suárez share a penchant for developing real-life characters whose eccentricities and behavior are marked by unforgettable—sometimes quirky and funny—characteristics, although Suárez depended less on caricatures. Cross-cultural influences from two sets of customs and languages as well as ways of thinking contribute to both authors' construction of personalities and plot lines. A new kind of America seems to dramatically emerge, as if recalibrating the scales of the normal and typical.

Most of Suárez's narratives are constructed around a metonymical barrio called El Hoyo. The sketch of that title functions as an emblematic gateway to his writings. Among the published stories, only "The Migrant" and "Mexican Heaven" take place outside of such an inner-city locale, although it could be argued that geographical similarities are still present. The characters are deliberately situated in the barrio, suggesting that it is an integral part of their existence. In other words, Suárez anticipates what Tomás Rivera later referred to as the urgency to "establish community" through literature, when he stated: "Chicano literature as it has flourished in the 50s and 60s revealed a basic hunger for community (*hambre por una comunidad*)."[7] Suárez clearly attempted to profile a new community, though only Chicanos recognize it as such.

Suárez's first eight stories made their landmark appearance in the journal *Arizona Quarterly* in the following order: "El Hoyo" (summer 1947), "Señor Garza" (summer 1947), "Cuco Goes to a Party" (summer 1947), "Loco-Chu" (summer 1947), "Kid Zopilote" (summer 1947), "Southside Run" (winter 1948), "Maestría" (winter 1948), and "Mexican Heaven" (winter 1950).[8] The remaining previously published stories originally appeared in the following literary anthologies: "Las comadres" and "Los coyotes" in *Con Safos* (1969 and 1972, respectively) and "The Migrant" in *Revista Chicano-Riqueña* (1982).[9]

In addition to the eleven published stories by Suárez, we have included eight other unpublished stories, thanks to the manuscript collection held by the Suárez family in San Dimas, California. The stories, introduced here for the first time, are as follows: "Doña Clara," "Life Is But a Tango," "Doña Clara's Nephew," "El Tiradito," "The Pioneer," "Something Useful, Even Tailoring," "Trouble in Petate," and "La suerte del pobre." The inclusion of unpublished texts completes the publication of the short fiction known and produced by the author. Other titles may have existed but then were misplaced or lost, although it is more likely that references to other titles represent different versions of a known story.

Another little known fact about the author and his overall literary production involves a quiet and cautious plan to create novels, particularly novelettes.[10] According to what he related to Allan Englekirk, Suárez traveled to New York in 1947 to try to interest a publisher in his manuscript "Cuco Goes to a Party," a short story that appeared in *Arizona Quarterly* in the same year. The manuscript was purportedly the basis for a full-length novel but resulted in a rejection by Macmillan. The editors had positive things to say about his writing, but the project never developed beyond a short story. Financial considerations made it impossible for him to pursue his dream further in New York, and he returned disappointed to Arizona. "Trouble in Petate," originally written in the summer of 1948, was also conceived as a novel. Based on Voltaire's *Candide*, it never came to fruition either, remaining as a long short story or a novelette. His third project, "A Guy's Worst Enemy," composed between 1952 and 1954, represents a short but complete novel of over 40,000 words about post–World War II life in metropolitan New York. But it appears Suárez wasn't fully satisfied with the final manuscript, and put it away in a drawer forever.[11] He admitted to Englekirk that he dreamed of combining his published works with the unpublished sketches in a single volume. In fact, Suárez is the one who originally proposed the title "Chicano Sketches," which we use here to honor his original idea. He told Englekirk that, subsequent to these attempts to break out as a writer, in 1975, he completed a draft of a fourth novel, to be called *The Kiosk*. Such a text has not been identified in his personal papers, although he described it as depicting the "experiences of some of the marginal people in the towns bordering Mexico and the United States." He even admitted that the draft still possessed several "'underdeveloped paragraphs and rough spots' but is confident that the work will reach the public once he eliminates these weaknesses."[12] From such comments, we can extract a sense of the writer's deliberateness and cautious composition. Other purported texts have yet to materialize in actual manuscripts.

A more complete picture of Suárez's literary production emerges by examining both his published and unpublished works. When combined into one collection, they more resemble a potential novel, or what Forrest L. Ingram has termed "linked stories."[13] What appears on the surface as a series of disjointed and fragmented narrative segments in fact represents a potential single manuscript containing multiple points of contact, similar to the now paradigmatic and canonized Chicano novels ". . . Y no se lo tragó la tierra" (1971) by Tomás Rivera, *Estampas del Valle y otra obras* (1973) by Rolando Hinojosa-Smith, and *The Mixquiahuala Letters* (1986) by Ana Castillo. Suárez clearly represents an important link—and precursor—to such works from the Chicano Renaissance, characterized by an underlying ambiguity and intertextual connections and commonalities through setting, characters, themes, and sometimes situations. These three classic works are also related to Suárez's *Chicano Sketches* in that they generated considerable critical discussion about their genre: novel, collection of short stories, or something in between.[14] Suárez wrote short stories to perfect his art of capturing precise depictions of barrio characters, but this did not preclude a future plan for attempting a larger narrative enterprise or a novel. He sensed the construction of a meta-text, that is, a larger text or series of stories in the form of a modern mosaic about a people whose fractional elements represented dots of their invisibility. Might his stories be taken as a prelude to the creation of a more expansive narrative project? Might he have thought: How can one tell these peoples' story if not through sketches or short realistic depictions, partly filled with humor or light needling in order to enhance their humanity? He must have also pondered how to give his characters life at a time when they were absent from the American mainstream and from the pages of American literature. It makes one wonder how and why he decided to give his literary phantoms a body and a face with a particular Chicano flavor. One possible source, which explains his penchant for realism, derives from the long-standing Hispanic tradition of the picaresque, with its down-to-earth qualities, roguish personalities, and deprecating humor and ironic twists. His intuition now seems sound and his vision prophetic. His literary project laid the foundation for the "future" production of Chicano literature almost twenty years later.

Analysis and Discussion of Published Sketches

The characters' Chicano identity in Suárez's stories resonates with originality and candor, including comic relief. This was definitely groundbreaking, even daring, for the 1940s. It is not by coincidence that his first two published sketches, "El Hoyo" and "Señor Garza," the most anthologized of his stories, contain much of the general barrio ambience, colorful characters, elements of quotidian life, themes, narrative structure, language, and mischievous attitude found in the subsequent narratives. These two sketches complement each other: the first concentrates on site or setting, while the second focuses almost exclusively on an individual, including a series of contrastive character traits. For example, "El Hoyo," meaning "the hole," establishes and frames the physical and social context by providing the geographical contours of the landscape and its people. Although near downtown Tucson, this rundown barrio on the margins defies its definition, being not a hole or pit, but simply an area described as the "river's immediate valley." Hence, the name "El Hoyo" contrasts well with the affluent parts of Tucson, but also contains sociopolitical implications of segregation. The name might have been a self-fulfilling prophecy, identifying a social pit, but in Suárez's hands becomes the opposite. In its ambivalence, the name might represent the pride of the inhabitants (a mildly subversive indictment), or a subtle form of dismissal or denial, encapsulating a metaphor for the end of the road or a place with an indentured existence. People can enter it with ease, but it is virtually impossible to escape from. The barrio also acquires features of a cauldron of peoples who have come together inexplicably, almost by chance, challenging easy classification or social homogeneity, thus presenting cultural diversity. For insiders, this place has a unique appeal because of its accepting nature: people let others live and be. As Charles Tatum has observed: "For Suárez, as for many Mexican American writers, the barrio represents a place of refuge and regeneration. Beneath its rough, shabby exterior, he finds the enduring soul of a people whose values and language have survived centuries of hardship, conflict, and social strife."[15] Without romanticizing, embellishing, or ridiculing its significance, the author describes the barrio as a place that permits peaceful coexistence, and camaraderie, where difference and otherness are negotiated with relative ease. It also represents a place where people become lost and forgotten as nonentities, sometimes irrelevant. As the omniscient narrator of "El Hoyo" observes: "Perhaps the humble appearance of El Hoyo justifies the discerning shrugs of more than a few people only vaguely aware of its existence." A place filled with the good, bad, and the ugly, it also tends to be forgiving, even protective, regardless of the licit or illicit characters' tendencies, including "harlequins, bandits, oppressors, oppressed, gentlemen, and bums." In other words, the place operates as a microcosm where Chicanos find some refuge thanks to its neutralizing and egalitarian character. It is not all good, but neither is it a hellish wasteland.

The story "El Hoyo" functions like a gatekeeper narrative, partly because it introduces the barrio (as a protagonist) and its people. Generally devoid of action per se, instead it faithfully recreates life in the barrio, that is, all that makes it a lively place of sounds, sights, and smells. The narrator seems concerned with capturing the essence of the place, where poverty fails to reduce the people to mere objects. Through a succinct, cross-sectional view, a completely sensorial impression emerges of what the place looks like, including some of its typical inhabitants. More importantly, this reflective sketch provides a philosophical rendering of what this place signifies and what constitutes it. Among the story's landmark qualities, (1) it offers, for the first time in literature, a definition of "Chicano" devoid of class distinctions; (2) it legitimates and validates the barrio as a viable subject that sheds light on the human condition; and (3) it inscribes and opens a new literary space from a barrio dweller's perspective. Using an approach ahead of its time, it looks at these marginal folks as regular people; in other words, the characters do not flaunt their ethnicity, but they aren't schizophrenic about it either. The term "Chicano" here transcends its often limited political definition, suggesting that these people were cognizant of who they were: "While the term *chicano* is the short way of saying *Mexicano*, it is the long way of referring to everybody." While "Chicano" is considered by some today a polemical term, the perspective espoused here is of an open-ended concept, a vehicle to synthesize disparate identities that don't correspond to facile labels. The barrio appears to integrate its inhabitants and mold them according to the Chicano experience, whether they are biracial (Mexican and Chinese, Mexican and Anglo, etc.) or simply some kind of working class. Those with vices enjoy anonymity by hiding in the barrio, while those with virtues share what they have. Criminals can be found alongside others who sense a sincere camaraderie or practice generosity. The ethnographic profile of "El Hoyo" takes on an unexpected universality, signifying a people's right to inhabit a place where they belong, despite its rundown appearance. It can also represent a point of departure of one's luck, a place that feels like home, or a locale worthy of returning to. The narrator clarifies: "El Hoyo is not the desperate outpost of a few families against the world. It fights for no causes except those which soothe its immediate angers. It laughs and cries with the same amount of passion in times of plenty and of want."

The narrator at the end proposes a carefully crafted culinary analogy to summarize and explain the barrio's essence, where difference and likeness intersect, perhaps paradoxically, without creating a contradiction. Referring to a favorite Mexican dish, called *capirotada*, the narrator emphasizes the people's heterogeneity: the ingredients and taste may change and vary, but a basic dish prevails. Although its preparation differs considerably from family to family, it retains a commonly identifiable flavor and substance: "Nevertheless it is still *capirotada*. And so it is with El Hoyo's *chicanos*. While many seem to the undiscerning eye to be alike, it is only because collectively they are referred to as *chicanos*. But like *capirotada*, fixed in a thousand ways and served on a thousand tables, which can only be evaluated by individual taste, the *chicanos* must be so distinguished."

The narrator's objective seems paradigmatic, by illustrating who and what these characters are: Mexican and Chicano are closely associated, while the author offers a useful working definition of the latter for his time. Suárez intimates a consciousness of the sort that would later be useful for the civil rights period of the 1960s. His discourse balances the subliminal with the overt in order to address—especially in 1947—notions of conventional anthropology by debunking stereotypes and obsolete characterizations of Mexicans. The author uses "El Hoyo" as the framing sketch to introduce a flexible ideology and definition to create his literary project. For that reason, we consider this first sketch deliberately emblematic and at the same time foundational in relation to the other stories.

The second sketch, "Señor Garza," also contains emblematic and foundational qualities, as something like the flip side of "El Hoyo." After "El Hoyo" provided an appropriate definition, a physical and social context, the next step was to populate this place with specific characters. With "Señor Garza," Suárez established the axis of these common folk, embodying the Chicano space as well as creating a compendium of wholesome traits. A single character is shown in his daily routine as a barber, occupying the center of activity, the social fulcrum, and thus revealing the spectrum of barrio inhabitants. Señor Garza, the barrio's middle-aged barber, and by extension soulful philosopher, fulfills that pivotal role admirably while serving as the center of the narrative. A gallery of diverse characters gravitate to Garza's Barber Shop, which is located downtown somewhere outside of the barrio's domain. In this way, the barbershop has multiple functions: it signifies a safe zone where these social "outsiders" can meet and mingle; and its insular quality permits the characters to encroach into the mainstream, if momentarily, while maintaining a sense of themselves. The sketch opens with an insistence that regardless of the barbershop's physical location, it too is an extension of El Hoyo.

"Señor Garza," much like the first story, concentrates on portraying an attitude about life:

> Garza's Barber Shop is more than razors, scissors, and hair. It is where men, disgruntled at the vice of the rest of the world, come to air their views. It is where they come to get things off their chests along with the hair off their heads and beard off their faces. Garza's Barber Shop is where everybody sooner or later goes or should. . . . To Garza's Barber Shop goes all that is good and bad. The lawbreakers come in to rub elbows with the sheriff's deputies. And toward all Garza is the same.

A place normally perceived as ordinary, a barbershop, acquires an extraordinary aura. Señor Garza, although far from perfect in personality and character, still stands out as a person of ultimate fairness, respect, consideration, and nonjudgmental morality. A kind of barrio "Saint Francis," he contributes to causes and to friends in desperate need. Depicted realistically, he is presented as a simple proprietor who doubles as barber, cashier, janitor, mentor, and guide. His approach to life seems uncomplicated yet far reaching, making his place of work and sphere of socialization an environment of absolute inclusiveness. Good natured and jovial, he expresses a philosophy that can be summarized by the adage that his job will not control him or dictate how he deals with everyone else. His schedule, for example, varies according to his mood and his relationship with his wife. He refuses to make barbering, or work, an end in itself, preferring instead to use it as a medium to satisfy others' needs. A neighborly chameleon, Garza's versatility is legendary. He changes his speech or behavior to fit the customer or situation: "When necessity calls for a change in character Garza can assume the proportions of a Greek, a Chinaman, a gypsy, a republican, a democrat, or if only his close friends are in the shop, plain Garza." Possessing picaresque charm, he relishes his surroundings, frequently taking breaks, flirting with the waitresses from a local restaurant, drinking with his friends until the wee hours of the night, and adjusting his routine to make himself available for small talk or idle gossip: "On most days, by five-thirty *everybody* has usually been in the shop for friendly reasons, commercial reasons, and even spiritual reasons" (emphasis not in original). Señor Garza is no saint: he seems to ignore his wife by catering to everyone outside his home. But the fact that a wide array of people show up at his barbershop can only be explained by his fun-loving, totally accepting, and generous person. The barbershop, depicted as a microcosm or refuge, becomes an ideal point of convergence, a modern-day melting pot. Zoot suiters, loafers, hen-pecked men, drunks, "bootleggers, thieves, love merchants and rustlers," all roam in and out of his shop, feeling more validated by their contact with him. As Englekirk notes, "Garza is a confessor, an arbiter, and a consultant,"[16] aside from being a counselor, a source of moral support, and an informal loan agency. His vocation is to cut hair, but his true calling is putting wisdom into practice and sharing his knowledge.

In addition, his unmatched humor blends with a didacticism derived from hard experience. For example, the narrator points out that he was born with so much hair that this later prompted him to become a barber. On another occasion he tried shearing dogs but had to quit because his house and brothers were becoming flea ridden. He also tried to make his fortune picking grapes in California, but ended up shedding twenty pounds and losing the hair under his armpits from climbing tall garbage cans. After numerous setbacks, he settled on barbering, an accident of fate that proved doubly profitable by allowing him to both philosophize and earn a living. He is in essence a man of experience who encourages others to pursue their inclinations while reminding them to seek a balance between ambition and realistic goals. Garza eventually attained a position of prominence, thanks to his entrepreneurship, doing something he genuinely enjoyed. With peace of mind and self-assurance,[17] he learns to control his destiny and is predisposed to share such a revelation with anyone. He possesses a deep understanding of human existence, reasoning that, at the end of life, nobody can take their material possessions with them. At its close, the sketch reiterates his fundamental precept: "Garza, the philosopher. Owner of Garza's Barber Shop. But the shop will never own Garza."

While Señor Garza imparts wisdom and knowledge to others, it is perhaps more accurate to say that he is the agent of transmission of information. He prefers matters related to the spirit, standing diametrically opposed to the temptations of the material world. Moreover, he acts as a generator of folkloric teachings, which he extracts from the gallery of characters through confessions and intimate conversations. He keeps the system and processes of culture alive by creating bonds among these fragmented people. He gives back what insights he has gained and transforms them into a tool of validation for these marginal characters to better prepare them for survival in a hostile social environment. In that regard, he represents a maximum expression of generosity by forgoing personal advantages and turning them to the benefit of others, thus exemplifying the best of what the barrio has to offer apart from simplistic idealizations.

The remaining stories, published and unpublished, resemble outgrowths or qualifiers, and serve to substantiate Suárez's literary project by adding to the gallery of barrio characters. The first two sketches exemplify his aesthetic method, a direct and unadorned realism, while the subsequent stories enrich and expand the core narratives. Although each sketch concentrates on one character, together they add to the horizontal panorama by giving body to an otherwise amorphous community that oscillates between the margins and fringes of a cultural mosaic. Each story stretches the horizon of a forgotten place, augmenting some of the characteristics, and personalities, found in the Chicano community, situated in a particular kind of place: the barrio.

The short narrative "Cuco Goes to a Party," for example, relates the troubled life of a Mexican immigrant named Cuco Martínez who one day goes against his monotonous routine and fails to go straight home to his wife. Señor Garza intercepts him and invites him to join Procuna, Lolo, and himself to celebrate Lili-boy's birthday with an improvised party and a few beers. Camaraderie and macho silliness swell with each beer, turning into fanciful simulations of bullfights. Lily-boy and Lolo tangle in a playful fistfight and later continue drinking with the others. Only Señor Garza keeps his wits as the designated driver, watching over his friends to prevent any mishaps. He gains a sense of satisfaction from his young friends' innocent carousing, which distracts them from life's hardships. The pretext is Lili-boy's birthday, but the real intent of the party is to reduce Cuco Martínez's anguish at home. Matters become especially tense after Cuco loses his underwear during the night of carousing and his in-laws use this as an opportunity to turn his wife against him. The sketch, then, is highly suggestive and somewhat mysterious and ambiguous. It is clear the unnamed in-laws and Cuco have conflicting cultural values, such as regarding what men can do in their free time. The conflict may derive from ethnic, class, or national differences. Garza, as the sage intermediary, is there to ameliorate the situation. If Cuco's in-laws are Anglos, then cultural differences can explain the drift. However, if his in-laws are acculturated Mexicans, then perhaps Suárez is pointing out the fundamental dissimilarities between this group and more recent (unacculturated) immigrants. Cuco decides to return to Mexico as soon as his wife, Emilia, gives birth, thereby avoiding further humiliation from his in-laws and conflict with Emilia. In that way, Suárez provides resolution to irreconcilable differences, but numerous questions remain. The story could have gained further dimension by developing the rationale for the wife's reactions.

Suárez's fourth story, "Loco-Chu," which resembles more a *relato*, or a short narrative, likewise connects with the previous stories and their barrio dwellers. As the barrio *loco* (town idiot or someone with a mental disorder), Loco-Chu possesses certain picaresque qualities, except for his weak intellectual faculties. The story emphasizes his homelessness by describing his everyday routine of roaming through the streets. Loco-Chu accepts any kind of coin given to him, but his passion for collecting nickels becomes almost legendary. He frequently extorts nickels and other favors by grunting, making faces, and shouting nasty words. He openly pesters and sometimes embarrasses people. A local nuisance, he is someone to avoid at all cost. When he obtains his desired nickel, he marches off smiling as if victorious. On the surface a local color sketch, the piece focuses on the poor fellow's resourcefulness and the general community's tolerance. Generosity emerges as the central idea: Lin Lew, a Chinese man who works in the Canton Café, feeds Loco-Chu, and Señor Garza gives him a penny and a newspaper to sell; others, however, treat him as an outcast or like the plague. With this story, the barrio's profile grows, as a place of peoples of diverse backgrounds and varying ways of being—some good, others less so. The idiot has no other place to go to and, to some degree, forms part of the natural landscape. He has no place beyond the barrio, which both tolerates and rejects him. Most of all, he has music as his ultimate refuge, a form of internal happiness.

In "Kid Zopilote" (1948) Suárez creates the first in-depth portrayal in American literature of the pachuco, or zoot suiter, preceding Octavio Paz's canonized version in *Labyrinth of Solitude* (1950). In contrast with Paz's distant and judgmental portrait of this barrio dweller, Suárez's is sympathetic, with folkloric resonance, as well as ironic and sad. The teenager named Pepe García, who unexpectedly became a pachuco, dons a stylized set of fancy clothes with a flashy hat. He adopted this 40s style while in California to overcome the loneliness and boredom he experienced while working in the fields. His metamorphosis is not well received when he returns home to Tucson, demonstrating an intolerance for and stereotyping of certain kinds of difference.

The sketch deals with how external labels, particularly *apodos* (nicknames) can envelop and redefine the individual. The epithet Kid Zopilote distorts Pepe's real being. He feels unaccepted or falsely accused of something he is not. Despite his resistance, his name takes over his identity, wiping out any possibility of integrating into his social environment, except with other pachucos. The narrator seems to regard these urban Chicanos with some awe, countering the prevalent negative impression of them. After explaining to Pepe the meaning of his nickname (essentially "Kid Buzzard"), his uncle provides him with a useful insight about assuming a different identity: "It is said a zopilote can never be a peacock."

Soon Pepe starts acting according to the stereotype of the pachuco, becoming a social parasite by trafficking marijuana cigarettes and pimping. As a result he ends up in jail, stripped of his pachuco identity; now with a shaved head and torn outfit, he is further ostracized. Estranged from his family and friends, his only redeeming quality is his guitar playing. Unfortunately, he remains a *zopilote* instead of a peacock, trapped in a vicious circle by his chosen lifestyle. Although Suárez's portrayal of pachucos shows a certain fascination with their flair, gaiety, and colorful argot, his final attitude seems ambivalent. Kid Zopilote is finally indicted for adopting a lifestyle foreign to who he is, given where he is from. The lesson seems to be: the barrio may have its pitfalls but it also possesses limits and dignity. Instead of an idealization of pachucos as a new kind of Chicano, we get irony: Kid Zopilote exemplifies someone unable to resist conformity. Trapped in his new identity, he experiences the double-edged sword of being and becoming.

In the sketch "Southside Run," Suárez experiments further with narrative by using a bus driven by Pete Echeverría as the instrument to tell the story. The bus functions like a movie camera that captures the physical layout of El Hoyo, and brings its people, architecture, and terrain into focus. The sketch takes the form of a journey through the barrio, with the image and impression of El Hoyo increasing dramatically as the narrator details the kind of people who inhabit the place. The sketch complements "El Hoyo," the gateway to Suárez's narrative world, but now we gain greater insight into the interior. The insistence on a realistic picture is noteworthy: street names are mentioned, exact landmarks are referred to, and common folk are described. The barrio comes alive as a place of ordinary people, with ladies chewing gum, men sitting in the shade of palm trees, shrines waiting to perform miracles, and houses rich with family history as "recorded in scratched walls and faded spots where the jelly left by small hands was unwisely washed off with wet rags." A view of the barrio emerges in which pleasant and unappealing things exist side by side. Pretty gardens abound next to junk piles; vice is rampant alongside virtuous behavior; urban projects "where everybody's private business is public topic" are around the corner from well-manicured homes. In other words, extremes and opposites are common. The bus tour provides a horizontal view of the place, but most importantly, an ethnographic biography where men and women, Chicanos and Chinese are neighbors and intermingle with ease. A vibrant milieu of noises and voices manifests itself with all its blemishes.

The tour, however, reaches a sociological conclusion by the narrator that Chicanos need to emulate the common Chinese store owners if they expect their businesses to be successful. The story is told of one Chinese land baron, however, who was so frugal that he became ill, emaciated, and was eventually eaten by his pigs. The message is that extremes in needs or desires can be harmful. The driver completes his route by making a U-turn to repeat the journey in reverse, thus forming a complete circle. The trip, then, provides an eyeful of bustling activities, people, and circumstances that shows the barrio to be a livable place where ordinary people cohabit.

Suárez's philosophical bent continues in the sketch "Maestría," which emphasizes the cultural custom of extending recognition to someone for their gifts and talents. A person is considered a "master" if he perfects a trade, whether it is socially redeeming or a folly: "It is applied with equal honor to a painter, tailor, barber, printer, carpenter, mechanic, bricklayer, window washer, ditchdigger, or bootblack if his ability merits it." A saddle shop *maestro* named Gonzalo Pereda resembles the character type of Señor Garza, that is, someone who works for a living but doesn't allow work to control him. "Life, he figured, was too short anyway." His true love is raising fighting cocks, and his fortunes improve dramatically after he receives a red rooster as a gift from a friend in Chihuahua. The rooster, later named Killer, possesses a pompous attitude, the good looks of a fine stock, and the instincts of an assassin. Gonzalo's hobby begins to consume his after-work hours. He parades the rooster on weekends from one cockfight to another, gaining considerable notoriety. When Killer finally meets his match, the *maestro* is devastated by his loss.

The rooster, a symbol of masculine prowess and bravery, serves as the vehicle for the narrator to comment on the passing of generations and express nostalgia for the good old days when life offered drama and danger. Immigrants from Mexico seem to be losing their customs, and previously cherished crafts and knowledge seem less appreciated in their new environment. The remaining real *maestros* are fading fast, forming a secret society where they honor their comrades. The sketch laments the passing of practices and customs in an ever-changing world. At first, this loss is perceived as something tragic; then, the narrator changes his mind and concludes with resignation: "Perhaps it is natural." What some critics might view as quaintness becomes a pragmatic realism about the nature of change in modern society. The sketch's didactic nostalgia offers consolation on the changing of the guard as older generations pass.

The sketch titled "Mexican Heaven" contains one of Suárez's best attempts at character development. The barrio priest Father Raymond is a foreigner whose insipid first sermons drove people out of mass before it was over. The priest and the people take some time to warm up to each other, given their differences. Putting aside his personal ambitions to become a bishop, Father Raymond makes a conscious effort to relate to the barrio community by attending every possible community event: weddings, baptismal celebrations, hunting trips, and one bullfight. In time he becomes a permanent fixture, and his rapport with his parishioners is exemplary. A genuine fondness grows between priest and community. He is more than part of their social gatherings; he becomes part of their lives. The locals are so pleased with his commitment and dedication that they see him as one of their own and call him Padre Ramón.

His greatest test of intimate bonding with the community occurs when he tries to convince a dying wino to accept the sacrament of Extreme Unction. The man refuses on the grounds that Heaven will lack the Mexican things he knows and cherishes. After a heated and challenging dialogue with the dying man, Father Raymond persuades him to take the sacrament by telling him that the Kingdom of Heaven "borrows some of El Barrio's finest aspects and even improves on them." The priest proceeds to humorously imagine a heaven where Saint Peter guards the gates attired in a Mexican *charro* suit and a big sombrero. Mexican angels play melodic guitars, people ride flying serapes, and pretty dark-eyed girls reside there who never become mothers-in-law. Enchiladas abound with tacos, tamales, beans, and other Mexican delicacies. Wide-eyed, the man relents, asks to receive the last rites, and then dies. The priest leaves with a heavy heart and returns to the rectory to say a rosary for the soul of the wino. The creativity by the priest validates a place he has come to love. The barrio, typically not perceived as having redeeming qualities, here becomes the savior thanks to the priest's clever imagination. True to Suárez's style, the sketch contains another irony: through the manner in which he saves the man's soul, the priest acknowledges that the Mexican community ultimately saved his.

The first eight sketches discussed and analyzed thus far establish Suárez as a precursor to an emerging Chicano consciousness. In his writings we detect a new mentality developing: a deliberate embracing of characters generally absent in American literature, namely those of humble barrio origins. These stories constitute the first cycle of sketches to create a group of outcast characters situated in a place that seems to exist outside of the American consciousness. Yet Suárez depicts them as possessing the same human virtues and frailties as any other group. Framed within a Chicano microcosm, the stories establish social types and archetypes with distinct inclinations. This Chicano writer's preference for capturing barrio dwellers, then, provides an in-depth vision of a wide assortment of people who range from ambitious to humorous, pathetic to generous. His next three published sketches, "Las comadres" (1969), "Los coyotes" (1972), and "The Migrant" (1982),[18] appeared considerably later as a second cycle, though the first two depict the same environment and people, and are written in the same style, as the earlier eight. It is unknown when, exactly, they were written, although the composition of the first two approximates that of the first cycle. The third sketch was probably composed at the peak of the Chicano movement, around the time of César Chávez's labor strikes in the 1960s and 1970s. It deviates from the representations of El Hoyo in the earlier sketches—probably in order to complement the previous pieces by incorporating a topic of current interest.

Suárez's ninth sketch, "Las comadres," once more examines barrio types, except that the perspective changes radically to focus on women. Kinship and familial bonding is portrayed through intimate women friends, who in baptizing each other's children strengthen their ties and trust. In this case Suárez does not shy away from the sensitive issue of domestic abuse at a time when it probably was a hushed topic. While the characterizations might appear to make light of the issue, the author gives it the same importance as other issues (corruption, infidelity, political machinations, indolence or lack of ambition, mental disorders, etc.). Anastacia Elizondo, a pretentious woman, is beat up by her husband for poor housekeeping. Her *comadre*, Lola López, always provides moral support and empty counsel by repeating: "He will change." The two women's frailties are exposed: the first is criticized for her apparent submissiveness, while the second is passive in her advice. The behavior is contextualized as something from the 1930s and 1940s, though the sketch does not condone the violence by the husband or the lack of action to stop it. The depression and the financial hardships put extra stress on everyone, particularly Anastacia's husband, Lazarillo, who resorts to intermittent violence. Anastacia feels trapped in her predicament. But after one more dreadful beating, she decides to flee with her children. She moves into a middle-class neighborhood, changes her appearance, and avoids contact with people from El Hoyo, whom she considers inferior.

The sketch is more about the durability of relationships than domestic abuse, although the latter probably has greater resonance today. The ties of friendship are tested when the two comadres are forced to reunite for a strange wedding ceremony between Lola's son and Anastacia's daughter, who unexpectedly delivers a baby immediately after the ceremony. At Lola's prompting, Anastacia returns to her husband, reforming her housekeeping habits. Her husband, however, responds with only indifference. The neighborhood is awakened one night by "wails, cries, and crashing furniture." The narrator de-

scribes Anastacia "lying in bed with a pair of black eyes and her hair dishevelled, bubbl[ing] on her pillow." A passionate encounter is intimated, alter-
ing our understanding of the couple's past conflicts. Although both man and
woman can be criticized (Lazarillo as a wife beater, Anastacia as an insecure
masochist), longing allows them one more opportunity to work out their differences and find a renewed sense of love. While domestic abuse is the central
topic, the actual theme of the sketch is the resolving of differences.

The subsequent story, "Los coyotes," presents the multiple meanings of
coyote, which in its narrow sense refers to someone who arranges the immigration status of others through any viable means, including scheming and blackmail. *Coyotes* prey on the hungry, the vulnerable, and the desperate. Through
numerous twists and turns in the action, the sketch indicts those who take advantage of people in need of some kind of intervention, assistance, or hope.
Ironically, Casimiro Ancheta had participated in the Mexican Revolution and
awaited the true revolution "to vindicate him as soon as the traitors and torturers of Mexican Liberty who now had the upper hand were overthrown."
Along with Pancho Pérez, Ancheta organizes a kind of affirmative action com-
mittee for "our race." The noble ideals of political power and economic security
are to be upheld on behalf of women whose husbands or sons are off to war.
Via methods of trickery and embezzlement (e.g., contributions, dues, quotas,
and assessments), the two swindler *coyotes* divert to themselves the allotment
checks sent home by men in the military. While the barrio people become
more desperately impoverished and depleted of resources, the two increase
their wealth and holdings. When they hear someone suggest a review of their
accounting methods and books, they fabricate a scene to make it seem as if
they have been assaulted by thieves in their office. They escape punishment
for their con game, but the barrio inhabitants mutter about the real culprits.
The sketch satirizes profiteering by social predators. The cynical view of such
scoundrels is summarized by Pancho's statement at the end: "I don't get mad
because they do it. It's just that . . . they don't invite." Suárez widens the definition of the *coyote* to a swindler of trusting people through shady organizations.

The last published sketch by Suárez, "The Migrant," is a significant departure from his previous stories. There is a change in sensibility and tone, as well
as in context, in this story of a farmworker named Teófilo Vargas in constant
search for work. Whereas the other sketches take place in El Hoyo mainly during World War II and the 1940s, this one occurs in the 1950s around the time of
the Korean War. Moreover, the previous sketches offer a lighthearted view of
barrio life, often filled with humor, satire, and burlesque descriptions of Chicano urban culture. And they contain a sense of hope because the characters
can always count on one another for support. In "The Migrant" pessimism and
tragedy seem unavoidable, couched within a deterministic vein where things
go from bad to worse. The leitmotif "Well, a man can't fight his destiny" haunts

the migrant worker, reminding him of an inescapable vicious circle. The work echoes Steinbeck's *Grapes of Wrath* in thematic thrust, but more closely resembles *The Plum Plum Pickers* (1969) by Raymond Barrio and *". . . Y no se lo tragó la tierra"* (1971) by Tomás Rivera in suggesting a cosmic struggle for survival. Suárez altered his focus from the barrio to the fields, once again addressing the needs of the most vulnerable and marginalized in their respective eras. If he in fact wrote the sketch in the 1950s, then it would distinguish itself for being an important precursor to the kinds of narratives that later emphasized the farmworkers' plight. More likely its composition dates to the 1970s.

The protagonist makes relentless futile attempts to escape migrant life in order to better provide for his family. The mechanical motion of such work reinforces the feeling of entrapment, and as in *The Plum Plum Pickers*, the condition of the shacks he occupies is referred to again and again, suggesting both social oppression and physical confinement. Similar to the situation described in the chapter "Cuando lleguemos . . ." in *". . . Y no se lo tragó la tierra,"* Teófilo comes from a family that had spent a good amount of its time migrating, continually uprooted, going from state to state and from one seasonal crop to another. He tries to change his life pattern upon marrying Natalia, but economic circumstances force them to seek the golden dream in California, where they fail. He again ventures out on the migrant trail on his own so as not to inconvenience his family further, leaving behind an unfinished house. However, his bad fortune is repeated, and he feels chained to what another worker once told him: "Once a picker, *mano*, always a picker." He joins a group of men to play a game of dice, an apt symbol for his life of mere chance. After numerous dead ends, his only alternative is to return to what he knows: Williams Farms, Camp Three, the starting point in the story. The story ends with his stumbling toward completion of this vicious circle.

One characteristic of "The Migrant" that distinguishes it from the other stories is its structure: less linear than the other sketches, its fragmented organization lends itself to capturing the protagonist's sense of confusion and entrapment. The use of dreamscapes complements the fragmentary narratives, suggesting that the character is often waking up from either a dream or a daydream, hoping for a better future but always ending up mired in the same cycle. The result is a narrative that captures the psychological dilemmas of a migrant whose fate is predetermined.

Analysis and Discussion of Unpublished Sketches

In the remaining eight unpublished sketches, Suárez adds to the gallery of characters he had already created and explores new topics that contribute to humanizing the barrio inhabitants. However, some of these stories are not situated in the barrio and focus more directly on a didactic aspect, as influenced by folklore (e.g., "La suerta del pobre"), or on a non-Chicano character (e.g., "Life Is But a Tango"). In addition, one longer work can be categorized as a long short story or novelette (i.e., "Trouble in Petate").[19] The variations in form, style, theme, and focus are quite noteworthy, exhibiting a versatile writer who is preparing these stories for final publication. Most of these sketches were probably written in the 1950s and went through various revisions.[20]

In "Doña Clara" Suárez develops a positive and credible female character. Something of a female version of Señor Garza, she possesses her own personality of noble spirit and boundless generosity. In contrast to the women in "Las comadres," Doña Clara asserts her independence and self-reliance. Her husband, on the other hand, is a womanizer, frivolous pretender, and irresponsible provider, who later abandons her and her two young children, forcing her to fend for herself as a landlord. Despite hardships, she proves to be highly resourceful and manages to overcome her economic difficulties through effort and determination. Although she loses her son at Pearl Harbor, she is able to persevere on the outside while crying inwardly, demonstrating an unbreakable spirit while continuing to comfort others who are less advantaged than she. Much like Señor Garza, she becomes the center of the barrio around whom others revolve, often depending on her for assistance and even refuge. Echoing Steinbeck, she calls the people her "*paisanitos*," the downtrodden who struggle just to make it. The first part of her name suggests her respect, dignity, and a sense of nobleness. At the end of the sketch, as occurs often in Suárez's stories, the narrator adds to the portrait: Doña Clara, the strong-willed optimist and protector of the disenfranchised, comes to represent the good Mexican qualities that still exist in the barrio. She offers a home away from home, "*un rinconcito mexicano*, a little Mexican corner.*" She becomes the archetypal mother figure, always willing to serve others.

In the second unpublished sketch, titled "Life Is But a Tango," Suárez leaves the barrio to situate the action in downtown Manhattan and in the world of one of his favorite sports: boxing. Simón Esperanti,[21] an Argentine national boxing champion referred to as "the conquering gaucho," has come to Manhattan to seek his boxing fortune. Impatient to reach the top, Simón has the misfortune to be matched against Spoiler Thomas, who knocks him out. The arrogant Argentine's opportunities dwindle to virtually nothing, and he loses his steak-eating lifestyle and fancy downtown apartment. His only recourse is to find someone who can support him. He meets a Puerto Rican young lady who offers him housing and food in exchange for teaching her how to tango. The philosophical moral of the sketch emerges at the end when Simón tells his friends that "life is but a tango. And one must dance it away." The carpe diem sentiment mixes with the melodramatic sadness characteristic of tangos.

The sketch "Doña Clara's Nephew" returns us to the affable Doña Clara. Her virtue as a generous person, already established as legendary in El Hoyo in the previous sketch "Doña Clara," is here underscored but also tested. Her nephew, a recent immigrant named Cuco Alonzo, has a tendency to take the easy way, knowing full well that his aunt will provide him with the basics, namely a roof over his head and meals. His job hunting always ends in failure, but she continues to show him sympathy while feeding him and giving him an occasional dollar for his expenses. She finds him a job with a contractor, for whom he does such things as carry hods and mix cement. She even declines his offer of his first check, recommending that he purchase clothing and save the rest in case he goes back to Mexico.

His aunt, however, soon sees his old habits re-emerging. She realizes he had "sold parrots for a living" in Mexico, an expression suggesting that he had avoided work by every means. Sure enough, he had scalped tickets to bullfights, bought and sold pawn tickets, served as a tourist guide, and become a "satisfier of whims and sins." He also became adept at loitering around cafés, bars, barbershops, and other places, generally peddling inside information for a commission. As a "parrot salesman at heart," Cuco becomes what Doña Clara feared most: a full-fledged hustler, taking advantage of anyone in his path. One night he challenges his aunt's generosity by allowing one of his drinking friends to stay overnight in his room, violating a basic rule. At her wit's end, his aunt asks him to vacate, but a few days later her guilty conscience compels her to ask his employer for Cuco's whereabouts. Unable to locate him, she concludes he has returned to Mexico. Later, however, she hears that he has married a girl uptown and moved in with his in-laws, taking a job as a pest exterminator.

Although the sketch lacks a well-defined conclusion, its lesson is that such a character never changes and is willing to adapt only according to his convenience. Doña Clara's tough love fails to alter her nephew's conditioned habits, basically because he is not predisposed to change. Nor is her abundant generosity enough to change her nephew, who is mired in vices. Virtue does not win out.

Suárez often resorts to the folkloric, as, for example, in the next sketch, "El Tiradito," which means "the fallen one" or someone forgotten. The aim of the story is to explain the identity of the man buried in the shallow grave marked with a wooden cross. The narrator underscores his story's oral source, pointing out that this version is only one of a reservoir of legends and "remnants of stories heard at childhood."

It is unlikely there is anyone living who knew Juan Can.[22] He was a man of great charm whom few women could resist, and men were, without exception, jealous of him. True to the variants in folklore and ballads, Juan is said to have been a stagecoach driver, a prospector, an Indian fighter, and an ore buyer, before finally becoming the proprietor of a bar. When he meets Teresita Ríos, he is smitten, but he is rebuffed by her father, who considers him of inferior social class. Juan Can dedicates the next few years to accumulating more and more wealth so that nothing, including Teresita, will be beyond his reach. As Juan's prowess and wealth grow in the region, Teresita's father becomes anxious. Failing to find an assassin to kill Juan, he creates a plan to deflate the suitor's growing empire. He contracts Pasquinas, the renowned gambler from northern Mexico, to challenge Juan in his favorite vice: a game of cards with high stakes. A carnival, with its fire-eaters, contortionists, and freaks, serves as the backdrop for the duel, and Pasquinas's disguise as a clown adds to the overall intrigue. At the end of the all-night game, Juan wipes his forehead in victory. But a figure outside the tent thrusts a knife into Juan's back, killing him instantly.

An epilogue explains how men and women began paying homage to his grave, turning it into a shrine for those in love, among others. Even if the true identity of the person lying within the grave is in doubt, people are convinced of one thing: "El Tiradito, the Fallen One, whoever he may be, grants wishes to those blessed with sublime faith." In a few words, Suárez describes how an anti-hero can become someone to whom prayers are addressed.

In "The Pioneer" the author returns to the theme of barrio predators, first seen in "Los coyotes." This short sketch follows the progress of a self-made man, carrying the mocking name of Maximiliano Torres Carbajalando. The name is a triple pun: "Maximiliano" to suggest aristocracy; "Torres" to underscore his ivory tower attitude; and "Carbajalando," which combines a typical name like "Carbajal" with a word meaning "goes working" or "pulling toward his side," or self-interested. Most people, however, call him "Güero Chulo," meaning light-haired, or blond, and handsome. He sneaked across the border illegally and encountered "Spanish Americans" who "smoked cigars, and spoke Spanish only sparingly." His sense of superiority leads him to mock these "self-styled pioneers." Although loath to take menial jobs, he is finally forced to go to work digging cesspools and mowing lawns, jobs he dignifies with the names of "geologist" and "landscape artist." Drawn to the mountains after hearing rumors of buried treasure, he witnesses two men hiding wooden crates in a hole. He discovers they are crates of imported cognac, and he becomes a dealer in bootleg liquor, an opportunistic thief during the Prohibition era. As the narrator observes, "His conceit grew with his ability." But that career ends one night when bootleggers set a trap for him and shoot him with buckshot. Still full of self-importance, he once again sets out to outdo the pioneers. He becomes a warworker, and as a sideline cashes the checks of migrant railroad workers "for a small fee," gaining a reputation for ruthlessness. The final irony is that he has become what he most despised: a Spanish American who smokes cigars and speaks Spanish only sparingly. The story's satirical perspective, although not fully developed, indicts this new kind of swindler.

A didactic strain reappears in the sketch "Something Useful, Even Tailoring," which borders on the folktale that teaches a moral lesson. In this case Luis Pereda, son of the town's tailor, tests his father's patience by always showing up late for his duties as a shop apprentice. The story depicts a generational clash. The father has a practical approach to life; he has chosen a vocation and become an expert in it. Luis, on the other hand, has lofty dreams about a baseball career. The father shows patience with his son, because he too had been a dreamer as a young man, longing to follow in the footsteps of the famous bullfighter of his time, Rodolfo Gaona. But a horrible period on a ranch and a shattered wrist suffered in a military assault during the Mexican Revolution end that dream. The father learned to distinguish between what is reachable and what is simply a fascination. Now with a son absorbed in his own dreams, Gonzalo recalls the words of his mentor tailor: "No matter their dreams, Gonzalo, when you have sons, teach them something useful, even tailoring."

The curious element in this sketch is that after the internal monologue by the father about his own youthful dreams, there is, perhaps, a hint of a transformation in the idealistic and somewhat rebellious son. Thus, perhaps the father's flexible and patient approach will pay off, and the son will eventually find in tailoring what the father found. At the end, when the father asks his son if he will bring some cold drinks for the two of them, the son responds "Good idea," suggesting a reconciliation between the two and indicating that the son may come to respect his father's practical vocation.

"Trouble in Petate" was created as a blueprint for a novel but remained only a long short story, the longest we have available by Mario Suárez. More a short story than a sketch, it nonetheless combines various elements from other sketches. The allegorical impulse is fundamental: to expose the human tendency to blur the boundaries between virtue and vice. An archetypal protagonist named Pepe (no last name) lives a simple life along with his dog Pulgas ("fleas"), his donkey Orejas ("ears"), his goat Enamorada ("sweetheart," or "in love"), his few chickens, and his little red rooster. He dedicates himself to leisure and avoiding worldly worries. For mild entertainment, he goes to the nearest town of Feria to visit his favorite local drinking joint (called a *chispa* station) and catch a glimpse of his love, Dalia. As a matter of routine, Pepe overdrinks and is sometimes arrested.

His simple approach to life turns into a string of misadventures. He finds out that Dalia is to be married off to someone else, then is arrested for assaulting that man, the *presidente municipal* (the mayor). A roaming stranger convinces

Pepe of greener pastures in a fantasyland called Petate City, a town filled with beautiful buildings, wonderful music, and lovely ladies. After Pepe is talked into selling his land, he sets out to see this illusory Petate City, whose name, which refers to a lowly mat made of straw, undercuts the city's reputation for glamour. Afraid people will laugh at him if he enters the city on a donkey, he leaves behind his beloved Orejas, though he does take his dog Pulgas. On the train to Petate City he encounters a gentleman with a high-sounding name of quasi-nobility and privilege, the highfalutin Octavio Claveles Villar[r]ica y Tostada. Fooled by the sob story of a "royal individual," Pepe buys socks from the man and later even exchanges clothes with him, for a price. Petate City turns out to be a place of extreme conformity and sham wealth. But Pepe dedicates himself to observing and practicing the customs of its inhabitants, such as by getting his hair curled and staying out of the sun. Much like a picaresque character, Pepe seeks worldly comfort and social status, but fails. After meeting Filomena Farsantina (her first name, meaning "beloved," is undercut by her last, which is a pun on *farsante*, meaning "fraud" or "fake"), his desire to conform becomes more intense.

The story assumes a Borgesian quality when Pepe encounters a waiter who looks like him, a kind of *döppelganger*, or double, who comes from a similar background. He warns Pepe that he will meet a similar fate: love gone awry, landholdings lost, and being accused of being a thief, trespasser, vagabond, and vandal. Pepe is rattled but remains determined to conquer Filomena. But just as he lost Dalia, Pepe loses Filomena to the butcher's son who won the lottery. Love, he again finds, is dictated by material wealth. He finally realizes that Pulgas is his only friend in this cruel world, and decides to rededicate himself to the simple life. But his vice of drinking too much *chispa* undermines his intentions. Walking home drunk in a bad part of town, he is mugged by a policeman, who robs him of his remaining money. Still in possession of the wedding dress and ring he had bought for Filomena, he is, however, unable to return them for his money or sell them to a pawn shop for more than a pittance. Finally, out of the blue, he is arrested on the street on the charge of burglary.

Pepe's picaresque adventures continue in prison, where his philosophical cell companion, Cornelio,[23] offers social criticism of Petate City. He tells Pepe that there are more honest men in jail than outside, and makes Pepe aware of the country's dictatorship. According to Cornelio, the only way Pepe can save himself is to join the military force controlled by the dictator, referred to as El Supremo. After a night of being bitten by bugs, Pepe resigns himself to join the army, while Cornelio stays behind to receive free room and board in jail.

Divided into ten narrative fragments, "Trouble in Petate" has the makings of an episodic novelette that Suárez could have expanded. It contains aspects of other sketches (e.g., the idea of fate, a desired simplicity, gullibility versus

deception, loyalty to real friends, and picaresque underpinnings). Although
the simpleton Pepe seeks a way out of his vicious circle of misfortune, he also
appears to be destined to repeat the pattern.

The last of Suárez's sketches included here, "La suerte del pobre," is distinguished by its having been composed in Spanish, apparently extracted directly
out of oral tradition, if we are to believe the note that credits Atilana H. Minjares
as Suárez's oral informant (fictional or real). Presumably Suárez recorded and
transcribed the anecdote, although we cannot dismiss the possibility that the
sketch is a total literary invention. Given the numerous typographical errors
and misspellings, and the fact that Suárez knew Spanish well, the extant version appears to be a very preliminary folkloric transcription still in the process
of becoming a text. It might also be labeled an "idea" piece, which could later
be transformed into a full-fledged sketch within the Suárez mold. The story
dramatizes a moral lesson about learning one's destiny, as conditioned by class
considerations and the prevalent misfortunes of the poor. Pedro, the destitute
protagonist, is always willing to provide any kind of service to make ends meet.
Constructed like a fable or fairy tale, the story begins with "Hace muchos años,
en un pueblo cuyo nombre no recuerdo . . ." (Many years ago in a town, whose
name I can't remember . . .), imparting greater fictionality to Pedro's town by
using a Miguel de Cervantes rhetorical formula.

One day, a rich man, interested in inquiring into his own destiny, hires Pedro
to go out and locate what fate has in store for him, instructing him above all to
tell his fate that he wishes to continue to have the same good fortune. After a
pleasant journey, Pedro finds his employer's destiny or fate, and says what he
has been instructed to say. Fate answers that it will always reciprocate as long
as the rich man treats his own fate well. After reporting back to the rich man,
Pedro decides to test his luck by searching for his own destiny, but he encounters nothing but obstacles: an inhospitable terrain, snakes, and hunger. Pedro
comes to an isolated hut, finds a dirty, emaciated, and disheveled woman, and
tells her he is in search of his fate. She retorts, "'Pues, aquí me tienes, grandísimo pendejo,' . . . la cual entonces lo mató a escobazos" ("Well, here I am,
you damn nitwit," . . . and she then attacked him, killing him with a broom).

The moral lesson resides in the absurdity of seeking one's destiny by com-
paring it with that of someone wealthy and privileged. His impoverished state
does not give him the luxury to pursue such a thing, and when he does, he
ends up worse off than before. The sketch may show how Suárez derived inspiration from folkloric sources such as proverbs and fairy tales. As a work of
social commentary, it suggests the double jeopardy of a poor man.

Conclusion: From the Quotidian to a Mischievous Didacticism

In sum, Mario Suárez is a creative and original storyteller, whose sketches often reveal a didactic impulse. His fiction intimates a new aesthetic plan to recreate a Chicano space by depicting characters from the barrio, embodied by the vibrant and sometimes paradoxical El Hoyo. These characters, often very ordinary but sometimes eccentric and always memorable, possess varying qualities that help form a microcosm of the human condition. What emerges is a multicultural community dealing with issues of assimilation, identity, and a sense of belonging. Also prominent in the sketches is the immigration experience, inspired by a steady stream of persons whose nomadic journey leads them to urban pockets in the United States, where they contribute to the creation of a social space while adjusting to and negotiating their new environment. Suárez is greatly moved by manifestations of humor, generosity, and tolerance as well as by class distinctions, concerns over social appearances, nostalgia, and folklore. Vice and virtue coexist and take on multiple forms and expressions. Yet Suárez avoids stereotypes by showing peoples' flaws, strengths, and mischievousness. His sketches, therefore, represent an important early development in Chicano literature by pointing toward a new consciousness and inscribing barrio inhabitants in a distinctively Chicano imaginary. He was ahead of his time: not for imagining Chicano characters, because they already existed, but for allowing them to come to life as literary constructs in their own terms. As a precursor to what has been termed Chicano literature, Suárez's sketches establish some of the most significant tenets and paradigms, focusing on characters from within as they measure their Mexican background and mold it to deal with their immediate circumstances. As his sketch "Mexican Heaven" imagines an afterlife of things Mexican where peace and tranquility can be found, his writings in general imagine a real Chicano place on earth. The sketches contained here describe, transpose, and recreate the soul of a place where Chicanos thrive and survive, thanks to their resourcefulness and gusto for life. These characters do not pretend to be heroic, but by their ordinary nature as real-life persons they acquire a boundless epic quality.

Notes

Introduction

1. These sketches appeared in volume 3 (summer), pages 112–15, 115–21, 121–27, 127–30, and 130–37, respectively.

2. The stories appeared in volume 4 (winter), pages 362–68 and 368–73, respectively.

3. The story appeared in volume 4 (winter), pages 310–15.

4. Only a few samples of this newspaper exist, in the Suárez family holdings. The circulation is indicated as 3,500. Suárez's journalistic development is clearly exhibited here; he doesn't mince words and demands authorities exercise a high level of ethics or face the necessary denunciations. In one article entitled "Alianza . . . ," he concludes by stating "Hay [sic] Alianza de mi alma, te asesinan sin que uno de tus hijos alce la voz en pro de su sagrada defensa" (*P-M*, 6 June 1958, p. 3; Oh, my dear Alliance, they attack you without having one of your sons raise their voice in your holy defense).

5. "Las comadres" and "Los coyotes" appeared in *Con Safos*.

The Stories

1. For the first eight published sketches, we use the original versions first published in the *Arizona Quarterly*. For "Las comadres" we use the version published in *Aztlán: An Anthology of Mexican American Literature*; for "Los coyotes" we use the version published in *Festival de Flor y Canto: An Anthology of Chicano Literature*; and for "The Migrant" we use the version published in *Cuentos chicanos*. Accents have been added, some spelling has been modernized, and minor changes in punctuation have been made. All previous publications of the stories are listed in the bibliography.

2. "Armistice Day" is the former name for Veterans Day.

3. Literally, "Foot Stomping Dance Hall." A hallmark of Suárez's lighthearted humor is the humorous names he gives places, or sometimes people.

4. Literally, "Yaqui Tomb" or "Yaqui Stomper," a politically incorrect name that suggests the liquor's "knock-your-socks-off" effect.

5. An island in the Philippines where an important battle took place during World War II.

6. *Frenesí* means "frenzy," but also a kind of profound influence on those who live in the barrio.

7. Here note Suárez's ability to capture what was then an emerging urban barrio slang influenced by African Americans as part of the pachuco era in the 1940s.

8. Star.

9. Owl.

10. The author once admitted to family members that Procuna is his alter ego in the stories. The name is believed to come from a famous bullfighter of the time that Suárez admired.

11. Literally, "plastered pal"—that is, someone who has overindulged in alcohol. The author is also playing with rhyme and alliteration.

12. The CCC, or Civilian Conservation Corps, was a New Deal program during the Great Depression that promoted greater employment.

13. Some critics have suggested that with this reference to a romantic dance from the nineteenth century, Suárez is resorting to facile local color or *costumbrismo*. In fact, the allusion seems a lighthearted reference rather than a superficial characterization of the social environment.

14. The nickname refers to an entire family of real-life bullfighters from Spain. Here, it specifically recalls Fermín Espinosa Saucedo, called "Armillita Chico," who was extremely popular during the 1930s.

15. Literally, "White Cat Café"—another playful place-name.

16. "Loco" is fitting for the character's mental states; "Chu" is short for *pachuco*, signifying a young Mexican American who was viewed as not adapting to either Mexican or American societies. A kind of rebel without a cause, the pachuco in the early 1940s began to carve out a unique identity through an invented language, a flashy form of dress, and a lifestyle of good times, defiance, and an accentuated pride. The pachuco phenomenon remained fairly popular until the 1970s.

17. The Asian name emphasizes the multicultural nature of El Hoyo.

18. Literally, "Kid Buzzard."

19. In this passage are numerous Anglicisms that have been Spanishized, which is common in barrio speech. But the author is also underscoring a bilingual modality in the speech patterns.

20. "Califo," slang for California, was popularized in the 1960s as "Califas."

21. Olvera Street is the old Mexican downtown area of Los Angeles that later became rundown until urban renewal in the 1960s turned it into a tourist spot.

22. Uncle.

23. Another Anglicism, meaning "relative."

24. The expression approximately means "hey, you guys."

25. The expression is immediately followed by its equivalent.

26. Like Canton Café earlier, the mention of the Italian bakery suggests a multicultural environment.

27. Here the reference to an ethnic political organization expands even further the profile of a place generally considered exclusively Chicano.

28. The reference is to the grave of a person whose identity is uncertain. The story of El Tiradito is told in a story of that name in this volume.

29. Suárez's use of these terms was quite ahead of his time.

30. *"Tú mirando"* (Look here). The misspelling is intended to represent the speech of an Asian who supposedly cannot pronounce the "r" sound. Considered culturally insensitive today, such transcriptions were commonplace shortly after World War II.

31. Here, where we would expect "El Hoyo" or the generic lowercase "barrio," Suárez uses the uppercase "Barrio" to accentuate its importance.

32. Note that throughout the stories Suárez likes to mention one of his favorite activities: bullfighting.

33. Literally, "old woman," but used here to refer to a wife or the colloquial "old lady."

34. Go ahead.

35. Someone who unquestionably thinks he has equal status with someone else.

36. A surely intentional reference to the novel *Lazarillo de Tormes* (1554), whose protagonist was the archetypal *pícaro* of the picaresque novel.

37. Literally, "monkey" coffee.

38. That is, Adolf Hitler. Schicklgruber was Hitler's grandmother's last name. Alois, Hitler's father, was her illegitimate son and bore her name for many years.

39. Apparently a literal translation from Spanish, it should be understood to mean "gossipmongers."

40. The sketch is filled with archaic names relatively uncommon today that have some comedic sense, such as Anacleto, Agripina, Ancheta, and Pancho Pérez, the latter comparable to "Joe Blow." Such names are reminiscent of the picaresque wordplay popularized by the novels of Miguel de Cervantes.

41. Benito Juárez is regarded as a national hero, having worked for the democratic reconstruction of Mexico during his presidency, 1861–1871. For three years he resisted the French forces led by Maximilian, culminating in the famous May 5, 1867, battle in which the French were defeated. Porfirio Díaz, on the other hand, is one of Mexico's most despised presidents, ruling (with the exception of one four-year period) from 1876 to 1910. After electoral fraud in the 1910 election, he was thrown out of office and into exile, marking the beginning of the Mexican Revolution.

42. The expression in Mexican Spanish, literally "dead flies," connotes someone who feigns meekness or hides his true character.

43. Somewhat equivalent to "bastards" or "sons of a bitch."

44. "Finished." "No more picking."

45. This Belgian city was a key strategic battleground where Germans and Americans fought between December 16, 1944, and January 14, 1945, to establish a critical military position.

46. Between 1942 and 1964, under the Bracero program, seasonal workers from Mexico were hired to make up for the labor shortage during and after World War II. Although the braceros were primarily farmworkers, *bracero* was also used to refer to Mexicans working on the railroad, in meatpacking factories, and so on.

47. "Hi," or more literally, slang for "what's up, you bastard." *Quiubo* comes from *Qué hubo.*

48. Slang for "kids."

49. Literally, "Damn Tough Guys Bar."

50. "Come here."

51. Short for *hermano*, or "brother."

52. A village in central Korea established in the demilitarized zone after the Korean War, it marks the site of the truce conference held from 1951 to 1953 between representatives of the United Nations forces and the opposing North Korean and Chinese armies.

53. The use of the nickname "Frog" creates a very Hispanic social ambience of humor and innocent needling.

54. Short for *compadre*, or "godfather of one's child," but more often a term for intimate friendship, referring to a kind of benefactor and a person in whom one can confide and have total trust.

55. A type of popular Mexican gumbo made with cow intestines, or tripe, with chile.

56. The strongest expression of aggression in Mexican Spanish, meaning "you motherfucker."

57. "*Ora*," short for *ahora*, here means either "well" or "now."

58. A colloquial form of *a dónde vas*, or "where are you going?"

59. "Son of a . . ."

60. A popular form of *salados*, signifying an excess of something, or in this case "screwed."

61. Like *compadre*, the term indicates kinship in extended families, in this case "godmother," but suggesting a person in whom one can confide and have total trust because of the commitment made to one's child.

62. The author often inserts references to things, people, or places he knew well, converting them to literary elements. Here he uses the name of the city near Pomona, California, where he lived until his death.

63. An intertextual reference to a social type found in John Steinbeck's writings, referring to fellow countrymen.

64. A reference to boxing, to which some men resorted to overcome their poverty.

65. The name is ironic, given the contrast between the boxer's self-centered mentality and an international language, Esperanto, created out of various languages.

66. The term is a put-down common in Argentina, meaning "arrogant" or "bum."

67. The term is used as filler, equivalent to "man" or "dude" in English, and bespeaks to the Argentine Spanish inflected from Italian. It is so common in Argentine Spanish that other Latin Americans called Argentines "*ches.*"

68. Aunt.

69. Another indication of the author's interest in bullfighting.

70. "North" ("El Norte") is a common reference in Mexico to the United States.

71. The reference suggests the author's literary tastes, which have clearly enriched his storytelling.

72. Note the simple pun of the name, "one can."

73. "Tecolote" means "owl," humorously suggesting a place where carousing lasts into the wee hours of the night.

74. The aristocratic-sounding name ends with an invented name composed of a common name, "Carvajal," with a gerund ending to humorously suggest "pulling" or "groping."

75. Another comical place-name—"Cat Hill."

76. The dog's name means "fleas."

77. The donkey's name means "ears."

78. The goat's name, meaning "in love," probably says as much about the owner as the goat, as will be seen later.

79. The town's name means "fair," as in a commercial fair, or market.

80. A *petate* is a humble mat made of straw where the poor sleep in place of a bed. The multiple mentions of Petate City (or "Straw City") augment the satire by mocking a city filled with self-indulgence and airs.

81. Literally, "spark." The drink is an apparent invention by Suárez to humorously suggest "firewater," or strong alcoholic liquor.

82. The term has various connotations, although here it seems to refer to a simple hot dog. Its root means "dog" but also may humorously suggest "feisty."

83. This could be an Anglicized Arizonan version of what is commonly known as "confetti," that is, an empty eggshell filled with small pieces of colorful confetti paper, also termed *cascarones*. Or, it could be a Suárez invention.

84. The names, meaning "Straw City" and "Little Straw City," enhance the comical quality, but also suggest a low-class ambience—in contradiction to their lofty self-promotion.

85. The statement is almost identical to that made by Simón at the end of "Life Is But a Tango."

86. The name of the currency is slang for "bucks" or "money."

87. "My dear, Pepe."

88. The narrator pokes fun at people with high-sounding, aristocratic names: "Octavio" implies patrician ancestry; "Claveles" means "carnations"; "Villar[r]ica" combines the Spanish for "villa" and "rich"; but "Tostada," although potentially a regular Spanish name, adds an element of mockery with its meaning of "toast."

89. An obvious though invented reference to Spain, from the old form "Hispania."

90. *Farsante* means fraud or fake, a jab at the family's aristocratic pretensions.

91. Dressmakers.

92. The name means "someone who swallows land"—in other words, a land-grabber.

93. Players of music for the kipop dance, previously mentioned. The name of the dance is made up, but suggests popular dances of the 1940s, possibly the jitterbug. It could also be barrio slang for such a dance.

94. The town's name means "little mouth."

95. Suárez often uses names to inflate or deflate characters.

96. We are respecting the author's sketch by reproducing it in its original Spanish version but also provide a translation immediately following. Only orthographic changes and minimal semantic corrections were made.

Discussion and Analysis

1. Paredes, "Evolution of Chicano Literature," 35.

2. For further discussion on the topic of literary history, consult A. Gabriel Meléndez's *So All Is Not Lost: The Poetics of Print in Nuevomexicano Communities, 1834–1958* and Francisco A. Lomelí's "A Literary Portrait of Hispanic New Mexico: Dialectics of Perception."

3. Paredes, "Evolution of Chicano Literature," 58.

4. For example, Chuck Tatum in *Chicano Literature* offers a cursory treatment suggesting that Suárez's sketches are picturesque character representations and little else. See page 33.

5. J. Allan Englekirk, "Mario Suárez," 253.

6. Luis Leal expands these points in his study "Pre-Chicano Literature: Process and Meaning (1539–1959)."

7. Rivera, "Chicano Literature."

8. Some of the stories have been reprinted in other anthologies or collections (see the bibliography).

9. Luis Valdez and Stan Steiner served as editors for the first book; Alurista, F. A. Cervantes, Juan Gómez-Quiñones, Mary Ann Pacheco, and Gustavo Segade for the second; and Rudolfo Anaya and Antonio Márquez for the third.

10. The writer confessed this to Allan Englekirk in a series of oral interviews from which Englekirk wrote the study "Mario Suárez."

11. The manuscript exists in the Suárez family collection, but there are no plans to publish it.

12. Englekirk, "Mario Suárez," 256.

13. See Ingram's *Representative Short Story Cycles of the Twentieth Century*, 17.

14. If we go back to the first studies of the works of Rivera and Hinojosa-Smith, we see that critics vacillated between calling them "novels" and "collections of short stories." By the end of the 1970s criticism accepted them as novels, for lack of a better term. Such categories have become further problematized in more contemporary discussions of postmodern literary production.

15. "Tucson, Arizona: El Hoyo," in *Mexican American Literature*, 244.

16. Englekirk, "Mario Suárez," 254.

17. Ibid.

18. The first two sketches appeared in *Con Safos*, the last in *Revista Chicano-Riqueña*. See the bibliography.

19. In his interview with Suárez, Allan Englekirk learned that Suárez intended to make this text a novel, as suggested by the length of the ten narrative fragments. See Englekirk, "Mario Suárez," 253.

20. The Suárez family collection contains various versions. We have chosen the one recommended by his wife, Cecilia Cota-Robles Suárez.

21. His name seems to suggest the universal language Esperanto.

22. Given Suárez's linguistic cleverness, the name is more than likely a pun on "one can." At the same time, the name might have an Asian origin, as occurs in other sketches.

23. Such a name contains hints of the puns and other rhetorical tools used in the exemplary novels of Miguel de Cervantes. Here Cornelio could suggest *cornudo* in Spanish, or "cuckold."

Bibliography

I. Published Primary Sources

In order of appearance:

Suárez, Mario. "El Hoyo." *Arizona Quarterly* 3 (summer 1947): 112–55. Reprinted in *Literatura chicana: Texto y contexto/Chicano Literature: Text and Context*, edited by Antonia Castañeda, Tomás Ybarra-Frausto, and Joseph Sommers, 154–56. Englewood Cliffs, N.J.: Prentice-Hall, 1972. Reprinted in *Con Safos: Reflections of Life in the Barrio* 1, no. 3 (March 1969): 36–37. Reprinted in *Mexican-American Authors*, edited by Américo Paredes and Raymund Paredes, 95–98. Boston: Houghton Mifflin, 1972. Reprinted in *Aztlán: An Anthology of Mexican American Literature*, edited by Luis Valdez and Stan Steiner, 154–57. New York: Knopf, 1973. Reprinted in *Voices in Aztlán: Chicano Literature of Today*, edited by Dorothy E. Harth and Lewis M. Baldwin, 13–15. New York: New American Library, 1974. Reprinted in *El Fuego de Aztlán* 2, no. 3–4 (1978): n.p. Reprinted in *From the Barrio: A Chicano Anthology*, edited by Luis Omar Salinas and Lillian Faderman, 101–2. San Francisco: Canfield Press, 1973. Reprinted as "Tucson, Arizona: El Hoyo," in *Mexican American Literature*, 244–49. Orlando: Harcourt Brace Jovanovich, 1990. Reprinted in *North of the Rio Grande: The Mexican American Experience in Short Fiction*, edited by Edward Simmen, 94–96. New York: Mentor Books, 1992. Reprinted in *Chicano Literature, 1965–1995: An Anthology in Spanish, English, and Caló*, edited by Manuel de Jesús Hernández-Gutiérrez and David William Foster, 104–6. New York: Garland, 1997.

———. "Señor Garza." *Arizona Quarterly* 3 (summer 1947): 115–21. Reprinted in *The Chicano: From Caricature to Self-Portrait*, edited by Edward Simmen, 268–73. New York: New American Library, 1971. Reprinted in *Mexican-American Authors*, edited by Américo Paredes and Raymund Paredes, 99–104. Boston: Houghton Mifflin, 1972. Reprinted in *North of the Rio Grande: The Mexican American Experience in Short Fiction*, edited by Edward Simmen, 96–102. New York: Mentor Books, 1992.

———. "Cuco Goes to a Party." *Arizona Quarterly* 3 (summer 1947): 121–27. Reprinted in *North of the Rio Grande: The Mexican American Experience in Short Fiction*, edited by Edward Simmen, 102–8. New York: Penguin, 1992. Reprinted in *The Latino Reader: An American Literary Tradition from 1542 to the Present*, edited by Harold Augenbraum and Margarite Fernández Olmos, 202–7. Boston: Houghton Mifflin, 1997.

———. "Loco-Chu." *Arizona Quarterly* 3 (summer 1947): 127–30. Reprinted in *North of the Rio Grande: The Mexican American Experience in Short Fiction*, edited by Edward Simmen, 109–11. New York: Penguin, 1992.

———. "Kid Zopilote." *Arizona Quarterly* 3 (summer 1947): 130–37. Reprinted in *North of the Rio Grande: The Mexican American Experience in Short Fiction*, edited by Edward Simmen, 111–18. New York: Penguin, 1992.

———. "Southside Run." *Arizona Quarterly* 4 (Winter 1948): 362–68.

———. "Maestría." *Arizona Quarterly* 4 (Winter 1948): 368–73; reprinted in *Mexican-American Authors*. Eds. Américo Paredes and Raymund Paredes. Boston: Houghton Mifflin, 1972. Pp. 105–10; *Literatura chicana: texto y contexto/Chicano Literature: Text and Context*. Eds. Antonia Castañeda, Tomás Ybarra-Frausto, and Joseph Sommers. Englewood Cliffs, N.J.: Prentice-Hall, 1972. Pp. 169–73.

———. "Mexican Heaven." *Arizona Quarterly* 6, no. 4 (winter 1950): 310–15.

———. "Alianza. . . ." *P[rensa]-M[exicana]* (Tucson), 6 June 1958, pp. 1, 3.

———. "Las comadres." *Con Safos: Reflections of Life in the Barrio* 1, no. 3 (March 1969): 38–40. Reprinted in *Aztlán: An Anthology of Mexican American Literature*, edited by Luis Valdez and Stan Steiner, 157–63. New York: Knopf, 1973.

———. "Los coyotes." *Con Safos: Relections of Life in the Barrio* 8 (1972): 43–46. Reprinted in *Festival de Flor y Canto: An Anthology of Chicano Literature*, edited by Alurista, F.A. Cervantes, Juan Gómez-Quiñones, Mary Ann Pacheco, and Gustavo Segade, 26–29. Los Angeles: University of Southern California Press, El Centro Chicano, 1976. Reprinted in *The Gypsy Wagon: Un Sancocho de Cuentos de la Experiencia Chicana*, edited by Armando Rafael Rodríguez, 15–22. Los Angeles: Aztlán Publications, University of California at Los Angeles, 1974.

———. "The Migrant." *Revista Chicano-Riqueña* 10, no. 4 (1982): 15–30. Reprinted in *Cuentos chicanos*, edited by Rudolfo A. Anaya and Antonio Márquez, 142–58. Albuquerque: University of New Mexico Press, 1984.

Unpublished Primary Sources

Suárez, Mario. "Doña Clara," "Life Is But a Tango," "Doña Clara's Nephew," "El Tiradito," "The Pioneer," "Something Useful, Even Tailoring," "Trouble in Petate," and "La suerte del pobre." A manuscript collection authorized by the Suárez family in San Dimas, California.

Secondary Sources

Barrio, Raymond. *The Plum Plum Pickers*. Sunnyvale, Calif.: Ventura Press, 1969.

Englekirk, J. Allan. "Mario Suárez." In *Dictionary of Literary Biography; Chicano Writers, First Series*, edited by Francisco A. Lomelí and Carl S. Shirley, 253–56. Detroit: Gale Research, 1989.

Flores, Lauro. "La dualidad del pachuco." *Revista Chicano-Riqueña* 6, no. 4 (fall 1978): 51–58.

Gibson, Arrell Morgan. "The Author as Image Maker for the Southwest." In *Old Southwest/New Southwest: Essays on a Region and Its Literature*, edited by Judy Nolte Lensink, 25–37. Tucson: Tucson Public Library, 1987.

Hinojosa-Smith, Rolando. *Estampas del Valle y otras obras*. Berkeley, Calif.: Quinto Sol Publications, 1973.

Ingram, Forrest L. *Representative Short Story Cycles of the Twentieth Century: Studies in a Literary Genre*. The Hague: Mouton, 1971.

Leal, Luis. "Pre-Chicano Literature: Process and Meaning (1539–1959)." In *Handbook of Hispanic Cultures in the United States: Literature and Art*, edited by Francisco A. Lomelí, 62–85. Houston: Arte Público, 1993.

Lomelí, Francisco A. "A Literary Portrait of Hispanic New Mexico: Dialectics of Perception." *Pasó Por Aquí: Critical Essays on the New Mexican Literary Tradition, 1542–1988*, edited by Erlinda Gonzales-Berry, 131–48. Albuquerque: University of New Mexico Press, 1989.

Madrid-Barela, Arturo. "In Search of the Authentic Pachuco: An Interpretive Essay." *Aztlán* 4, no. 1 (spring 1973): 31–60.

Meléndez, A. Gabriel. *So All Is Not Lost: The Poetics of Print in Nuevomexicano Communities, 1834–1958*. Albuquerque: University of New Mexico Press, 1997.

Morales, Alejandro D. "Visión panorámica de la literatura mexicoamericana hasta el Boom de 1966." Ph.D. diss., Rutgers University, 1976.

Ortego, Philip D. "Backgrounds of Mexican American Literature." Abstract in *Dissertation Abstracts International* 32 (March 1972), 5195A (New Mexico).

Paredes, Raymund. "The Evolution of Chicano Literature." In *Three American Literatures: Essays in Chicano, Native American, and Asian-American Literature for Teachers of American Literature*, edited by Houston A. Baker, Jr., 33–79. New York: Modern Language Association of America, 1982.

———. "The Image of the Mexican in American Literature." Ph.D. diss., University of Texas at Austin, 1973.

Rivera, Tomás. "Chicano Literature: The Establishment of Community." In *A Decade of Chicano Literature (1970–1979)*, edited by Luis Leal, Fernando de Necochea, Francisco A. Lomelí, and Roberto G. Trujillo, 7–17. Santa Barbara, Calif.: Editorial La Causa, 1982.

———. "... Y no se lo tragó la tierra." Berkeley, Calif.: Quinto Sol Publications, 1971.

Robinson, Cecil. *With the Ears of Strangers: The Mexican in American Literature*. Tucson: University of Arizona Press, 1963.

Rodríguez, Juan. "El desarrollo del cuento chicano: Del folklore al tenebroso mundo del yo." In *The Identification and Analysis of Chicano Literature*, edited by Francisco Jiménez, 58–68. New York: Bilingual Press/Editorial Bilingüe, 1979.

Tatum, Charles. *Chicano Literature*. Boston: Twayne Publishers, 1982.

———. "Tucson, Arizona: El Hoyo." In *Mexican American Literature*, 244–49. Orlando, Fla.: Harcourt Brace Jovanovich, 1990.

About the Editors

Francisco A. Lomelí is chair of the Department of Spanish and Portuguese and professor of Chicana/o Studies at the University of California, Santa Barbara. He has published extensively in Chicano and Latin American studies, focusing primarily on literary expression. His areas of expertise include cultural studies, literary history, border studies, theoretical questions of aesthetics, and general literary criticism. He is a leader in the promotion of Chicano literature internationally, having participated as co-organizer of various conferences in Bordeaux, Málaga, Alcalá de Henares, and Naples. His publications include *Chicano Studies: A Multidisciplinary Approach* (with Eugene García and Isidro Ortiz, 1983), *Handbook of Hispanic Cultures in the United States: Literature and Art* (1993), and *Nuevomexicano Cultural Legacy: Forms, Agencies, and Discourse* (with Víctor Sorrell and Genaro Padilla, 2002).

Cecilia Cota-Robles Suárez was raised in Tucson, Arizona, the tenth of eleven children. She attended Tucson public schools and the University of Arizona, and she taught first grade in Tucson public schools before moving to California to teach in Whittier and La Mirada. She left teaching for Head Start, where she held administrative positions. She later earned her doctorate in education at the University of California, Los Angeles, where she also worked in Chicano studies. In 1970, she developed one of the first bilingual Head Start training programs, which served five community colleges. She worked for twenty years at California State Polytechnic University at Pomona, where she ran the early childhood program. On retirement in 1982 she stayed active in her community, administering a City of Pomona grant through the Academy of Community Achievement. Dr. Suárez was working on several books on Mexican history when she passed away in March 2004.

Juan José Casillas-Núñez is a doctoral candidate in the Spanish and Portuguese Department at the University of California, Santa Barbara. Currently he is Assistant Professor at Santa Barbara City College, where he teaches Spanish for Heritage Learners, Latin American Culture, and Chicano literature.